Risk
of a
Lifetime

Enjoy the read!

Risk of a Lifetime

Claudia Shelton

This book is a work of fiction. Names, characters, places, and incidents are the product of the author's imagination or are used fictitiously. Any resemblance to actual events, locales, or persons, living or dead, is coincidental.

Copyright © 2014 by Claudia Shelton. All rights reserved, including the right to reproduce, distribute, or transmit in any form or by any means. For information regarding subsidiary rights, please contact the Publisher.

Entangled Publishing, LLC
2614 South Timberline Road
Suite 109
Fort Collins, CO 80525
Visit our website at www.entangledpublishing.com.

Edited by Tracy Montoya
Cover design by Fiona Jayde

Print ISBN 978-1503118584

Manufactured in the United States of America

First Edition April 2014

*To my very own blue-eyed hero
—my husband John—
who shared a lifetime of love and excitement with me.
I miss you.*

Chapter One

"I need to go to the bathroom," Marcy Bradley said, loud enough to get the attention of everyone in the First Missouri Capitol Bank of Crayton.

All five of them. Six, if you counted the robber, Leon Ferguson, a bully from her fourth-grade class twenty years ago. These days, he clocked in at well over six feet, two-hundred-fifty pounds of sweaty stink mixed with a stale odor of wood smoke. He'd gotten their attention when he slammed the bank president to the floor. Even more when he'd shot the exit sign. Now his mud-crusted boots made a path in front of the teller windows, back and forth, back and forth.

Any other Friday morning, Marcy would be composing poetry in her mind as she waited in line to make the weekly deposit from her counseling business. Instead, she lay cheek down on the shiny, cold marble floor of the eighty-two-year-old building as Leon continued to hold everyone hostage. When this was over, she'd drop a note in the suggestion box about cleaning the baseboards.

For the past twenty minutes, Leon yelled about the "cost of gettin' by" and bragged about the last time he went fishing. From all appearances, his tolerance level for whatever drug he was high on today had long since passed. His mean side had flashed when he'd cold-cocked the janitor with his fist for not getting down on the floor fast enough. That explained Leon's wife's many "accidents" the woman had told her about during their one-on-one counseling sessions. No wonder the woman ran away.

The stock market ticker tape flicked across the ceiling-mounted television. Scrolling words flashed on the screen. An antiquated fan in the opposite corner fluffed Marcy's hair with each back-and-forth rotation.

A few alternatives to lying on the floor skimmed through her mind. Run. She could run for the door and… A gunshot wound didn't rank very high up on her agenda for life experiences. She also decided this wasn't the time to make one of her sarcastic remarks about how Leon had flipped her skirt up in junior high and squirted her hot-pink panties with a water pistol.

This wasn't the time for anything except figuring out a way to keep breathing and make it to her thirtieth birthday two months away.

"Excuse me." She really didn't need to go to the bathroom. But, if that's what it took to get out of the situation, so be it. Anything beat being held hostage. Almost anything.

The robber glanced around.

She waved her fingers from the floor. "It's me. Marcy."

By now, Leon would have usually blacked out if he was only drunk. Today was different, though. Today his demeanor reeked of disorientation and violence. Today he might blow her away before he realized he'd picked up a real gun instead of a toy.

She'd been around enough guns to know this was a Glock, a Luger, or something like that. Big and dangerous in the wrong hands. Leon's were definitely the wrong hands.

Rule number…one…four? Didn't matter what number. One of the law enforcement rules she learned from drop-dead-gorgeous JB, her almost-used-to-be husband and one heck of an FBI agent, was "don't upset the perp. Be his friend." She could do that. Be a friend…kind of…maybe.

She sorted through everything she'd learned in her psychology Master's program. With a little luck, she could talk Leon down. After all, she was a marriage counselor. Even had a seventy/thirty rate of success. Of course, the seventy percent had ended in divorce.

Eyelids pinched to slits, he waved the gun in her direction. "Did you say something?"

"I said I've got to go pee." She inched to a left-elbow lean. Smiled sweetly. "Please."

A few feet away, Joanie Reynolds gave her a *you're-nuts* look from where she'd fallen on a deposit from the previous evening's receipts at Joanie's Pizza, Pub, and Pool Room. Marcy had seen the bag of money disappear beneath her friend's well-endowed body and knew there was no way Joanie would give up the stash without a fight.

"Nope. Go where you are." He turned back toward the teller window.

"What do you mean 'nope'? This is the first day I've worn these brand new, skinny-leg jeans. And they weren't cheap, let me tell you."

He turned back around, his gaze scanning her legs.

She eased to a sitting position. "You're right about everything being so expensive nowadays. Do you know how high gas is? I mean—who can afford to drive anymore? My car's gas mileage is a joke. What about yours?"

"Eighteen miles a gallon. You got to know how to keep your vehicle running good." He leaned back, smiling his gap-toothed grin. Decay pitted the teeth that remained. "I got me a *Chilton's Guide to Automotives* and a set of wrenches from Sears."

She wished she hadn't eaten those blueberry pancakes for breakfast. They weren't exactly sitting right in the pit of her stomach. Besides which, it was time to use his momentary camaraderie to her advantage. She rolled onto her hands and knees, then crawled past Joanie toward a chair next to the counter.

He stepped over her friend and kept pace with Marcy's slow movement. "Where you think you're going?"

Using the seat for leverage, she pushed herself up enough to sit down in it. Her hand plucked at lint on her denim pants, and she sighed. "There, that's better now. I think I need the next size up in these jeans. They were beginning to bind down there on the floor. Okay if I sit here?"

"Long as you don't move around no more. Shut up, too. I got to have some quiet to think what I want to do with this here opportunity." Brow furrowed, lips pursed to a scowl, he paced between the front door and the counter.

Marcy wished she'd paid closer attention to robber personality types in her college behavioral classes. She'd been more focused on marriage counseling—and revenge-killing profiles. Her dad had been killed by a hate-filled man with a vendetta against any FBI special agent that stepped in front of his gun. Her dad had been the first agent out the front door of the Bureau's Regional Office building that day. She'd turned eight years old the week before he died.

Of course, she knew how Leon's thought process worked from the few times he'd shown up at her office for court-appointed counseling. That should at least give her an edge up on the situation. Except his thinking wasn't always great on a good day, and this was a bad day. A real bad day so far.

The new-as-of-two-weeks-ago president of the bank cowered in the corner where Leon had told him to sit. The teller on the early morning shift stood stone-still behind the counter. Except for the fact her eyes were wide open and rounded like silver dollars, she'd have looked like she was waiting for the next customer.

Outside, cars honked at the two drive-up windows. They apparently didn't know there was a robbery in process. If they needed money for lunch today, they weren't getting any here.

From across the room, Leon cleared his throat, waving the gun in Marcy's direction once again. "What do you think?"

"Me?" she asked.

"Yeah. You got all them fancy degrees. What do you think I should do with this opportunity?"

Opportunity? What opportunity? He was robbing a bank. She glanced at the teller. No help there. She looked at Joanie. None there, either.

Well, hell, she might as well come up with something herself. "You're right. A person doesn't get many chances like this in life. You've got to be careful what you choose. Maybe—"

"We know you're in there, Leon." Deputy Evans's voice vibrated from outside the bank through a bullhorn. "We're gonna tow your truck if you don't come out of there right now. I ain't got time for your shenanigans today."

Her uncle, Cal Davis, the Sheriff of Crayton Police Department, was out of town on a much-needed vacation until next week. He'd left Evans in charge. Nothing wrong with that, except this wasn't one of the usual pranks Leon played around town.

Leon fiddled with the blind at the front window. Rubbing his palm against his pant leg, he appeared confused. His jerky head motions didn't make her feel any safer, either.

Someone might get hurt before this was over. She wished her uncle was the one waiting outside in the street. In fact, she wished it was—

"You gonna come out, or do I have to come in there?" the deputy said.

Evans had a wife, three little kids, and a mother to support. Marcy had to think of something before the situation turned to tragedy.

She eased to her feet and leaned against the counter, quiet and nonchalant. "Why don't you ask for a bullhorn of your own?"

Leon swung around. His gun arm veered up shakily as he focused on her. "What did you say?"

"Ask for a bullhorn. The teller could call to tell them you want one. She could go outside to get it for you." At least that would be one less hostage in the bank.

"Why would I want a bullhorn when I've got all this money?" He lowered the gun back to his side. His head jerked repeatedly.

She glanced at Joanie, then the bank president, then the guard who hadn't moved since he'd crashed to the floor. She realized she appeared to be the only one thinking in the room. Or the only one about to get sent straight to heaven for mouthing off.

"That way you could talk to them about what you'll need for your getaway," she said.

He wrinkled his forehead. Sweat beads popped on his upper lip. "Good idea. 'Cept you make the call, and you go out to get it."

That hadn't gone as she planned. She nodded and made the call before heading to the front door.

Leon stepped in front of her, gun pointed at Joanie. "If you don't come back, nobody else is leavin'. Got that?"

"Got it."

. . .

Marcy stepped out the door into the brisk warmth of a fall morning. The clock at the corner of Third and Main struck the half hour. Her eyes scanned the scene in front of her. Two police cars stationed across the street sat silent, but their lights flashed a warning.

The stocky, sandy-haired deputy and one other cop stood behind a police cruiser directly in front of her. On her left, the tall, lean rookie crouched on the far side of the second car, his gun drawn and steadied on the top of the trunk.

Another man, likely law enforcement, although not in uniform, leaned against the far, rear fender of a car a few spots down. The man ignored the events on the street. Back to the bank and on his cell phone, he looked as if he dared anyone to bother him.

Her insides twisted when he moved away from the cruiser. Even from that angle, his six-foot-one stance and the dark-brown hair skimming the collar of his leather jacket were more than familiar. Familiar enough to make her insides zing with recognition.

Stretched taut across his back, the coat moved with him as he walked away. She knew every muscle beneath that jacket. All the scars. Didn't need to see his face, she'd recognize those shoulders anywhere—Jean Bernard Bradley.

JB to the world. More than JB to her.

Bullhorn in hand, Deputy Evans trudged from behind the car and stepped in her direction. He looked more agitated than concerned. From the slump of his shoulders and the lines in his face, he'd probably been up for hours getting the kids ready for school while his wife fixed breakfast.

"This isn't a prank. Leon's got a real gun. Loaded," she shouted as she stepped into the street.

JB stopped. Straightened. Hard-stretched his fingers a second before rolling them into fists. The moves meant he remembered her voice. He'd do whatever it took to save her. No matter what the danger. She doubted he'd changed. He'd always took the lead, took the bullet, took the victim to safety.

She had to make sure saving her didn't get him killed. 'Cause she damn sure couldn't live with that. Hell, could her day get any more complicated?

He turned his head with that chin-down tilt she knew so well and zeroed in on her with a penetrating look over his shoulder. The blue of his eyes wasn't visible from where she'd stopped, but she knew the intensity even if it had been close to three years since she'd last felt the heat. Her pulse notched up a few more beats. He always had been one gorgeous, sexy man. Nothing had changed there.

Deputy Evans ducked back behind the patrol car and reached for the radio. Backup would be on the way.

She stared at JB and said, "A real big gun. With a high-as-a-kite hand on the trigger."

He barely nodded, but she knew he'd heard the warning.

Already he'd unzipped his jacket. In the process of shucking the coat, she saw him slide his shoulder holster off, but not before he slipped his gun behind his back. Only seconds had passed, yet he'd taken charge of the situation just as though he'd never left town. Like he was still the deputy of Crayton instead of an undercover FBI agent assigned to parts unknown.

"Evans, get down behind that car," he said.

The deputy paused, then squared his shoulders. "My town. My responsibility."

JB nodded, strapping on the bulletproof vest a patrolman tossed to him. "I understand. Just thought you might want the Bureau's help. I've dealt with hostage situations before. Have you?"

The deputy paused only a second, then slid the horn toward JB. "The Crayton Police welcomes the FBI's assistance."

JB unbuttoned the sleeves on his white oxford and rolled the cuffs a couple of turns. Tugged them straight. She knew his battle mode. His routine.

Once he took on an assignment, he was tenacious. Nothing and no one got in his way. He'd get himself shot over her if they weren't careful. Much as she didn't want him back in her life, she couldn't bear to think of him gone forever, either.

He scooped the bullhorn from the pavement and held his arms out to the side at shoulder level as he walked forward. When he stopped a few feet in front of her, his gaze barely scanned her face before he returned his attention to the bank building.

"How bad is it?" he asked.

"Bad. He's all junked up on something." She reached for the horn. "Be careful. Please be careful."

His fingers brushed against hers as he released the horn. "Almost sounds like you care."

"You wish!" She forced herself not to blink. If she did, she might grab him and hold on for dear life.

His eyes zeroed in on hers. What passed between them

was private and personal and unspoken. She'd let him go—kicked him out, in fact—when he'd threatened to take the same job that had killed her father. Never in her wildest thoughts had she imagined he'd take her up on her offer of freedom.

One month after she'd set his suitcase on the front porch, a letter with no return address had arrived. It said he'd done everything he could to prove himself to her and he was sorry he hadn't been good enough. He'd told her to just send him the papers, and he'd give her her freedom. She'd called him at least once a month after that. Left voice messages asking him to return her call. No reply.

A year later, there'd been a message on her voice mail saying he'd be out-of-contact for a while. She should get on with her life. Find someone new. She could only wonder when the hell had he been in contact over the past months? A few days later, an envelope had come addressed to her. Confidential. It included a form stating she was JB's next-of-kin, a power of attorney to make health and financial decisions for him if he was incapacitated, and an insurance policy naming her his beneficiary. She hadn't wanted those; she'd wanted him.

That's when she'd hired an attorney from outside Crayton and sent divorce papers. Even scribbled in bright red ink "Come home or sign these papers" across the top of the first page. Thought that would force him to make a decision. It had worked. He'd signed the papers and sent them back with a black-marker line slashed through the "Come home" part. That was the last she'd heard from him until now.

"Don't go back inside." The corner of JB's mouth twitched as he refocused his attention on the bank door. "I'll take one step forward and to the right. You jump behind me."

"I can't. Joanie's in there, plus three others. Leon said he would shoot them if I didn't return."

"Leon may be a bully, even mean, but that doesn't sound like something he'd do." JB's stare remained fixed across the street.

"Most days, I'd agree. Not today. He's juiced. Head shakes. Crazy eyes. Sweating." She lingered a second. "Don't go getting yourself killed before I can give you a piece of my mind."

A hint of a smile jerked at the corners of his mouth before he clenched his jaws. "Wouldn't dream of it."

Damn it to hell, even after all this time, he still made her insides quiver with just a few words. Why hadn't he come home and talked before he signed the divorce papers? Her uncle had told her it was the way she'd pushed JB away—the whole packing his bag and leaving it on the front porch deal. That's all he would say. To this day, she still didn't know what that meant.

But she'd decided if that's the way JB wanted it, then it was okay with her. She'd done just fine on her own the past few years. She would continue to make it without his help… except for now. She'd be more than grateful if he could get her out of this situation without getting either one of them hurt.

She walked back to the open bank door and stepped inside. Leon grabbed her from behind, shielding himself with her body as he stood in the doorway.

"Hold that bullhorn up to my mouth." His grip wrenched tighter across her chest and shoulders. He wrapped his arm around her and forced her further outside to the edge of the sidewalk.

Her hand shook as she raised her arm. JB still stood

where she'd left him.

"Press that damn speak button before I blow your lover boy away," Leon hissed in her ear. "You think I don't know who he is?"

She searched the metal with her fingers for the button. "It's on. Don't do anything foolish. It's on."

His gun arm straightened as he aimed at JB. "Back off," he shouted, "or I'll shoot you where you stand."

JB didn't move except to slide a hand behind his back.

Her uncle had once told her about a hostage who'd stood so still, the SWAT team was able to take the shot at a kidnapper. Right now, that was all she could think about. *Stand stone-still.*

Leon swung the gun back at her. "Maybe I'll shoot your off-again, on-again, off-again wife. What about that?"

JB backed all the way to the patrol car. "Far enough?"

...

JB focused on Marcy. At five-foot-six and what still looked to be one-hundred-thirty pounds, she wasn't much of a shield for Leon's frame. She didn't move. Good girl.

Taking a shot at the bully wouldn't serve any purpose. Not as long as there was a chance he could talk him down. His gun would be the last resort.

This wasn't the way he'd planned on seeing Marcy again. In fact, he'd hoped to be in and out of town before she even got wind he was around. So much for that plan. Three years was a long time, and he'd learned how to live without her. Still, he wouldn't stand by and see her hurt, either.

Leon shoved the gun against the side of her head. "No. All the way to the building behind you."

After feeling his way around the hood of the car, JB

continued backwards until the cold brick of the building bit into his shoulders. She'd been right. Leon's haggard look spoke of bad home brew mixed with meth or something stronger.

Coming back to Crayton had been a mistake, but his dad's estate needed to be settled. The thought of handling everything by mail had entered his mind, but his undercover assignments weren't all that conducive to signing papers with a notary. He'd learned that with the divorce. So here he was, caught between what might have been and the reality of Marcy with a gun pointed at her head.

The drugged-out man's day was about to get a whole lot worse if he hurt her. JB would take him out in a flash and make it look like self-defense. FBI training might have been intense, but in-the-field operations had taught him things not mentioned in Quantico's hallowed halls. Like how far he'd go to stay alive. Or to save someone he loved. Had loved, in this case.

Leon leaned forward and set Marcy on her feet. Yanked back a handful of her auburn hair. A quick flash of fear shadowed her face as she gasped. He laughed, low and menacing.

Right now she looked like a small, defenseless woman. JB knew different. She could be a hellcat when she wanted. Her eyes, the color of dark chocolate, held fear today instead of their usual warmth. He didn't like that. Didn't like it one bit.

"Hey, JB, I think I'll have me a little taste of what you had." Leon yanked harder on her hair, then leaned in and licked her cheek from her chin to her forehead. "Not bad. Maybe I'll have a little more once we get out of town."

The sonofabitch had no idea how close he was to being blown away. All JB needed to do was roll and yank the gun from his back waistband. Gun up, pull the trigger, gun down. Situation resolved.

His insides edged in that direction, but his training said negotiate. Try another tactic.

Marcy closed her eyes and flinched. She clenched her fingers around the metal of the horn. JB knew she was afraid now. Mad and afraid. Not a good combination for her.

The veins on JB's forearms pulsed to attention, and the muscles in his biceps hardened like steel. "You're okay, Marcy. You hear me? I've got you."

Her body eased as she opened her eyes and stared into his. The expression on her face softened. Even her lips had tipped upward, parted a bit. He knew that look. Surrender. Trust. Come what may, she'd put herself in his hands. He tore his focus from her. Cemented it on the man with the gun.

He relaxed into the role of negotiator. "What do you want, Leon?"

The bully waved his gun around. "A truck. And…a…a…bag of money."

"Okay. You want a Ford or a GMC or—"

"Ford. A black Ford. And two bags money. Two big bags."

"If we give you the pickup truck, what do we get in return?" JB stood away from the wall, took a couple steps forward.

Marcy closed her eyes again. Not in a fearful way, JB realized, but so as not to distract him.

Leon tightened his grip on her. "That bank guy. I'll give you the bank man."

"Why not Marcy?" JB took a couple more steps. "She's already outside."

"No! She's mine." Leon jerked his gaze upward as if caught by a movement. "I'm gonna—"

A shot rang out. Leon's body recoiled, and she lurched to the side as his hold released. She screamed as he crumbled.

"Who fired that shot?" Gun drawn, JB vaulted over the hood of the patrol car and raced toward her. "Hold your fire."

She turned to him, and a second shot echoed through the air. A cry of anguish escaped her mouth as a bright red trickle snaked down her arm where the bullet had grazed her. His back to the line of fire, JB caught her before her legs bent and cradled her in his arms. He knelt, shielding her with his body. Her head flung back, and her eyes went half-lidded. Was she reacting to the sight of her own blood or a wound he hadn't seen?

He clutched her hand. "I'm here, sugar. Hold on."

She responded with a soft press of her fingers.

Another bullet clipped through the air. Ricocheted off the concrete. Crashed through his shoulder. Her body sagged, wilted.

"Marcy? Marcy!"

He felt like the shots were directed at them instead of Leon. Why? The force of his fear for her grabbed his heart and shoved it into his throat. He scanned the area for a safe, quick path to a barrier. Nothing. Moving was not an option.

What had he heard? Silencer. What had he seen? Nothing so far. Of course, the silencer could lower the flash. This wasn't the police taking shots. This was a sniper. The rifle scope might be off, or the guy might be nervous shooting in such a confined area, or maybe this was his first job as a hired gun, but there was one thing for sure—the guy was a damn pro.

Who in this sleepy, little town had that kind of training except for the police? And, him?

Who?

Chapter Two

Phone shoved against his ear, JB paced around the commandeered office of Dr. Crowley at Our Lady of the Lake Medical Center while speaking to his boss Kenneth Wilson at the FBI's Regional Office in Kansas City.

The paramedics had brought the three victims of the shooting here. Thankfully, Marcy's injuries were mild compared to what might have happened. No bullet wound—she'd been hit by a few chunks of pavement. She was somewhere down the hall being prepped for exploratory surgery on her shoulder to make sure they got all the fragments out.

The bullet that had hit him had only grazed his shoulder, a flesh wound that had already been cleaned and stitched up.

"That's what I said. No one from the sheriff's office fired the shots that hit the robber or my ex-wife. Evidently, Leon's made some enemies in town." He didn't half believe his statement, but until he had more proof, he wouldn't bring up the possibility of a sniper. "The local police asked if I'd be available to help them out on a small task force to work through the bank robbery and shooting."

He figured the frown on his boss' face had just deepened. And, truth be known, he didn't want to stay in town any longer than he had to.

"Afraid I can't let you do that since you're emotionally involved." His boss sucked in air and cleared his throat on the release. "I'll send Dwight Landon to work with them. You remember him, don't you?"

"Yeah. We worked a drug bust in Springfield last year." Even though JB's main FBI office was located in Kansas City, Missouri, the satellite offices stretched from Garden Center, Kansas, to St. Joseph, Missouri, from Jefferson City to Springfield, Missouri.

Landon seemed okay, but the idea of someone else on his own Crayton turf didn't sit well. Besides, the agent didn't compare to his first FBI partner, Albert Jennings, whose death was still an open case. Leads might have faded, but to JB, that case would always be active.

He scrubbed his palm across his hair and glanced through the open doorway into the hall. Sadie Dawson, Marcy's mom, leaned against the wall, staring at him as if he were the only person she could count on at the moment. He nodded. She nodded in return. Her fingers trembled when she moved them to cover her quivering chin.

Locals referred to Sadie as a resilient, stand-up broad. The tall, willow-thin woman with carrot-red hair would do anything for anybody in need, even the few in town who bad-mouthed her. Right now, she looked scared and needy herself.

A nurse approached her with a handful of papers and a pen. The women talked, then Sadie pointed at him. An uneasy feeling grabbed him as the two walked in the office and stopped. He could feel the hard ache at the involuntary clench of his jaw. He turned and moved to the window, then scanned the parking lot and the surrounding area.

"You still there?" his boss asked.

"Yeah. I don't know about Landon. There may be a problem with him fitting in around here."

"Give the guy a chance." Wilson cleared his throat. "I know you looked up to Jennings, but he's gone. Move on."

JB cringed. He'd move on when his partner's killer rotted behind bars. "Landon's a shadow. Stays to himself. And if you ask me, which you didn't, he comes real close to crossing the letter of the law a lot of times. I don't like working with someone like that."

He heard what he'd just said and cringed. Hell, *he* was someone like that. The words he'd just used hit awfully close to home.

"I hear you. For now, see how this goes. Let me know if he gets in the way more than he helps."

"Hey, I'm not staying around here. I'd planned to be in and out of town in one day, but this robbery has put a hitch in those plans. Once I've consulted briefly with the police, I'll be on my way." JB raked his fingers through his hair, heaving a loud sigh.

No way in hell was he staying in town. From the letters Sadie had dropped him every so often, Marcy was doing just fine without him.

Wilson cleared his throat. "Don't you think your wife—"

"Ex-wife!"

"Okay. Don't you think your ex-wife may feel safer with you around for a few days?" The man paused. "Women are funny that way. Hate you one minute. Can't live without you the next. Besides, you never know when your expertise may be needed."

"Then put me in charge of the case." JB was amazed at the inconsistencies being bantered around in this conversation. His boss never seemed to make up his mind lately.

"What do I have to do to get this through your head?" Wilson's harsh tone gave no room for discussion. "Special Agent Landon will be lead on this."

JB fingered his wedding band tucked in his jean's watch pocket. He had planned to leave it in an envelope at the sheriff's office before he left town. JB glanced at the nurse and Marcy's mom waiting just inside the office doorway. Maybe he should stay a few days. Make sure evidence wasn't being ignored. Man-up and give the ring to his ex-wife in person.

He turned back to the window, braced his hand against the frame. No way would his boss change his decision. No way would Landon come close to knowing how to talk to the locals. No way the Crayton Police Department had the resources or guidance to follow through on leads. Especially with the sheriff being out of town.

Might not be JB's case, but this was his town, and he wasn't leaving until the pieces fell into place. Besides, he'd already been wavering about his job with the Bureau. "Remember last month when you put a warning in my personnel file for a no-brainer infraction? Said I needed to be more careful at following your boss's orders."

"Sure. I remember. No big deal." Wilson's tone sounded less than straight forward.

"Wrong. Being called on the carpet for no good reason was a hell of a big deal in my book." JB focused on the life-changing words he'd mulled over for the past few weeks, ever since he put in for a transfer. "You know that resignation letter you're holding for me? The one I gave you in case my transfer request didn't go through?"

"Now hold on there. I've got a good idea what you're going to say, so take this piece of advice before you speak. Don't make any rash decisions. You've got a career to think about. Your future." Wilson's flat, non-conciliatory tone sounded about as sincere as dirt.

"I already thought." JB steeled his resolve around his next words. "Pull the resignation out and file it. Effective. Immediately."

Enough said. He ended the call. Protocol would have been to handle the leaving in person, but unusual times called for unusual means to an end.

After clicking to his e-mail files, he pulled out a copy of the resignation and forwarded it to Wilson and Wilson's boss as added assurance that they both knew he quit. Whatever he needed to do to protect Marcy and this town would be his own call. Not the Bureau's.

The phone rang as he turned back to the women. Caller ID showed his boss—ex-boss. JB powered the handset off with a long, hard push of his finger. So much for a career with the FBI.

Sadie joined him by the window, and he draped his arm across his ex-mother-in-law's shoulders, pulling her into his hold. She'd kept him up-to-date on Marcy for the past few years. Never asking why they were apart. Then after the divorce, Sadie'd still dropped him a note every so often.

"How you doing, Sadie?" He owed her an explanation. But how would he explain that the suitcase on the porch that last night before he'd left town had been an echo from the past that he couldn't handle?

She leaned on him for a moment, then straightened and blinked her eyes to clear the tears. When a couple trickled down her cheek, she brushed them away as if daring anyone to say they existed. "This nurse needs to talk to you."

"Okay." He looped his thumbs in his back pockets. "What can I do for you, ma'am?"

The woman in scrubs placed the papers on the side table then held the pen in front of him, impatience etched across her face. "Dr. Crowley wants these forms signed by the next of kin before we operate on Marcy Bradley."

He stepped back. Waved his hands in front of the paperwork. "You got the wrong person here. Her next of kin is her mama. Marcy divorced me a long time ago. Besides, she didn't look bad enough that she can't sign."

She'd always wilted at the sight of someone else's blood. Especially his. Evidently, his fleshy bullet wound had been enough to cause her to faint earlier. Sure, hers needed to be explored, cleaned, and sutured, but there hadn't been enough blood for the injuries to be life-threatening.

Clearly irritated, the nurse slammed the pen to the table and headed out the door. "Dr. Crowley said one of you had better have signed that form by the time Ms. Bradley's ready to roll into that operating room."

He held the pen out to Sadie, but she shook her head.

Marcy's older sister Betsy, the spitting image of their mama—tall, thin, and red-haired—charged into the room and into the conversation with the ferocity of a caged lion. "So what I heard is right. You sorry excuse for a man aren't back in town half an hour before you get yourself shot again."

"There was a robbery." Sadie reached for her daughter's arm. "He saved Marcy from being hurt worse than she is."

"That still doesn't give him the right to be signing any papers for her." Betsy grabbed the pen, but her mother took it from her.

"I really doubt anyone needs to sign those papers. Marcy wasn't hurt so bad she can't give permission."

With the air of authority, Dr. Crowley entered his office, gently nudging the women aside as he lumbered firmly to the table. "While you three are arguing, there's a woman down the hall heading to the operating room. Now sign the forms, JB."

"I signed the papers." Sadie held the form out to him.

Dr. Crowley glanced at JB, then narrowed his focus on Sadie. "This the way you want it?"

She nodded her head.

Dr. Crowley blew out a long, loud sigh. "You do realize I'm the deacon in the church you sometimes favor us by attending, don't you?"

Sadie straightened, staring him down. "Yes, I do. And as such, it is your responsibility to do what is in the best interest of your congregation."

"You and your daughters will be the death of me yet, Sadie."

"Don't include me in this." Betsy shook her head as she rested her hands on her hips. Then, she turned her face toward JB. "And you can just pack up and leave anytime."

"Not now, Betsy." JB held his hand up to stop her words. Inside, his control churned hard and fast to be free. She must have felt it, because she shut up. He straightened, easing back. "And not until your sister's well, either."

He wondered what the hell had just transpired with the doctor, but some things weren't his business. One thing for sure, though, he didn't plan to leave town until the robbery and shooting were well on their way to being solved. Even if it meant staying around longer than he'd planned.

That would give him time to consider which job to take next. The police department he'd applied to in Texas? Or the covert ops he'd been asked to be a part of a few months back? Both thought he was good enough. Both wanted him.

And both locations would keep him away from Crayton… and the only woman who'd ever made him smile morning and night.

Only she hadn't been strong enough to let go of her father's death and face the fact JB's job would always be in law enforcement. Too bad they hadn't realized the fact before they were married. Would have saved a lot of heartbreak on both sides.

"Where's Marcy?" he asked.

The doctor grabbed the forms and headed down the hall. "They should be rolling her into surgery about now."

JB charged past him. Past the nurses' station. Past Truman, Marcy's stepfather. Past a waiting room full of familiar faces. He had to see Marcy, touch her. Later, if she didn't remember him being there, that would be okay. He'd know. He could live with knowing. She might not be his wife, but keeping her alive and well was his top priority the next few days.

A gurney edged out of her hospital room.

"Hold up!" JB shouted to the orderly.

Grasping her hand, his breaths came ragged—and not from the short sprint down the hall—as he stroked wisps of hair from her forehead. Damn, even the antiseptic smell of the hospital couldn't cover the remembered scent of her jasmine shampoo.

He leaned in close. "How you doing, sugar?"

"I'm cold." Her eyes fluttered open. "It hurts. A lot."

"Doc Crowley's going to fix that."

The orderly tried to move the gurney forward, but JB braced it in place with his body. His lips brushed her temple. "Oh, Marcy. Marcy, Marcy, Marcy."

"JB." She opened her eyes full force. "Why'd you leave?"

Give her the truth. Tell her how much her words made you

feel you weren't good enough for her. How you couldn't stand to see her frightened for you every day you left for work as a lawman. Or that you needed to prove something to yourself.

No. This wasn't the time or place. Maybe it never would be.

"Because you let me go." He swallowed hard then brushed a kiss across her forehead. "Don't forget you're the one who locked me out."

Her eyes closed and her breathing weakened.

"Why'd you send the divorce papers?" He needed her answer. Needed to know what or who had taken his place.

"I figured you'd get mad and come back…and we'd be like before." She loosened the hold on his hand. "Didn't work. You never came back."

Like before? They'd been young and naive. Not anymore. He'd developed an edge that went with the job. One she'd never be able to understand. And her? From the letters Sadie sent him, Marcy had regrouped and moved forward. But she'd still never left Crayton except to go to college.

Like before? Nothing could ever be like before.

A nursed opened the doors to surgery, and the orderly pushed Marcy into the cool hallway. The doors slowly closed back into place.

He braced his head against the doorframe. A whole lot had happened in the last eight hours since he drove back in to Crayton. One hell of a lot.

Sadie touched his shoulder. "You two could try again."

"It's not that simple. Marcy couldn't stand the thought I might be killed on the job like her dad. It tore her apart every time I got hurt." He shoved his hands in his pockets. "Can you honestly tell me she's gotten past that in the past few years?"

"She was only eight. A thing like that sticks with a kid."

"Hell, do you think my childhood was a damn picnic? Not hardly. Doesn't mean I didn't have to grow up and stop making excuses long enough to move forward." JB quirked the side of his mouth with a sarcastic grin. "Or in my case, move out of town."

Sadie set her hands on her hips, a mirror of Betsy earlier. "So move back."

"I'm sorry, Sadie, but that's not even on my radar." JB shook his head and headed for the waiting room. There was no way to explain to anyone how much he needed the excitement of the chase and apprehension that went along with his career. He was good at what he had become—a loner who got the job done. Sure there were times he ended up in a bad situation, but he always found a way out. Worked smarter the next time. Got stronger.

Did he think he was invincible? Hell, no. But he knew he'd fight to the end. The day he finally went down and didn't get back up, no one would say he hadn't given everything he had. No big deal. That was the risk he faced every day.

After all, what good was life without a little risk?

Chapter Three

The morning nurse shooed JB out of Marcy's room so she could change her bandages and give the bed a quick clean-up. He took the opportunity to grab some breakfast in the hospital cafeteria. Focused on his third cup of strong, hot, black coffee, his eyes were at least open.

Last night had been long and uncomfortable in the recliner next to her bed. He'd spent most of the time calming her moans and scared mutterings. Even with medications, she still tossed and turned. Might even help if they took her off some of the pain killers.

He didn't like sitting around doing nothing. The nurse had said to give her an hour. By his watch, that hour had come and gone fifteen minutes ago. Time to get back. Marcy's scream met him as he turned the corner. He charged through the door to her room.

A man stood next to her bed while she flailed her arms at him. Blood trickled from the IV in her hand. The man lowered his forearm across her chest, and she clawed at his face.

JB grabbed the man from behind and flung him across the room. Dropped him to the floor with one swift maneuver. Braced his hand and arm against the back of the intruder's head and dug his knee into the man's back. "Don't even think about moving."

Dr. Crowley charged in to the room and pushed the call button. "Get security down here stat. And a nurse."

"Cool it, JB. It's me." The man on the floor didn't fight back. "Agent Landon."

JB eased his hold. "Landon? When did you get to town? Better question, what the hell are you doing in here?"

"Trying to find you. Wilson said this job was top priority, so I drove in last night. I thought you might be able to help when I interview this Leon guy." The man stood up, brushed himself off. "One look inside the door told me something was wrong. She was ripping at her IV. Banging her head against the side rails. Already had the oxygen tube tossed away."

"Help me. Help me." She backpedaled on the mattress. Her feet slipped. She got nowhere.

The doctor worked to calm Marcy down as the nurse cancelled security.

JB rushed to her side, lowered the bedrail, and climbed in beside her. "You're okay, sugar. Everything's okay."

She clutched at his shirt as he folded her in his arms.

"I'm right here, Marcy." He stroked her hair, kissing her forehead. He needed to stop doing that. And for damn sure stop calling her sugar.

"JB?" Her breathing slowed as her body wilted against his. "Am I okay? Did you get him?"

He gripped her closer. "You'll be fine. Your IV needs a little repair work, though." He fingered the blood on top of her hand where the needle dangled from the tape strapped across her skin.

The nurse rushed to her side and worked to stop the bleeding.

Landon approached the end of Marcy's bed, and she cringed, grabbing onto JB tighter. The fear on her face made him take a second look at the man.

Tall and built like a defensive center, Landon could be an imposing presence. Never mind his squarer-than-square jaw, a twice-broken nose, buzz-cut hair, and heterochromic eyes—one blue, one brown. Even with his tinted contacts to correct the coloring, his look disconcerted a lot of people the first time they met him.

"Could be she simply had a reaction to the medication." The nurse re-hooked tubes to the machines. "Happens."

The doctor nodded.

JB worked to remain objective. What was she seeing? What had happened before he burst into the room? Hallucinations? Delirium? Something had her terrified.

"This is FBI Agent Dwight Landon. He's here to help with the bank case." JB soothingly palmed her cheek and glanced at his previous work associate. "This is Marcy Bradley. My ex-wife."

Landon reached out his hand. "I figured as much. Nice to meet you, Mrs. Bradley."

"Marcy. Just Marcy." Her voice trembled as she pushed herself up further in the bed, moaning with each little move.

She scrunched her legs against herself. Like a frightened child, she eased her hand into JB's. One look said she was seriously afraid. Like victims he'd consoled right after a vicious attack. Terrified. Panicked.

His instincts revved, focusing on Landon. "How did you know this was Marcy's room?"

"The nurse told me."

Dr. Crowley stopped his check of the beeping equipment. "Which one?"

Landon's expression hardened at being questioned. "The male nurse assigned to this room."

The nurse working on Marcy's hand glanced up. "There are no male nurses on this floor. This is my room assignment for the shift."

JB moved closer to the other agent. "Maybe you should explain how you got in here."

Landon stared at the bedrail and didn't flinch. "I know you're upset seeing as how it's your wife."

"Ex-wife." JB countered.

Landon sighed. "Okay, ex-wife. But don't push me, or you'll end up with another write-up in your personnel file."

"Too late. I already quit."

The agent looked up in disbelief. "Now why the hell would you do that?"

"Gentlemen." Dr. Crowley stepped between the two men. "Please take this outside the room."

"First things first," JB said. "What did this male nurse look like?"

"Six-two. Green shirt. Heavy, black-framed glasses, grey hair, mustache. Pushing a cart loaded with books and magazines. Needles and syringes," Landon said.

"That sounds more like a volunteer, except he wouldn't have sharps on his cart. Must have been pens." The nurse worked at getting the bed sheets back in place. "They all wear a pale green shirt."

Landon eased his shoulders. "Look, I got off the elevator, and this guy was standing there at the nurse's counter. I asked where the Bradley room was, and he pointed me in this direction."

"Without checking the room assignments?"

"The man said he'd just left a book in her room. Then he got on the elevator, and I came down here."

"No one brought me a book." Marcy's focus flitted from Landon's face to his hands then to his pocket and up again. "You...you tried to hurt me. Said you'd kill me...enjoy killing me."

"Me?" Landon scowled, picking up a magazine from the rolling tray by the bed. He held it up for everyone to see. "All I did was keep you from getting hurt."

"He was trying to help you, that's all." JB folded his fingers around hers. Her uncontrollable quivering told him she was about to lose control again. Shock couldn't be far behind.

"I know what I'm saying. He tried to rip my IV out." Her voice rose in volume and anxiety. Her fingernails dug into his arm. "Don't leave me alone with him. Please don't."

JB had been around enough people who'd shot up to know that someone skewered by a drug reaction responded like this. They'd swear things had happened one way when surveillance clearly showed another.

"I'm not going anywhere. It's the medicine," JB said. "They've pumped so many meds into you, you didn't know what was happening."

"I did know." She grabbed the doctor's hand. "Why won't anyone believe me?"

JB caught Landon's attention and motioned to the door. "Maybe you should wait for me at the nurses' desk."

"Sure thing." The man walked up beside JB and Marcy. "I hope you feel better soon, Mrs. Bradley."

Her breath accelerated, coming out in escalating pants. "Go away. Please go away."

JB pushed Landon aside with his body. What was wrong

with the guy? Couldn't he see his presence upset her? Working his jaw to control his response, JB tempered his words but used his back-off tone to get the point across. "I said wait at the nurses' station."

The agent raised his head, staring into JB's eyes. Challenged. JB didn't blink. If need be, he could toss Landon across the room again. Bash him through the door. And kick him down the hallway like a soccer forward scoring a goal. He'd rather not but would if the man didn't move of his own accord… and soon.

"Now! Right now." JB pointed to the door. "By the way, when you talk to Leon Ferguson, find out if he saw the shooter. And call Leon's attorney. He needs to be there before you talk to Leon."

"Wilson said he already got the clearance to talk to him." Landon walked out into the hall, closing the door behind him.

Marcy's grip tightened on JB's hand. "Don't leave me alone with him. Please. Please. I know what happened." Her breathing had leveled, but her eyes pleaded with him to believe her. "Who else would it have been?"

He leaned in close, careful not to jar her wound. "Landon's never coming back in this room. I promise. You'll never be alone with him again."

Sadie pushed the door open and stepped inside, followed by Betsy. One look at Marcy's face, and the two of them rushed to her bedside, barging between the doctor and Marcy.

"What's going on?" Sadie questioned.

Doctor Crowley shook his head. "Your daughter needs some rest. Time to heal. We've got to keep her relaxed."

"Those drugs are doing a job on her." JB cringed at the scene he'd witnessed when he walked in the room. Lucky she hadn't hurt herself worse. "You're doing more damage than good right now."

Betsy rubbed her sister's arm as her mama stroked Marcy's forehead.

Sadie looked to JB. "Is she okay?"

Marcy's face flushed. Intensified excitement, imagined or real, meant intensified blood pressure. She pounded the mattress. "No, I'm not okay. Why won't anyone listen to me?"

The doctor ordered the nurse to restart the IV in the other hand.

"I asked if she's okay." Sadie glared at JB.

"She will be." He didn't release his hold on Marcy, easing between her and the nurse.

"Move, so the nurse can put the needle back in." Dr. Crowley scowled, puffing himself up to his full, commanding presence.

Not going to work this time. "What for?" JB asked.

"She needs an IV needle inserted. The staff needs to be able to give her something fast if something like this happens again." Doctor Crowley scribbled on the chart. "IV's the fastest way. In fact, I've ordered a sedative for her as soon as we get the bag going again."

"No sedative." He glanced at Marcy. "Didn't you tell me once that you had a bad reaction to anesthesia when you had your appendix out? That when they gave you a sedative, things just got worse?"

Marcy nodded in return.

He centered his stare on the doctor. "So no sedatives. You can give her the pain medicine orally."

She focused her eyes on the doctor also. "I'll ask if I need anything."

JB pointed at Marcy's mama, her sister, and then himself. "One of us will be in this room all the time. Day and night."

The women nodded. They might not know why, but they knew to follow his lead. Betsy might be mad as hell that he'd come back to Crayton, but even she wouldn't fight him on anything that had to do with protecting her sister.

JB rolled the sleeves of his shirt up to mid-forearm and tugged them into place. "Doc, you need to go take care of the rest of the hospital. We'll take care of Marcy."

• • •

Once his wife calmed down, JB handed her off to Sadie and Betsy. He needed to get out of the room and calm down. Following up with Landon would at least give him something to do besides being surrounded by women who were all on pins and needles with him sitting there.

Many times, he saw families in stressful waiting rooms become uncooperative. This was the first time he found himself in that position. Desperate. Pushy. Defensive. He didn't like the feelings that had raged through his body. Never again would he look at a victim's agitated family member in the same way.

He shook his head. In less than fifteen minutes, he'd blocked the nurse from her job, made the doctor mad, and ordered another FBI agent out of the room.

Way to go, JB. Way to go.

• • •

Marcy had stared at the door ever since JB walked out a few minutes ago. So much for thinking she'd never see him again.

It had taken weeks for the lawyer to track JB down when she'd sent the divorce papers. Then, out of the blue, the papers arrived back, signed. The FBI's only comment had been to say they didn't disclose the whereabouts of their undercover agents. After her attorney had left the papers with her that day, on the promise she'd sign and get them back to him for filing, she'd sat down in JB's chair and bawled herself to sleep.

That had been over a year ago. And she'd been perfectly fine all by herself.

Then last week, when she'd first heard he would be back in town to settle his dad's estate, she'd thought about taking a trip. Why hadn't she followed through on that idea? Gone over to the lake. Booked a room for a couple of days at the fancy-shmancy lakefront hotel. Instead, she'd opted for a highly unlikely chance encounter. Now, look where that had landed her.

Sadie brushed Marcy's hair back from her forehead with a damp cloth. Offered her a cold drink of water. Rubbed lotion on her hands and arms. The tension from her body began to ease.

"Thanks." The motherly attention felt good to her today.

All the while, Betsy had stood looking out the window. Her sister didn't like hospital rooms...too many memories from her time spent in one years ago. Yet here she was being part of what the three women had always been. Strong and always there for each other.

Sadie sat back down in the chair by the bed. "What are you gonna do?"

"Nothing." Marcy shook her head, making the room spin for a moment with her grogginess. "Nothing at all."

"You've got to tell him." Betsy turned and walked to the bedside, leaning over the rail. "As much as I dislike JB, he deserves to know."

Marcy turned away. This couldn't be happening. Her life had been perfect just a little over twenty-four hours ago.

Well, maybe not perfect, but at least it was what she had decided to make of her life. She'd gone her own way. He'd gone his.

If the people who knew her secret—Sadie, Betsy, her uncle Sheriff Davis, and her church deacon, Dr. Crowley—just kept quiet for as long as JB was in town, everything would be fine. With luck and a little time, she could set everything right.

"You understand, don't you, Mama?" She stared into Sadie's eyes.

Her mama sighed, lifting her lips into a weak smile. "I understand you made a choice that's turned into a messy situation. Agreed?"

"Maybe. But, I can fix this." She turned back to her sister. "Just promise me you won't say anything. Promise…please."

Betsy turned and walked back to the window, shaking her head. "Sure. Sure, I'll be quiet. When have I ever been anything but quiet when it comes to what you do with your life?"

Not good enough. Marcy knew her sister too well. "Promise, Betsy."

"I promise."

She gripped her mama's hand tighter. "Now you. Promise?"

"You know me, I hate making promises. Might have to break one."

Chapter Four

JB stopped at the nurses' station. "Has anyone seen the man who was supposed to be waiting for me here?"

"He asked what room Leon Ferguson was in." The unit secretary didn't look up, just pointed down the hall.

"Thanks." From being a Crayton deputy in the past, he knew the location for secured hospital rooms and headed in that direction. No need to ask for a guard on Marcy's rooms. The police would tell him she was just an innocent bystander. That they didn't have the finances or manpower to secure every room in the hospital.

That was okay. He'd secure the room himself.

Nearing Leon's room, he didn't recognize the patrolman stationed outside Leon's door except as the one who tossed him the Kevlar yesterday. Of course, there'd probably been a lot of changes in the past three years.

The cop, Patrolman Kennett from his name badge, stepped in front of him. "May I help you, sir?"

"Has FBI Special Agent Landon been here yet?" JB

flashed his badge, even though he knew he shouldn't, given that he'd resigned.

Kennett was about his own age, early thirties. Same height, lean, and broad-shouldered. Cropped, dark hair with even darker brown eyes. Pressed uniform. Polished shoes. Overall, the man seemed professional in all regards. In fact, JB found it hard to believe he was only a rookie.

The cop stepped aside. "He's been in there about fifteen minutes."

"Did you offer to go in with him?" JB pushed the door open a slight crack.

"Yes, sir. He said that wouldn't be necessary." Kennett raised his eyebrows in question.

He let go of the door and waited until it closed before he locked eyes with the cop again. "Has Leon been assigned a lawyer?"

"Yes, sir. Said he waived his rights for this conversation." Kennett leaned in close enough to garner attention to his statement. "Said he was among friends. Then he motioned Agent Landon over to his bed."

Evidently, Leon thought this was some kind of game. JB remembered him being smarter than that. Of course, the man had walked into a bank the minute it opened and pulled a gun. Not smart. Then again, he'd always been a schemer, but what could he possibly be angling for at this stage?

JB planned to stay out of any interaction with Leon. Since, to hear Wilson and Landon talk, he was already too biased to be anywhere near this case. "What friends?"

"Beats me," Kennett said.

JB sighed and cricked his neck. On one hand, he was glad to see Leon talking to the FBI without an attorney regulating the conversation. On the other, something didn't set right with the idea that legal representation wasn't present. "Maybe I'll hang around. See if Leon changes his mind about the attorney."

"You won't have long to wait." Kennett nodded down the hall. "The court-appointed attorney just stepped off the elevator."

The lawyer marched up to the two men, a scowl cemented to his face. "I'm Garrett Watlow. Leon Ferguson is my client."

JB held out his hand, flashing his shield in the other. "I'm Jean Bradley. My friends call me JB."

"I'm not your friend, Mr. Bradley." The attorney ignored the offer of civility. "What were you doing questioning my client without my permission?"

Kennett opened his mouth as if to defend him, but JB held up his hand then looped his thumbs in his front pockets. Non-confrontational.

"Well, Garrett, you were my friend in high school." He leaned back against the wall. "You better get your facts straight before you blow steam in my direction." He nodded at the cop.

"JB hasn't talked to Leon." Kennett said. "Special Agent Landon is in there."

Garrett didn't offer an apology. Instead, he barged through his client's door. "Don't say another word, Leon."

Landon swung around. Surprise shot across his features, and trepidation coated his expression.

JB watched from the doorway.

Leon's expression went from carefree to anxious. "What are you doing here, Watlow? I didn't call you."

The attorney ignored his client and faced Landon. "Get out of here now. I'll be lodging a complaint with the Sheriff's Department and your superior, too."

Landon glared at him as if he were a gnat to be swatted

away.

No fear etched Watlow's face, either. "If I find out you've compromised this case then I'll have you before the judge by this time tomorrow. You'll be one case less than you started the day."

Leon smiled. "Me and Mr. Landon were just having us a friendly conversation. Isn't that right?"

Landon's shoulder twitched as he swallowed. "That's right. My boss said he spoke with Leon, and no attorney had been requested."

"That right?" Watlow zeroed in on his client.

Leon fidgeted with the sheet, looking every place but at his attorney. "I don't rightly remember."

JB catalogued every move, tone, and expression in the room. What was he missing? "Get out of there, Landon. Are you trying to blow the case?"

The agent balked and shot Leon a hard look, nodding even harder.

"Come on, Landon." JB braced his arm against the doorframe to keep from charging into the room and extracting the agent. "Now."

Landon stormed out of the room. "Don't push me, JB. You quit, remember? So you don't get to tell me how to do my job."

Leon's laughter echoed from the room. There was something strange about this whole scenario.

Garrett Watlow walked across to the door and extended his hand to JB. "Sorry about before. Good to see you again."

No need to shun the apology. Might have done the same himself in Garrett's place. He shook the man's hand. "Good to see you, too."

"Aw, now isn't that sweet." Leon lazed against the back of the bed as if he didn't have a care in the world. "My attorney and an FBI agent... No, make that the ex-husband of my hostage and my attorney standing in my room, making nice and polite."

JB turned toward the hallway.

"Hey, how's Marcy doing?" Leon cackled.

JB stood stone-still.

"Let me know if there's anything she needs. I can always make a quick trip down the hall." Leon made kissy sounds. Laughed. "Anything at all."

JB flexed his fist, then eased his fingers and walked away.

...

A couple days and a whole lot of coffee later, JB leaned back against the hospital wall and waited patiently...kind of. Marcy'd been a regular bad, high-maintenance, impatient patient. Insisting she could do everything when she couldn't. Then double insisting she'd go home today. Even Sadie had noted her daughter had always been a quick healer.

His trips away from the hospital had been few. Mostly for a quick shave and shower his friends at the Crayton Police had offered, plus dropping in at the local department store for a change of clothes. At this point, he wanted a long, hot shower and a good night's sleep. Was that too much to ask?

The past few days had been stressful. The past few months, horrendous. And the past few years, one never-ending series of tense negotiations with his judgment, his ego, and his stubbornness. Never mind on-the-job parlays, real or in-character.

As soon as Dr. Crowley would allow, JB would tend to Marcy at home. He didn't want her in this hospital any longer than need be, even if it meant putting up with Marcy's sass as she stormed around the house. And, no doubt about it, she would storm around the house.

Not being able to do what she wanted for a few days would accelerate her agitation. Him being there would launch her sky-high. She liked being in control. Everything within her sight would be fair game for cleaning or change—dust bunnies, cobwebs, smears on the windows, out-of-date food in the refrigerator, clothes that fit, clothes that didn't fit, the heat, the a/c, curtains open, curtains closed. Nothing would be safe from her scrutiny…including him.

Dr. Crowley finished his examination then signed the release papers. "I'm only letting you go home because JB's there in case you need anything."

...

Marcy shot up in bed. "JB's where?"

Oh, no, no, no, no, no. He was not going home with her. She'd go sleep on the street before she'd face the possibility of what he might find at the house.

"At our house." JB cricked his neck from side to side. "Seems the paperwork isn't right to finish up my dad's estate, so I'll be in town a few more days."

She tucked her hair behind her ears as she slid gingerly to a standing position. Effects from the medications still lingered. A few rapid blinks of her eyelids focused her vision enough that she could point at him. "Who said you could stay at my house?"

"Our house."

Wincing from the fact she'd raised her arm with the stitches, she lowered it just as fast. Next time, she'd be more careful. Our house? What did he mean…our house? She lightly shook her head to clear the fog clouding her thoughts as the air between them hung heavy in the room. Was it just her that felt the weight of this so-called outcome? Because this situation had never entered her mind when she decided to keep certain things a secret.

"I told him he could stay there. Now if you have a problem with the arrangement, then the three of us can discuss other options." Sadie shot her daughter a warning look. "That is, once everyone is on the same page about you and JB's relationship."

"What does that mean?" Marcy asked.

"Nothing." Her mama smiled all sweet and nice…almost sugary. Sadie was not the sugary type.

From the corner of her eye, Marcy saw the furrowing of JB's brow. He'd picked up on the wording. Wouldn't take him long to start asking questions. Then all heck would break loose.

"I don't know what you're talking about." She needed to cover her mother's insinuation there was anything out of the way going on in Marcy's life.

"Really?" Sadie lowered her voice and continued, "Then you don't mind if we talk about those divorce papers and how they never…"

Marcy took a couple steps toward her mama, weaved, and then braced against the side of the hospital bed. "You wouldn't."

Sadie cocked her head and raised her eyebrows. "Wouldn't I?"

She could tell JB had tilted his head, trying to hear their quiet conversation.

"There's no other place for me to stay around here." JB appeared as if he didn't have a care in the world. "I hoped you'd help me out. Let me stay. For old times' sake?"

"There are at least five hotels in the area," Marcy

reminded him.

She watched his expression tighten with the narrowing of his eyes, the lift of his chin, the squaring of his shoulders.

"You don't need to remind me of hotels." His too calm and quiet tone emphasized the moment. "But may I remind you that my name is still on the property. And I plan to stay in my house while I'm in town."

She'd forgot about his one demand in the divorce decree. That his name would stay on the deed to their home. She hadn't fought him since that was the only thing he asked for. Besides, from the moment they walked into the house years ago, she'd known how important having a place to call home meant to him. All well and good, but, she hadn't expected him to ever be back in the house…with her…not even on a temporary basis. This could be a problem.

"I could stay with my mama." She looked at Dr. Crowley, hoping for agreement. None there.

"I'm busy. My house is too small. May be going on a trip." Sadie walked over to the window. "Might even paint the living room. Strip the woodwork. Or something."

"I get the idea, mama. You think I should go home."

Sadie turned to her daughter, grinning a genuine Sadie-smile. "I think you should go home. Let JB take care of you for a few days."

Marcy grabbed the release form from the doctor and signed. "Okay. I'm going home." She pointed at JB. "You can stay. A little while."

He nodded. "Whatever you say, sugar."

The nurse entered, followed by a volunteer pushing a wheelchair.

"No. No wheelchair." Marcy took a step toward the door and teetered.

JB swooped her up in his arms and deposited her in the

wheelchair.

She sighed heavy. Tired. Defeated. Ready to go home. "Thanks."

He flicked the foot rests down and stepped behind the handles as she raised her feet into place. What was that about one step starting the rest of your life? Not today. Their life together was over. This was nothing more than a momentary inconvenience that she could handle. After all, she'd sent the divorce papers. He'd signed them. This was nothing.

She bit the inside corner of her mouth. Nothing…except for that one little problem she hadn't told him about.

Sadie held the door open as he pushed the wheelchair into the hallway. "See you later."

"Bye, mama." She folded her hands nice and neat in her lap as she slumped back in the chair.

"Get ready for the ride of your life." He walked faster, pushing a smooth, slow curve from side to side. Not enough to give her pain, but enough to give her spice. That's what he used to call doing anything just outside the line of propriety.

Marcy grabbed one arm rest, then the other. "JB what are you doing?"

"Are you in pain?"

"No."

"Then hold on and enjoy the ride." The wheels on the chair spun faster when he broadened his stride, increasing the pace.

Volunteers hugged the wall. Dr. Crowley stepped back into a room. The janitor buffing the floor spun in a circle with his machine. The automatic doors slid open a second before he careened through them and onto the sidewalk in front of the hospital. He stopped at the edge of the curb, right next to his truck, and flipped the wheelchair brakes in place.

"You're crazy, JB Bradley." She looked up at him with feistiness. "Down right crazy."

"Learned everything I know from you, sugar." He rested his hand on her shoulder.

"Stop calling me sugar." She jerked around and stabbed him with her back-off stare.

He backed off. Grinned.

That had probably been a mistake. Now he'd do it just to spite her. She might as well face the fact she'd screwed up on a lot of levels. But all she had to do right now was make it through the next few days. Keep her mouth shut, and stay away from anyone in town who knew her secret. Because if JB found out, he'd be livid.

She sucked in her breath and eased out of the wheelchair. How was she ever going to spend even one night alone in that house with him without slipping up?

Chapter Five

After the days spent recuperating in the hospital and at home, Marcy's insides still felt jumbled from the surgery. Plus the incision hurt more than she wanted to admit, even though she'd always been a quick healer. Really, she'd have been fine at home by herself, but JB had insisted she might need help. The doctor agreed. Her mother agreed. And even her sister agreed.

Four against one, she hadn't stood a chance of being alone, but she'd laid out her ground rules the moment the two of them walked in the house. JB had his room. She had hers. Yes, he could cook meals for her. Yes, he could do the laundry. Yes, he could pick up her medicine and groceries and even help her straighten her clothes. But helping her bathe or tucking her in bed at night was off-limits.

He'd agreed. Hadn't stopped him from looking sexy as hell in a tight, black, muscle T-shirt as he brought her a bowl of soup. Nothing unusual, just what he used to wear. Then her senses had perked up real fast to his clean, male scent every morning. And the thought of him in the shower had stripped her composure to its limit.

But her tipping point had been yesterday afternoon as she'd watched him clean her car. Damn. She'd never realized how many positions a person had to use to reach all that pesky dirt. Of course, he'd caught her looking, grinned, then turned around and ignored her as he finished the car. She knew, because she hadn't been able to tear herself away from the window.

This had to end before she ripped her clothes off and said "take me now." Or before she made a slip up and confessed everything she'd made her sister promise not to reveal. Which would be worse, she wasn't sure. Of course, not once had he looked at her like a man even the least bit interested in taking up where they left off. Good. She wasn't, either. She wanted him out of Crayton for good.

Evidently, her talk with him last night had finally convinced him that cabin fever was setting in, and she needed to get out before her pleasant attitude got the better of her. He'd laughed. Said he'd think on it. This morning, he'd relented, and now here they were parked in front of her counseling office.

She winced as JB lifted her down from his truck. Even the mere feel of his hands around her waist made her core quiver with what-ifs. Anticipation. No...no need for anticipation. What-ifs weren't going to happen...not now... not ever again. She had her own life now, and as soon as she got everything straightened out, she might just take up the dinner offer from the high school math teacher in the next town over. He'd been asking her out for the past six months, and truth be told, he wasn't half bad—for someone who didn't like fishing, hunting, or anything that involved being in the sun.

"I can't believe I let you talk me into bringing you to your office." JB placed her on her feet like a fragile piece of crystal. "You get one hour. No more. Then I'm taking you home where you still ought to be."

"Two."

His expression said he wasn't happy, but he'd give her two hours.

After allowing him to open the front door and carry her briefcase, she brushed past him, knowing full well he could have given her more space in the doorway. The room smelled musty, felt close, and for an instant, she realized this outing might not have been the best idea. But she'd e-mailed her clients to let them know they could reach her at the office today. So, like it or not, she'd stay.

He wandered from the front room to her consultation area to a small private office in the rear. He looked in the direction of the turquoise sofa and quirked the side of his mouth. "See you've still got that same squeaky make-out spot."

She didn't favor him with a reply, but a bitterly cold Valentine's Day with the two of them making enough heat on that sofa to start a fire flooded her memory. That had been the first of many afternoon memories. She felt herself smile, then flattened it out. "Are you satisfied there's no one here? I'm not a child, you know. You seem to forget I took care of myself for the past few years."

His jaw worked into the same clench he used to block his feelings every time something inched close to the truth. Turning toward the front door, he inspected each closet along the way. "Two hours at the most. I'll check back sooner. You got your phone turned on?"

She patted her hip pocket and nodded, then shoved him toward the door.

"Lock up behind me," he said.

"I still don't know why you think someone was shooting at me. Leon's the one with a million enemies, not me." Doing what he said was not going to happen. She needed to make a point and make it now, that she was her own woman. "My office is open for as long as I stay."

"Don't argue with me on this. Besides, I'll be out of your hair soon, so humor me on this while I'm here." As he stepped outside, he motioned to the button he'd drilled into the brick the first day she'd opened her business five years ago. "They can use the buzzer."

That had been a day filled with dreams for their future. Seemed like a long time ago. Even longer, the two of them had been Crayton's high school sweethearts. The state football star and the cheerleader. After graduation, they'd been Crayton's dream couple. They lived together through college before inviting half the town to their wedding.

Later on, the town had watched them flounder. By then, he was a Crayton deputy, and she the county's only marriage counselor, but he wanted to join the FBI. Knowing he'd never leave of his own accord or follow his dream without her, she'd shoved him out the door with more than a few unkind words.

All because she had freaked out every time he got the least bit hurt. And then, when he'd ended up shot, her resolve had broken. He'd healed fast. Walked it off like the wound was nothing more than a scratch from falling off a bike. Put on the badge and gun and headed back to work in less than a week. She'd been the one who needed longer to heal.

The memory of her father being killed in the line of duty with the FBI had stepped in front of her like a roadblock before a blast zone. She had refused to face the possibility of living through the same pain she'd seen her mother experience the day she opened the door to the news. She and her sister had stood beside their mom at the grave, walked beside her into an empty house, and moved back to Sadie's hometown of Crayton.

But, that hadn't been the worst part. That came as Marcy lay in bed at night listening to her mother cry after she thought everyone was asleep. One night, she'd edged to the corner of the living room doorway and seen her mother curled up in the seat of her dad's chair. Looking just like a baby being held and rocked by a loved one. She'd been quietly sobbing with her cheek pressed against the back of the seat. Marcy'd run from the scene. Hidden under her covers to silence the emotion she'd witnessed.

Looking back, JB's chair had been her own breaking point. He'd left for an undercover assignment, and she'd panicked. Curled up in his chair, sobbing because he wasn't there and she was afraid for him and she was…afraid for herself. Emotions were too hard to handle, so she'd shut them out. Steeled herself to the fact she could never allow herself to go through what her mother had gone through.

Sure, eventually her mama had married Truman, a real estate investor. He might be away on business trips a month or so at a time, but otherwise, they all lived a normal life in Crayton. He called her and Betsy "his girls." Made life safe for them. Made Sadie happy.

But, in her thinking, a good counselor knew her own limits. She was a good counselor. And painful emotion was her limit. Her own self-evaluation told her she'd never be able to move forward if something happened to JB. Better to have kicked him out and known he was alive than chance loving him and then losing him forever. That was too scary. Too outside her box to even consider.

He pecked on the glass in the outside door. "Hey. Stop

your daydreaming. What are you thinking about?"

"How damn annoying you can be." She tilted her head, smiled sugar-sweet, and tapped in return.

His expression conveyed he wasn't amused.

Eyes half-lidded, he lifted his chin. Sometimes she really liked that look, used to know where the rest of the evening was headed. Other times, the expression meant he was set in his ways, and nothing or no one would change his mind. That was this time. He didn't smile, just motioned to flip the deadbolt. Evidently, he wouldn't leave until she complied. Fine. The minute he drove away, she'd undo the lock.

She flipped the handle then rolled her eyes at him. "Satisfied?"

"For the moment." The corners of his mouth edged up a bit as he shifted from one foot to the other. For an instant, she thought he'd ask her to reopen the door. Come back in and…what?

His gaze swept over her, slowing at spots on her body that used to drive him crazy. Her insides quavered as her fingers inched toward the lock. It would be so easy to open the door. To fall against the man she craved and drag him to the sofa…if they made it that far. There'd never been any man in her bed but JB. And he knew every little touch that made her happy. She knew his, too.

"Maybe I should hang around." His eyes held a question.

"No!" She shook her head. The sooner she got him out of there, the less likelihood she would make a fool of herself. She pointed at his truck. "Go."

"Okay." He eased away from the door. "I'll be back. You've got my number if you need me."

The FBI seemed to have instilled a no-nonsense attitude in him. A new intensity filtered through his shoulders, into his eyes at times. Or he used a tone that stopped refusals most times. Not with her, but with others. What else had he learned? Done? Had there been other women? After all, he'd signed the divorce papers. Maybe he'd even— No. She wouldn't let her imagination go there.

"Please leave so I can get to work," she said.

Grudgingly, he walked to his truck and drove off.

She smiled at the retreating vehicle as she unlocked the door again. Halfway down the hall to her office, the phone rang. Once. She checked the caller ID. Nothing. Five minutes later, the phone rang again.

"Hello. Marcy Bradley's office."

No one answered.

"Look, I've got more to do than play answer the phone today, so stop calling."

Heart racing, she felt gripped by a cold nausea as she hung up. She flattened her back to the wall, palms plastered against the paint. Panicked, she glanced up and down the hallway again and again and again. There'd never been a time she hadn't felt safe in her office. This was just anxiety raising its ugly head because of the robbery and everything else the past few days. She walked back to the front door and reset the deadbolt, then stumbled to the bathroom and splashed water on her face.

JB was right. People could ring the damn bell today.

Forty-five minutes passed, and the only call had been from her secretary wanting to know if she should come into the office. Marcy declined her offer. She phoned Cross's Tattoo Parlor next door to let them know she was in the office, see how they were doing. The answering machine picked up with a message saying the shop was closed for a week of vacation.

Once the mail arrived, she reviewed the monthly bank statements. Not good. Neither was the line-up for future appointments. Her shoulders slumped. No matter how much she cared for her clients, her marriage counseling business wasn't working. Before she and JB split up, her client list paid the bills and grew their savings. Now, she barely paid her office and personal bills each month. Guess people trying to hold their marriage together didn't put much confidence in a counselor who couldn't do the same for her own.

The phone rang, causing her to jump. JB's cell number showed up on the caller ID display. A glance at the clock showed 10:33. He'd given her one hour and five minutes before he called.

She wouldn't give him the satisfaction of knowing she had his number programmed into her office landline phone. "Hello. Marcy Bradley's office. May I help you?"

"Hey." JB's words came through the same way he always started their calls. "You doing okay?"

"Of course." Why couldn't she admit she felt less than okay? Felt like a failure. Felt like she'd lost control of her world in that bank lobby and couldn't find her new center. "Of course, I'm okay. Why wouldn't I be?"

"Doesn't sound like it. What's wrong?"

"I'm tired, that's all. Don't worry. I can take care of myself." She doodled a tree on her notepad. A heart. Damn. She scribbled through the heart hard and fast. Control, she needed to stay in control of her emotions.

"Yes, you can take care of yourself. Yes, you have taken care of yourself. And, yes, I've been a…a…" His heavy sigh growled with release. "Well, I'm here now, so let me help you."

She could refuse, but he sounded genuine. In fact, that was the closest she'd ever heard him come to saying he was sorry about anything. Except in the letter where he mentioned not being good enough for her. Of course, he was good enough for her...for anybody. That wasn't the problem.

Might as well let him come pick her up. Being out of the house and in her office hadn't made her feel any better. Nothing would make her feel better until he left town. "Maybe you're right. I'm ready to go home whenever you get here."

"I'm just a few minutes away. Wait inside, and I'll load the boxes you wanted to take home."

"Ring the buzzer when you get here."

Call ended, she shoved her paperwork in the briefcase before heading to the reception area. She'd work from home tomorrow, give herself a few more days to get her strength back. Her forehead felt warm against the palm of her hand. Hair a little damp across the hairline. Guess she should have turned the air conditioning on.

She figured she'd have just enough time for a cold root beer from Pete's Soda Fountain and Deli across the street before JB arrived. Stepping outside, the autumn breeze wafted through the leaves of gold and red and caressed her cheeks. Fall had turned out beautiful this year. Of course, cold weather would drop in without warning soon enough.

Entering the deli, she waved to the proprietor, old papa Pete Patrellie. He and his family were a town staple. From halfway across the store, the soda fountain beckoned to the sound of oldies music. She liked having her office in this area of town. The tattoo parlor, bakery, flower shop, Pete's, and her own office made up a tight little market district.

"What can I do for you today, Ms. Bradley?"

"Two large root beers to go." Much as she hated to do anything nice to encourage JB to stick around, she couldn't imagine getting herself a drink and ignoring him.

"Drinking heavy, are you?" The fizz of the foam as it filled the cup sounded the same now as it had when she was ten years old. She loved this shop not only for its nostalgic red, white, and black counter and stools but for Pete himself.

"Nope." She smiled and laid a five on the counter. "Guess you heard JB's in town for a while."

Noncommittal, Pete nodded.

"Well, he's been acting like a mother hen the past few days. Today he's chauffeuring me around."

Pete tightened the lids on the cups and poked the striped bendy-straws in the tops. "Seems like yesterday the two of you would come in after high school. Just like clockwork, you'd go sit at the last booth in the back of the store and huddle over one root beer float for the two of you. You ever think about those days? Laughing as your foreheads bumped and—"

A roar like two jet planes crashing into each other rattled the air. The building shook. Pete's front window shattered. Bits of glass prickled her skin. She reactively flung her arm across her face and turned away. She turned back as the rain of glass pinged onto the floor. Fluorescent orange and red flames roared into the sky from the rubble of what used to be her office. Used to be the adjoining tattoo parlor.

Pete edged up from behind the wooden counter, holding his arm where an ominous chunk of wood lodged. His wife ran from the back room to help her husband.

"You okay, Marcy?" he shouted.

She nodded, picked up the two empty cups of root beer from the floor, and shivered. Shivered again harder. Her face grew clammy. The cups fell from her hands. Numb and on auto-pilot, she stumbled toward the scene. Toward what used to be her front door.

JB's truck did a 180 as it screeched to a stop, and he bolted for the shifting mass of destruction. The sight of him running straight toward the dust-settling pile of rubble shook her back to the moment.

"Marcy! Where are you?" He raced across the debris as if he didn't see or hear or feel the heat while he side-stepped the spot fires. "Marcy? Marcy!"

"Nooooo, JB!" She charged after him across the shattered bricks, the shards of glass, the chunks of asphalt and concrete littering the street. "Stop. I'm here. I'm here!"

He disappeared in to the section of her office that was still standing. A moment later, a second blast rocked her world.

Chapter Six

JB barreled toward the flames. "Marcy!"

His lungs filled with the acrid smoke, choking his senses. Heat crushed his movements and singed the hair on his arms. And the few angry, lingering flames beckoned him to test his strength. Resolve pressed him forward.

Find her. Find her. Don't stop, find her.

A secondary explosion blew on the far side of the building. He flattened to the ground, covering his head with his arms. A rain of fragments dropped down. A couple of larger chunks found him as a target. No chance. There was no chance Marcy might have survived the second bomb.

His heart broke. His agonizing shouts mixed with the hiss and crackle of the settling debris. He stumbled to retrace his steps.

Sirens screamed closer. Blue sky merged with murky heat waves. Burning coughs racked his lungs. He collapsed to his knees in the debris. Marcy was gone. Enfolding his head with his arms, he rocked back and forth.

Make this a dream. A nightmare. Please, dear God, make this a dream.

Soft hands grabbed his and pulled. Stronger hands lifted his feet, others supported his middle. Voices merged in the background for a stretcher and medic. And someone pounded the smoldering material on his legs as he was placed on the cart. Within seconds, the stretcher jerked as the paramedics slid it into the ambulance, then placed a plastic mask over his mouth and nose.

Oxygen.

"No! Leave me alone." He shoved the lifesaving air aside again and again while his lungs fought to suck deep, racking breaths. Exhausted, he pushed against the fingers stroking his forehead. "Leave me alone."

"It's Marcy. JB listen to me."

Softness against his cheek.

"I'm okay. Look at me, I'm okay."

He pushed the mask aside. Marcy?

A kiss, then another, then another. His tongue licked the salty wetness that caressed his lips. The fog of his mind craved the feelings flooding through the break. He'd do anything if she were alive. Quit law enforcement. Move back to Crayton. Anything. Even leave her alone if that's what she wanted.

"Look at me, JB. I'm okay." Her voice cracked as the hand holding his trembled.

Sucking in the clean air, he fought to open his eyes. "Marcy?"

She nodded, curling her fingers through his hair. Tears flooded across her soot-covered face, joining his as she burrowed her cheek against his.

"I thought I'd lost you." He pulled her against his chest as the ambulance doors closed behind them.

Her fingers gripped his shirt. "Me, too."

He kissed her hair. Her forehead. His lips skimmed hers as he thumbed away the soot from her cheek. "I thought I'd lost you."

...

JB's few hours in the trauma unit pushed him to his exasperation limit. Talking to Marcy had tested his last iota of composure. "Yes, I heard what you've been saying for the past five minutes. Can we get past this?"

"Not until you tell me what I said," she stated.

Ultimatum? She thought she'd issue an ultimatum to him. Hell. Even stone-cold killers had balked at issuing him ultimatums. He was only one turn of a key in his truck's ignition away from leaving Crayton far behind for good. "Let it go, Marcy. I agreed with you, so let it go."

She took a step in his direction. "So what did I say?"

Marcy seeing him in the hospital's so-called gown didn't sit right with him. Made him appear weak. Wrong, if that's what she thought.

"You basically said you still can't stand to be in the same room with me. That you had a moment of weakness when you thought I was gonna die, and that I shouldn't get any ideas you meant anything you said or did out there." He fought to control his tone.

"And?" Hands on her hips, she pushed to get her answer.

"Listen lady, I'm not going to stand here and repeat everything you said. Just know that line of thought goes two ways. This is just another case to me. And you are just another victim to protect." He gritted his teeth and glared in her direction. "Now, where are my clothes?"

Dressed in a set of blue scrubs the staff had given her

after she'd cleaned up, Marcy eased into the chair by the window and leafed through the same magazine she'd been looking at for the past hour. "They smelled to high heaven. Betsy's taking Mama to the house to pick up clean ones for you."

"Sadie had better be back soon, or I'm leaving this place the way I am." JB kicked the sheet off the bed, tugging the gown's hem down to mid-thigh. "Do you think there's a law against walking out of a hospital wearing nothing but one of these?"

"I wouldn't know." She tossed the magazine in the chair next to her. "You're the big, fancy FBI agent around here."

"Ex-FBI agent."

"That may be, but you'll always be a lawman. Just like I'll always be a counselor. We don't know how to do anything else." She sighed. "Besides, you're damn good at what you do. The world needs people like you who risk their own lives to save the rest of us."

JB needed to solidify his position. Make sure she didn't get any ideas about him being her own personal hero of the moment. "I'm trained to protect people, among other things. It just happened to be you this time. Next time might be somebody heading into witness protection. All the same to me."

Dr. Crowley walked in, carrying a file. "JB, the trauma unit says you're tied for first place as the worst patient they've encountered in the past ten years."

"What's the prognosis? When can I get out of here?" Showered, shaved, and shampooed, JB still had the smell of soot and grime permeating his senses. Brought back memories of a drug bust explosion last year where the factory blew up right as they entered. Took forever to feel clean again.

"If you pipe down and let me recheck your wounds, I might let you leave." The doctor poked and prodded, pressed on JB's ribs, hips, chest, and back. "Got any blurred vision?"

"Nope."

"Headache?"

"Nope."

"Ringing in your ears?"

"Nope."

Doc looked at his paperwork again, then found the right spot to retest with his fingers, hard and to the point. Raw hellfire and brimstone cranked into JB's lower back, shooting up his spine.

"Any pain?" Doc asked.

JB's brow furrowed, along with the powerful clench of his teeth. "Nope."

"Would you tell me if you did?" The elderly doctor released his pressure point.

"Nope."

Doc glanced in Marcy's direction. "He still staying at the house?"

She nodded.

"I'm concerned about a possible concussion, but I'll sign the release since she's there to keep an eye on you tonight." Doc sighed, flipping the chart closed, then he turned to JB. "And, don't you think for one minute I believed your denial about pain in your back."

"Wait one minute." She sprang to her feet, hands propped on her hips. "You forget. I'm not responsible for him anymore."

The doc raised his eyebrows and lowered his gaze on her. "Is that so?"

She bit her lip and nodded. "That's so."

"Marcy Marie Bradley, did you forget I'm the deacon in

your church? Birthed both of you. Know most everything goes on in Crayton. And I'm not past divulging non-medical information when push comes to shove."

"Oh, all right." She sat in the chair again and picked up the magazine, thumbing nonchalantly through the pages. "I'll call the ambulance if he incapacitates himself during the night. But I'm not waiting on him hand and foot. He can make his own breakfast, scrub his own back, and take care of any other bodily needs by himself."

Took great restrain on JB's part not to burst out laughing as doc's face reddened. The old guy shook his head and stomped from the room, muttering something about "respect for a religious man."

"Now where are my clothes?" JB rolled to a sitting position and dangled his legs down the side of the bed. His body hurt more than he planned to admit to anyone else. The spot doc pressed might bear watching.

A tap on the door caught their attention, and Marcy stood.

"Here's a shirt, jeans, and a pair of socks," Sadie said through the opening, pushing her arm into the room with the clothes. "Forgot the underwear."

"Commando's fine with me." JB offered.

Marcy shot him a can't-believe-you-said-that-to-my-mama look before she took the stack from her mother. "Thanks."

"You need anything else?"

"No, we're ready to head home. I really appreciate you doing this."

The red-haired woman reached through and gave Marcy a hug. "I'm glad you're both okay."

"Me, too."

"Thanks, Sadie," JB said.

The door closed with her goodbye before Marcy brought the clothes over to the bed, laying them next to him. When he stood, the world shifted for a moment, and he steadied his leg against the mattress then ripped the hospital gown off.

She grabbed his arm, flicked her glance in a quick once over of his body, then dropped her hold. "You sure you're okay to go home?"

Their looks met for a long, steady moment. The heat from her hand on his arm had touched more than his skin. From the flush of her cheeks, she'd felt it, too. She turned away, and he pivoted toward the bed.

"I've been hurt a lot worse than this. Get your stuff together, so we can get out of here." Glancing over his shoulder, he grinned as she walked to her chair. "And, don't worry, sugar, I can take care of my bodily—"

Damn, he'd done it again. Called her sugar. He needed to stop, even if he did like to see her fume every time he said the word.

The door banged open, and in barged Betsy.

"Do you ever knock?" Marcy asked.

If he thought turning around would get her sister out of the room sooner, he would. Instead, he stayed facing the bed then looked back over his shoulder.

Betsy let her gaze rest right where it landed. "Looking mighty good from the backside, JB."

Too late, Marcy dashed to block her sister's view.

"Glad I got your approval." Naked and cold and still a little wobbly on his feet, he didn't move.

Betsy cleared her throat. "I wanted to make sure you both were okay."

"We're fine. Is there anything else we can do for you?" JB squared his shoulders. "If not, then you may want to leave, because I'm gonna turn around in about three seconds."

Marcy spun to face him, her look one of jealous indignation. "You wouldn't dare."

JB grinned. "One. Two."

Betsy turned and walked out the door while Marcy followed her, blocking any chance of reentry.

"You sure everything's okay?" Betsy asked through the barely open doorway.

"Everything's good." Marcy pushed the door closed inch by inch. "Thanks for taking mama to get the clothes. I'll see you tomorrow."

The door finally met the doorframe, but a second later, it reopened a couple inches. Better not be someone with a wheelchair.

"Marcy?"

"Yes, Betsy."

"Be sure you keep an eye on those ugly bruises on JB's side and back. They don't look good, if you ask me."

He glanced in Marcy's direction as she walked back in the room. Buttoning and zipping the jeans in place, he could feel the weight of her stare. He quickly dragged the black T-shirt over his head. Winced as he stretched his arms into the sleeves. Damn that hurt.

As he eased the shirt down his body, his wife's gaze lingered on his chest. He figured she saw the bruises. Maybe even the still red and puckered scars from his last case. He didn't plan on talking about those any time soon. He shuffled into his boots and laced them up. The faster he got himself and Marcy out of there, the less likely she'd ask questions.

"You ready?" His fingers brushed a strand of hair behind her ear when he stepped in front of her.

Her lips parted. Her eyes focused on his for a moment before they lowered to his shirt again.

"Don't worry. It's nothing. A couple of bricks hit me in that second blast." He turned her to the door.

"What about the other—"

"Not now, Marcy. We'll talk later."

She let him steer her as she stared straight ahead. At one point, she swiped away a couple of tears that had the nerve to roll down her cheek. She'd always said women who cried were weak. Not always. He'd learned that emotions can do strange things to a body's reactions. Tears were just one of many coping mechanisms.

Sometimes against pain. Sadness. Joy. Or, being glad for another breath, hour, or day. Being tortured made you realize what you had to be thankful for. Surviving made it even more apparent.

His grip tightened beneath her elbow as he guided the two of them out the door. "Let's go home."

Eyes unfocused on the empty air between them, she nodded.

The vicious, puckered scars across his chest would need to be explained. Along with the brand. Not today, though. And not unless he felt she could handle what he had to tell.

Chapter Seven

Hours later, JB stormed into the Crayton Police Department's new two-story brick building. He'd spent the last hour arguing with Marcy about whether he should stay home and rest or go rattle the police to see what the hell they'd found out on the bombing. Finally, he agreed to make the meeting short and eat a bowl of minestrone soup when he got home. Evidently, she'd added being nearly blown to smithereens as something cured by her famous minestrone, right along with broken legs, gunshot wounds, and the common cold.

No one better try to convince him the explosion had been caused by the water heater blowing up or a gas main rupture. No doubt that's what the evidence would show. He'd bet money against it. Whoever was behind what was going on in town had crossed the line when they'd involved his ex-wife.

"Where's Deputy Evans?" he asked the grey-haired sergeant behind the front desk.

"He and that FBI friend of yours are over at what remains of your…uh…" Awkwardness didn't begin to describe the expression on the sergeant's face as he cleared his throat. "At what's left of the tattoo parlor and counseling office."

JB thanked the man and bolted to his truck. He should have gone by there first, and he would have if his head didn't hurt so damn bad he couldn't think straight. And the nausea rumbling through his stomach didn't speak well of the night to come.

A couple minutes later, he parked his truck parallel to the police tape stretched across the street a block away from the scene. Deputy Evans and Special Agent Landon were deep in conversation a few feet away from the broken down building that used to be Marcy's office.

Deputy Evans held out his hand as JB approached. "Glad you're okay."

The cop's grip felt firm and genuine.

"What are you doing here, deputy?" JB scanned the area for markers.

"Watching the arson and bomb people do their job. The sheriff will want a full report not just on what they find, but one from me on how they performed."

Sounded like something Sheriff Davis would insist on. The man always dug deep and then even deeper once he was involved in a case. Plus, being the uncle of one of the victims meant he was involved on an entirely different level.

Landon walked into the conversation. "Good to see you're still walking around. Shouldn't you be home resting?"

JB shot him a glance. "Still hanging around I see."

"I figure since I'm here on the bank robbery, I might as well see if I can lend a hand on this case."

Might be the appropriate thing to do, but JB wasn't

convinced Landon was being entirely truthful. "Maybe you should let the Crayton Police Department take care of their business. They know when and who to call in for cases involving experts they don't have on the force. Isn't that right, Deputy Evans?"

"Right." Evans agreed as Kennett stared into the air.

Just thought I might be of help." Landon walked into JB's space. "What are you doing here anyhow?"

JB might have felt like his head might explode, but his ex-partner provided all the incentive he needed to stay in the moment. "I plan to see who bombed the building where Marcy has...had her office. If that means sticking my nose into the investigation, then so be it."

Landon poked his finger in JB's direction. "You're too damn personally involved to think with anything but your—"

"You might want to stop before you finish that sentence." JB's hand fisted as he stepped within an inch of the loudmouth. "Otherwise, I'm gonna plant you in the ground."

Kennett, the rookie, eased to the side of the combatants.

Deputy Evans cleared his throat. "It's been a long day, men. Maybe we should take a step back and wait for the experts' conclusion."

"All I'm saying is you're making a lot out of some tattoo parlor getting blown up." Landon glanced at JB. "Unless you think this is tied into that whole bank robbery episode."

"Don't tell me the thought hasn't crossed your mind." JB relaxed his stance.

"I don't plan to tell you anything since you're no longer part of the FBI." Landon shook his head. "Damn shame."

"What?"

"I said it's a damn shame. I thought you were smarter than that." The special agent narrowed his focus at JB. "And just for the record, I was going to say you were thinking with your heart instead of your head. That'll get you in trouble every time. Got your last partner, Jennings, killed."

JB realized Landon was right. Jennings had gone on the last police call to meet an informant. Some young girl who'd come up to him on the street and said she was being used in a child slavery scheme. She'd agreed to meet him the next day with more details but had been so scared she didn't trust anyone else coming along. Jennings had gone by himself like she wanted. Thought with his heart…not his head. He'd been ambushed and killed at the meeting point.

Evans finished his notes and tucked the pad in his pocket. "What makes you think the target was the tattoo parlor?"

"May be a long shot, but look at the facts," Landon said. "Their business is closed for a few days. The owners are out of town and can't be reached. And, from what I've heard around town, Cross's Tattoo Parlor caters to some real lowlifes around the area."

Kennett straightened.

Landon ambled along the perimeter of the crime scene tape. "Probably nothing more than payback for a bad drug deal." He crouched to eye something on the ground, then straightened and walked away as his phone rang.

JB turned to the deputy. "What can I do to help?"

No response. He opened his mouth to ask again, but Landon walked back in to the group, so JB decided to wait.

"Just for the record, I'm the one in charge of this case until the sheriff gets back. So don't go trying to pull anything over on me or my men." Deputy Evans pulled out his pen and pad. "That goes for both of you."

JB nodded in recognition. Guess he and Landon had just been put in their place.

Evans looked up. "By the way, JB, Sheriff Davis

requested you stay in town until he gets back. Just in case there are any more…problems."

"Problems? Don't you find it a little coincidental that Marcy's been in the line of fire twice ?" JB stepped in front of Evans. "Maybe you ought to see what her uncle thinks."

Hands on hips and jaw set, the deputy made it clear he didn't like being told what to do or his decisions being questioned. "The sheriff and I discussed matters when we spoke a few hours ago."

"And?" Landon asked.

"Her uncle said he's cutting his vacation short. Should be back by the end of the week." The deputy lowered his voice. "Coincidences do happen, JB. But I'll have a cruiser drive by her house every so often."

JB looped his thumbs in his jean pockets in an effort to appear non-confrontational. He shook his head as he scanned the heap of destruction from the office building.

Evans walked away. "Kennett, call the Crayton Hardware store and have them hold all their tarps just in case we get some rain before the investigators are finished. In fact, take a couple of guys over and pick them up."

"Before I go, I've got something to say about the tattoo parlor theory." Kennett took a deep breath and blew out a long sigh. "Cross's is a second-generation business. Never had any trouble with them as long as I've been here."

Sounded the same as when JB'd been the deputy of Crayton.

The rookie's clear voice rumbled strong. "Second, the owner got called out of town two days ago because his father had a heart attack on a hunting trip in the Canadian outback. They went to bring him home. They weren't lured out of town." Kennett thumbed his finger at the debris. "So Special Agent Landon may want to rethink his assumption."

JB nodded his aching head and cleared his vision momentarily. The rookie was okay. He'd keep him in mind when knowing who to trust came to the forefront. A lawman never knew when he'd need someone not afraid to say what they think.

Landon stepped up beside JB as they watched the police walk away. "So, what's your take on this?"

"Nobody better try to tell me it was a faulty water heater or a propane leak. Not unless they've got good evidence, and nothing else is in the pipeline of possibilities." JB might not be cozy with this agent, but anything he could do to get info, he'd do, including sharing theories. "You?"

"Like I said before, it's a damn shame you quit the Bureau." The man smirked, then turned and walked away.

Sonofabitch. Guess he needed to work on his let's-be-friends attitude if he wanted any answers from him.

Landon stopped and glanced back. "By the way, how's your wife doing after this?"

"Ex-wife." JB wondered why the man was concerned with the health of Marcy. "Fine."

"Tell her I asked about her. Hope she's okay."

No way in hell would he mention Landon to her. "I don't think that's a good idea seeing as how you didn't exactly make a shining impression the first time you met."

Landon stepped to leave. "You're probably right. Forget I brought it up."

Chapter Eight

Marcy glanced at the kitchen clock one more time as she braced her foot on the chair rung, bouncing her toes in time with the passing seconds. JB never knew the meaning of a short meeting or assignment when he had been a Crayton deputy and evidently hadn't learned in the time he'd been gone. She didn't plan to let herself be overcome with wild what-ifs like she had three years ago when he didn't show up for two days, though.

If he didn't show up soon, she planned to dump the pot of minestrone she'd made earlier into a few containers, stick them in the freezer, and go to bed.

After pouring another cup of coffee, she devoured her third cupcake. Moist, yellow cake with chocolate, fudge icing just the way JB liked them. So much for letting her emotions get in the way of her better judgment. For all she knew, he'd left town and wouldn't be seen for another three years. She peeled the paper from another cupcake, ate the icing, and tossed the rest in the trash.

The slam of JB's truck door interrupted her thoughts. She'd make him have to ring the bell while she took her time in answering and considered whether to unlock the door or not.

Easy as anything, he stepped inside. She jerked to her feet, frowning, eyes rounded, and mouth open.

"You forget I still have a key to our house." He grinned along with his gotcha wink. "I'm surprised you didn't change the locks when you divorced me."

"I'll get that done first thing in the morning."

"No need. If you want the key, I'll give it to you." He walked into her space. Braced his arms on each side of her against the kitchen counter. Leaning toward her ear, his breath whispered through her hair. "Do you want the key, Marcy? Should I leave it on the table?"

JB smelled like JB, and she tilted her head in his direction. Would be so easy to… She jerked back. Too close…he was too close. Bobbing under his arm, she walked to the stove and filled a bowl with minestrone, setting it on the kitchen table.

"I'm not hungry." He held his hand to his stomach.

"Should have known you were out with the guys having pizza." She placed a spoon next to the bowl in case he changed his mind. He'd always loved that soup. Was one of the few things she made halfway decent.

"No." He sighed, ragged and hard with a hitched groan.

Glancing over her shoulder, she saw him steady himself against the table with one hand, the other arm curled tight against his ribs. "What's wrong?"

"Nothing." The clench of his teeth told a different story as he lowered himself to the chair.

"Don't give me that. You forget I know your cover-ups." She filled a glass of iced tea for him.

"Long day. I've been at the scene then police headquarters all this time." JB downed the drink in one long gulp. As she'd expected, he picked up his spoon and dug into the soup. "The local department seems a little overwhelmed, but they'll be okay. Landon tried to bulldoze his way into their investigation."

"Why?"

"I don't know, except he's a know-it-all. I'll keep an eye on him. By the way, looks like I'll be around a little longer."

"Should have known." She sat a jar of crackers on the table.

"Not my idea. Deputy Evans said Sheriff Davis asked me to stick around until he gets back in town. Got a problem with that?"

She sighed heavily in return. "No problem. I'm sure my uncle has his reasons. I just figured you'd rather be on your way."

He mindlessly crushed a handful of crackers into the bowl of soup. "Smells good, thanks."

She nodded and continued to putter around the kitchen.

"No more soup." His cheeks puffed with a sigh of air as he pushed the bowl away. "Think I need to go to bed. I'll see you in the morning."

Marcy watched him walk down the hall and turn to go in their bedroom. "Hey, bucko. Wrong room."

"Sorry. Force of habit." He stepped down the hall.

"Hasn't been much of a habit the past few years, now has it?" She swore she wouldn't give him the satisfaction of knowing she might still care.

Too late.

"We need to talk." He staggered, stopped walking, then did the slow-turn glance over his shoulder. "Not tonight."

She opened her mouth to make one of her sarcastic

remarks, but he slumped against the wall, and she darted to his side. "Dizzy?"

Nodding, he straightened. Eyes wide open, he wobbled with each step. She looped his arm around her shoulder and wrapped hers around his waist. Together, they stumbled to the side of the bed before he lowered himself down.

Elbows braced on his knees, head lowered to his palms as they scrubbed his forehead, he grunted, accentuating his current state. "Where're those pain pills the doc gave me? My head feels like it'll explode any second now."

After rushing to the kitchen, she brought him one with a glass of water. "You need to be in the hospital."

"No." He downed the medicine and stretched out across the bed. "I'll be okay."

"Let's get you out of those clothes and under the covers then."

"I'm okay like this."

"JB Bradley, you never once slept in a lick of clothes in this house. And you're not starting now." Where the heck had that come from? She might as well have opened the door to her bedroom. The man she knew would pounce on that suggestion's implication.

Nothing. No movement. No comment. He did nothing to indicate he even realized what she had said. Not even that sexy wink or bite of his lip that could entice her to hell and back. He must really be sick. Or done and over her. Maybe both. Didn't matter. They were nothing more than two friends thrown into circumstances beyond their control.

She pulled him up until he sat on the side of the bed again.

"Go on. I can undress myself." He pitched toward the floor.

Shaking her head at his stubbornness, she braced her

body against his to keep him on the bed as she bent down and tugged his boots and socks off. He leaned into her side, steadying himself with his hand against her hip, and her core flashed with recognition.

Down girl. That is not a pass.

"Stand up, so we can get you in bed."

He stood, flicked the button on his jeans, and unzipped. She tugged the pants downward, and they fell to the floor. Her insides tingled on her intake of breath. The air in the room grew heavy with need. He hadn't changed since they left the hospital. Still commando.

She lifted the edge of his T-shirt, but he shook his head, pushing her hands away.

"I saw the burn marks at the hospital. And the slash marks. Which we will talk about later. Now help me get this off of you." She grabbed the shirt one more time, successfully pulling it over his head with his help.

Her gaze flowed down his lean, muscled body from his shoulders to his chest to the tan line riding low on his hips. She fought to keep from following the dark line of hair from his belly downward. After all, the man was sick. They were divorced. He'd made it clear he wasn't back in town for her. Wasn't planning to stay. She shouldn't…she damn well shouldn't.

She lost the battle as she skimmed the rest of the way down. He was still the hottest man she'd ever seen. Not that she'd seen anyone else but JB in her life. Damn it was hot in this room. She flicked on the fan switch on the wall.

Turning back the covers on the bed, she pushed him to sit. "Now lie down, and go to sleep. If you aren't better by morning, I'm taking you to the hospital."

"No. No more doctors." As he slid under the sheet, his hand covered hers. "Stay with me, Marcy."

Stay?

She eased her hand away. "Probably not a good idea. Get some rest."

Looking at JB, all muscle and need and the man she loved, she knew it would be more than easy to slide alongside him. Easy to give everything she had to him again. In fact, her body pulsed and ached with the thought of what his words meant. Did she? Did she dare let him know the power he held over her?

No.

He'd broken her heart twice already—the second time when he'd signed the divorce papers. The first time had been when he'd told her he wanted to join the FBI.

After her dad had been killed on the job, her mother had moved the family back to Crayton. Nothing bad would follow them to such a small town. Especially one where the sheriff was the girls' uncle. Being young, she hadn't realized what her mother meant. Being grown-up, she knew exactly what that statement meant.

Marcy wanted children, and she didn't ever want to have to worry over things like that. She didn't want to wonder every night if her children's dad was just late getting home or if the unthinkable had happened. No, she wouldn't give JB any sign that she might still care. Even if he wasn't a Bureau agent any longer, he'd still head to another job with law enforcement once his dad's estate was signed off on.

Unless he decided to stay in Crayton. Join the police department again.

Now wouldn't that be just dandy? She'd always known there were plenty of women in town who'd love to take him off her hands. Some single…some not so single. What if he chose one of them, and Marcy and the happy couple ended up living down the street from each other? That would mean she'd see them holding hands, kissing, dancing so close everyone would know what was going to happen at home that night.

Damn. Damn. Damn. What was wrong with her? With those thoughts bouncing around her brain, not only did her shoulder ache from her wound, so did her heart. That was one of the hardest parts about filing divorce papers—the thought of him in another woman's arms.

The sound of his already-asleep breathing made her smile. Almost with a mind of their own, her fingers lightly brushed through his dark hair. Down his cheek. Across his shoulder.

Whew. She needed to walk away fast. Take a shower. Scurry into a sleep shirt and tonight, even into a pair of panties.

She left his door open a bit in case he needed anything later. Tomorrow morning he should be better. If not, she meant what she'd said about the hospital. How she'd get him there she didn't know, because he was one stubborn man when it came to doctors. He'd always been stubborn.

Then again, so was she. After all, she had taken her own advice and let JB go. Let him follow his dream. Let him stay gone. She could have gone to find him, but...

Finally feeling tired enough to sleep, she locked the front door and turned out the lights. She climbed into bed and scrunched her pillow before snuggling into the softness.

"Marcy! Marcy, where are you?" JB's anguished shout filled the air.

In the darkness, she rushed to his side and flipped on the bedside lamp. Still asleep, his head rolled from side to side. His face a contortion of pain and panic. His arms flailed at the covers.

"Marcy!"

"I'm here, JB. Open your eyes, I'm here." She crawled in bed beside him, grabbed one arm, and soothed his face with her other hand. "You're dreaming. It's only a dream."

He jerked awake, then engulfed her in his arms. His soft kisses pressed into her hair. "I couldn't find you. I searched everywhere, but you weren't there." His voice echoed his emotions. "I thought I lost you for good."

"No, JB. You didn't lose me." She felt herself swept into the moment and stayed close by his side. In all likelihood, he'd just relived the explosion in nightmare form. "I'm right here. See? Right here."

He rolled out of bed and made his way to the bathroom. The sound of running water filled the air. Wiping his face with a towel when he returned, he looked awake and alert.

"Whatever's in that pain med zonked me good." He lay down in bed and offered his arm for her to snuggle inside his hold. "Stay here tonight. I promise I won't try anything. Just stay here with me."

"Okay." Sometimes her mouth had a habit of speaking before she thought things through. Oh, well…one night wouldn't hurt. And JB always kept his promises.

Still, how could she be sure? She was about to backtrack and tell him no way when her traitorous body folded against him, her leg automatically slipped across his, her cheek nestled into the crook of his shoulder, and her hand rested on his chest. It might have been three years since she'd touched his bare skin, but her body remembered the markers, the paths, the man.

Oh, how she remembered the man…

His arm folded around her curves, pulling her tight against his rock-solid body. Nuzzling his face against her hair, he softly groaned. "You feel so good. I've missed you, Marcy."

The words and the heat from his skin against her own

rekindled her desire. She fought to control the urge to push his promise to be good aside. Roughness from the branding mark on his left, upper chest caressed her fingers with each breath he took, and without thinking, she softly kissed the spot. She leaned closer, sliding her knee between his thighs, moving her cheek to rest against the mark.

She didn't feel the sharp, jarring worry of sympathy-pain she had felt all the times before when he'd been wounded. This time, she felt strong and proud to be the woman lying by this man who had suffered so much, yet held her with such tenderness. She brushed her lips across the mark again, then laid back against his chest.

Still, she couldn't go back to the way things had been before. She couldn't.

He sighed heavy, yet peacefully. "Goodnight, Marcy."

"Goodnight, JB. Sweet dreams."

Chapter Nine

JB opened his eyes to a symphony of aches and pains, plus a dingy white ceiling that needed a fresh coat of paint. Foggy from the restless night, he was still all-too aware of the softness snuggled against his side. He smiled. Marcy had stayed. No, the last thing he remembered before falling asleep was her walking out of the bedroom. So how come she was here now?

The medicine. The nightmare. Now, he remembered. The promise.

He stroked her arm, then let his palm slide down her side. Would be so easy to move his fingers to all the places that were sure to bring her even closer. His body ached, throbbing with memories of other times, other mornings. He took a chance and circled his fingers on her hip.

"Ummmmm." She sleepily eased his hand aside, keeping her fingers between his and her body. "No…you said…"

Even though she pushed him away, her lips still tickled against his skin as she drifted back to sleep. Damn that promise he made not to try anything. Never mind the one he made himself before he came to Crayton.

He'd played out the scenario of what would happen if they happened to see each other and she wanted to get back together. There'd be a serious talk. Lots of listening on both sides. Even then, he doubted they'd ever be back together. Nonetheless, if any of that talking and listening ever transpired, it needed to be accomplished with their clothes on.

All the soft mewy sounds she made in her sleep, coupled with her jasmine-scented hair, were more than he could take at the moment. He slid his arm from beneath her and rolled out of bed. They had to stop acting on emotion, because sooner or later, they wouldn't stop.

He damn sure needed to stop making promises. And not just to her. Now he'd agreed to hang around Crayton until the sheriff got back in town. Of course, he'd planned to do that anyhow seeing that two coincidences involving Marcy were too much for him to turn and walk away.

She moved only enough to wiggle into the vacated warmth of his spot and burrow into the covers. The sheet slipped a little, and the rise and fall of her breasts with each breath worked to his core, pushed his resistance to the edge.

Hell, they'd both feel better if they got this out of the way. Might even stop jabbing at each other so much, if they could part as lovers. If she nudged him away again, no problem, he'd head for the shower. He reached for the covers to slide back in beside her, then stopped.

No.

They were divorced. Plain and simple. There'd be no sex. No pretends. No for-old-times-sake hook-up. A good, cold shower, that's what he needed. Of course, his body would feel better with heat. Maybe he'd flip from hot to cold and back again until his brain centered in his head.

Stepping into the shower stall brought back memories of him and Marcy up against those same beige, ceramic and glass tiles. More memories than he needed right now.

He turned and braced his hands against the shower wall. As the water beat a rhythm on his back, his muscles loosened, and he did his damnedest to concentrate on the past days' events. He wasn't sure the two cases were tied together, but he planned to find out.

His mind walked through the evidence. Leon likely hadn't targeted Marcy when he'd decided to rob the bank. The man probably hadn't even realized the seriousness of his actions. He'd gotten juiced, needed money, and had gone to the bank to make a withdrawal…sort of. Of course, the gun jumped the incident to a felony. Conclusion…Marcy and the robbery were purely accidental in JB's way of thinking.

The shooting was another story. Why hadn't the shooter finished the job as Leon lay exposed on the ground three feet away from her? Instead, the bullets had veered closer to her with each shot, the last one grazing JB to get to her. Out-of-line rifle scope or expert marksmanship?

After toweling off, he glanced at her sleeping form in the bed as he headed to what had been his side of the closet for a shirt and jeans. Her long leg looped around the edge of the sheet. A tiny bit of hot pink panty peeked from beneath her sleep shirt. His groin sprung to life, and his towel tented. The cold shower effects hadn't lasted long.

He grabbed his boots from beside the bed, then focused straight ahead until he got out of the room. He needed a distraction, along with some cool, morning air.

Thirty minutes later, he walked back into the bedroom. "You gonna sleep all day or what?"

Smiling, she lazily stretched like a woman waking up to

tease the man beside her. A woman ready for some morning love. A woman who'd forgotten whose bed she'd slept in.

Her eyes popped open, hands pulling the sheet to her neckline. She pushed herself upright and inched back in the bed. Her hand slid beneath the covers and, from what he could tell from its movement beneath the sheet, she checked to see what she still had on.

"A promise is a promise, sugar. Everything's just the way it was when you went to sleep. Shouldn't have asked you to stay with me last night, but I was feeling none too good at the moment." He sat the drink carrier on the nightstand, along with a bag of donuts fresh from Art's Bakery via the local convenience mart. "Large coffee, three creams, three sugars. Right?"

"Right." She peeked into the sack.

"One chocolate Bavarian cream and one chocolate iced vanilla cake donut. Right?"

Already biting into the gooey icing, she let the sheet slide as she swung her legs over the side. "Right."

He headed to the door. "That's okay. Don't worry about me being hungry."

"I'm sorry," she mumbled through a mouthful of donut, holding out the sack. "I figured you already ate yours on the way back like you always did."

"Only three." He chuckled. "Think you know me pretty well, don't you?"

Her expression shied as she sipped her coffee, eyes darting any place but at him. His gut clenched a warning to bide his time. In the window's reflection, he watched her pad across the carpet with her bag and cup of coffee. She paused, looked over her shoulder, and he glanced over his.

Clearing his throat, he went to the window. "I forgot how beautiful the leaves around here can be in the fall. By the way, there's a nip in the air, so you may want to dress warm."

"Thanks for the donuts and coffee." She walked out the door.

Instinctively, he followed her into the kitchen. "If you've got time once you get dressed, I'd like to talk."

She turned to face him, her expression unsure. "Maybe later. Betsy and I are going shopping about noon."

"Where?"

"The Outlet Mall."

"Who's driving?"

"Me."

He needed her in sight until he figured out what was going on. "Maybe I'll tag along."

She rounded, laughing. "You, me, and Betsy? Are you crazy?"

Evidently. But he'd contend with her sister if it meant keeping Marcy safe.

"Why all the sudden concern?" She finished off the last donut, then concentrated on her cup of coffee. "I've been taking care of myself for three years. What makes you think I can't now?"

"Well, for one thing, ever since I got to town, you've been on the verge of extinction." He leaned his shoulder against the wall.

"Never had a problem until you showed up. Maybe you should leave town again." She lifted her eyes to look into his. "Seems like danger always follows you."

That hurt. "What do you mean?"

She ignored his question and turned away. "Forget I said anything. I'm going to get dressed."

Bumping her elbow on the doorframe to her bedroom, coffee sloshed out the hole in the lid. She bent to wipe up the mess with the napkins from the donut bag. Her top inched up her thigh, her hip, and her backside.

Unable to control the heat in his core, he walked away while he could still manage to move. At the kitchen counter, he stared out the window over the sink. The yard looked the same except she'd replaced their old, wooden swing with a wicker-look one complete with brightly striped cushions. He wondered what else she might have replaced.

Him? Had he been replaced by someone new and bright and shiny? Just because he hadn't seen any sign of another man didn't mean one didn't exist. Maybe she'd picked a businessman like Truman. Could be the guy was simply away on a trip. Except, Truman's "work-related trips" were undercover for the U.S. government.

JB knew that for a fact, so did Sadie. He doubted more than a few others in town knew the man's secret, though. Doubted Marcy ever realized her mother had married another man just like their father, remarried the FBI. Only this one led two lives, public and private.

Years ago, once JB had started investigating how to become an agent with the FBI, Truman had revealed that he'd been a Special Agent with the Bureau at one time. Said since his retirement, he only "consulted," as he'd called it, when the undercover assignment would be short term. Most people thought he was just away at a real estate workshop or partnering on a new development in other parts of the world. The arrangement worked good for him, Sadie, and the girls. Kept his family safe and out of sight in this sleepy town, but allowed him to still feel useful in protecting the country.

In fact, the straw that broke JB and Marcy's marriage had happened the week before she'd shoved him out the door. He'd gone with Truman on an assignment as part of a police-FBI joint operation, just to see if he really might be cut out for the Bureau. The agreement had been JB would stay out of the way. An ambush had negated that agreement.

When he'd walked in the front door the next day, Marcy had been livid. Had looked like hell from crying as she'd worked herself into a frenzy imaging a million things that had happened to him. Sure, he hadn't told her exactly what he was doing, just that he'd be helping out in another town department for a few days. He damn sure hadn't mentioned the FBI because of the way she'd reacted to his talk of becoming an agent one other time. Wouldn't have mattered if he had.

She'd demanded he never leave Crayton again. Yelled about him being in law enforcement. Berated him that he was hurt...again. It had been only a scratch, not even really a wound. And she'd called him a few names he hadn't even known she knew.

She'd been a wreck.

He'd followed his career choice on a test basis, and she'd fallen apart. From what he saw, she'd never be able to handle it. Something changed between them that day. That was the first night he'd slept on the couch of his own accord. She'd kicked him out a couple days later.

After downing the dregs of his coffee, JB crushed the paper cup and tossed it in the trash. He should have known coming back to Crayton would only be a rehash of old conversations. Maybe deep inside he'd started to hope she had missed him as much as he missed her. That being apart had been enough for her to face her fear of danger. Of death. Of anything to do with being a lawman.

Evidently not. He was a fool to have imagined different.

She walked into the kitchen dressed in jeans, a sweater, and her back-off attitude. Leaning against the counter, she challenged him with her stare. The woman who'd snuggled against his side last night and kissed the scar on his chest was nowhere in sight. Evidently, she'd run from her feelings again. Hidden herself behind her stronger-than-strong female attitude once more. She'd quickly forgotten how she ran her fingers over his body last night when she thought he was asleep. Pretended she was sleeping, too.

Okay. There'd be no more time spent in the same bed. But he'd be damned if he let her blame everything that happened in the past few days on him. If she wanted a challenge, she'd get one. "So, you think the bank robbery, the shooting, and the explosion all followed me to Crayton?"

"I'm saying there was nothing going on in this little town until you arrived. Ergo, common sense says to look at what's different." She tilted her head to the side the way she always did when analyzing something. "You. You came back to town, and all hell broke loose."

He stepped in front her, a couple feet away. If this was going to be the talk, then they'd hold it eye-to-eye. He hooked his thumbs in his side, jean pockets. "You've got all your psychology and analyzing to feed your thoughts. How about using a little common sense for my world?"

"Such as?"

"You want to know why I never came back after you kicked me out?"

She didn't look away, just slid her palms into her back pockets. "Okay. Why?"

"No man likes to have his wife tell him he's not good enough for her."

"I never said that."

"Might not have been those exact words, but you let me know every time I ended up hurt on the job that you couldn't stand to be around a man who couldn't protect himself." He reined himself in, walked to the door. No need to bring up how she'd told him he didn't love her, that he'd never put her through all that pain if he did. He'd been ready to give up the law just to prove his love. She'd made that unnecessary with the suitcase on the front porch.

His strength, stamina, and will to live had never been a doubt in his mind. But from the moment his dad had taken custody of him, picking him up at the bus station and telling him he wasn't worth the price of the ticket, he'd doubted his worth. He'd been twelve years old. Twelve years old, and no one wanted him. Too damn bad. He'd decided then and there no one was ever gonna keep him down. But the doubts dug in for the long haul.

The next six years had been hell on earth what with trying to stay out of the way of his old man's punches, work enough to keep food on the table, and go to school. Sports, school, and thoughts of the future were what kept him on the straight-and-narrow. That plus Sheriff Davis, who'd become like a dad to him. Of course, once his old man had found out about his mentor, he'd pounded JB even more.

The day he'd finally stood up to his dad and gave him punch for punch back hadn't squashed the doubt. That was the last time either one of them had laid a hand on the other. Even as his old man had lain on the floor and spit the blood from his mouth at JB's feet, he'd mumbled that JB still wasn't worth the price of a ticket. Then, he'd told him to bring home a pint of whiskey after school.

That was then, and this was now.

"You were always coming home injured. How do you think that made me feel?" She'd folded her arms across her chest. To her, she'd made her point, and the conversation was over.

Not this time. This time he would stand up for himself…

even to Marcy.

"So you're saying because I was hurt, you were in pain. Well, let me tell you about pain." He grabbed his coat from the hook and stepped onto the porch, glancing back over his shoulder. "Pain is being shot and your wife going to the other room to sleep."

"You needed your rest."

"When you finally came back to our bed, you turned away every time I reached for you. Was that also because I needed my rest?"

She bit the side of her lip. Tightened her crossed arms.

"Your games aren't going to work with me, Marcy. Not then. Not now." He held his tone even, calm. "I got a Criminal Justice degree to be a lawman. I plan to be one the rest of my life. Being punched, kicked, spit on, or even shot are hazards of the job. If you can't handle that, then you're right, I need to leave. Is that what you really want? Because I won't come back again."

She didn't answer. Didn't move.

"Okay. Once these cases are settled, I promise I'll go." He closed the door behind him and stepped off the porch.

The door opened, and she padded softly across the porch planks. "Where are you going?"

"Now or later?"

"Now."

"I'm going for a walk."

"JB?"

He stopped.

The top step squeaked as she stepped on it. "You only know one way. Fast and protective. It's just the way you are. You're always the leader. First in the door. Last to leave the job. It's one of the reasons I fell in love with you. But every time you came home hurt was like being stabbed in my heart."

He couldn't argue. Nothing could change how he approached life. He also understood not every woman was cut out to be married to a lawman.

"All I wanted was for you to change jobs so you wouldn't get killed. I thought kicking you out might make you change." Another creak. Another step. She sighed. "From the looks of the scars on your chest, that didn't happen."

"Not hardly." This conversation needed to end before the what-happened questions began. He glanced back over his shoulder. "At least my mother left a fifty and a one-way ticket to Crayton when she threw my gym bag on the porch, locked me out of the house, and shipped me to my father. I was only twelve years old. Guess I wasn't good enough then, either."

"I never said you weren't good enough." The whisper of her voice echoed across the yard. "Never."

"That's what I heard. Loud and clear."

...

Marcy stood at the kitchen window, watching JB run the perimeter of the cleared area of their property. She'd never known what happened to bring him to live with his dad in Crayton. He'd always been vague on that point, no matter how hard she'd pressed him. Vague about his mother, too. All that had ever been said was that his mother couldn't take care of him. Marcy and everyone else in town assumed she must have been ill. No one was surprised when two years later, word came of her passing.

Of course, everyone knew what a bastard his dad had been. The sheriff even tried to get JB to file charges for the beatings, but he always said he'd tough it out. That every day he made it through was one day closer to being out of that house for good. All he needed was a football scholarship. He'd worked hard. Studied hard. Got a scholarship. And earned every hard-fought scrap of his degree.

She'd never been so proud in her life as the day he tossed his mortar board in the air and yelled he loved her. Her world had been complete knowing she'd share whatever he'd give of his life.

Now...now, she wanted to know more. *Needed* to know more. She'd counseled a lot of people who'd been hurt in some way during childhood. Surely she could help him make peace with those memories.

Clenching his arm tight against his side, he stepped inside and grabbed a glass of water.

"What's the matter?" she asked.

"Nothing. Just leaned wrong and got that bruise to hurting." He headed to the living room. "I'm gonna catch a little of the game 'til you and Betsy leave for the mall."

"Mind if I join you?"

He clicked on the television, motioned her to come on in. Fifteen minutes later, he had his feet up on the ottoman, and she was curled into the corner on the opposite end of the sofa. Neither had said a word.

She reached over and muted the set, then turned to face him, back straight, hands in her lap, like a skilled listener. "If you ever want to talk about your mom or anything else, I'd be happy to listen."

His feet hit the floor before she could blink. "Is that all you got out of what I said?"

"I just thought I might be able to help. After all, I do have some background in this sort of thing." What was he so angry about? "You know, people pay good money for my advice."

"I'm your ex-husband. Not your client." He clicked the TV off and headed to the hallway.

"I know that."

"Do you? Do you even know what that means?" He braced his hands against the doorframe. "And, just for the record, I've faced my past and moved on. Maybe you should do the same. Stop being a counselor with straight A's from college, and just be a woman. That doesn't mean you're giving up your independence. It's about being a person who loves life and lives it one step at a time."

"I've tried." She traced her hand across the horticulture book on the table. For the past few months, she'd tried to learn how to grow things. Maybe that would help her not always analyze everything to the nth-degree. "But I can't seem to figure out how."

He headed down the hallway, then came back to the living room doorway. "You knew when you married me that I'd be involved in the law."

Her mind was racing. She'd hurt him before and wanted to make sure that didn't happen again. "I hoped you'd decide to be a lawyer or a teacher."

"Can you really see me standing in front of a classroom of kids who've been up half the night before playing video games? Who'd rather be any place in the world but in that chair listening to me?"

Soft and real, she laughed. "I guess that does stretch the imagination."

He walked over and engulfed her in a gentle hug. "Sugar, you can't change my career choice any more than I can stop you from trying to help people live a better life. Understand?"

She did understand, and that was part of the problem. Loving someone when you couldn't accept who they were cut out to be meant making both of you unhappy. As a counselor, she should be able to figure out a solution. Three years ago, she'd done just that with two outcomes to consider—end their relationship or accept the dangerous what-ifs. She chose the one she could live with—she'd kicked him out.

Now that he was back in town, the question was whether she'd be able to make a different choice this time. Because the last few years had been hell without him next to her.

He stepped back. "I know you've got me and the law and your dad's death all whipping around in that pretty, little head of yours. Always has been. You think I'm gonna end up like him, and you'll end up a widow like your mother. Right?"

She nodded. Truth was the truth.

"Damn it, Marcy. I could walk outside and get hit by a falling tree and be just as dead as being hit by a bullet."

"That would be different."

"How? I'd still be dead."

She shook her head, the answer only a thought away. "Because a tree would be an accident. Being shot would be from the danger of the job. Don't you understand? Danger walks with you every time you put on a badge. And I don't want to live with that always on my mind."

He headed toward the living room, the cords in his neck taut against his skin. "Then why the hell did you even marry me in the first place?"

Chapter Ten

"I still don't like you going off without me." JB leaned against the fender of Marcy's car. He hadn't been able to stay mad at her. And sooner or later, they'd probably end up in each other's arms. But at the end of the case, he'd keep his promise. He'd leave.

"Honestly, you act like someone's out to get me." She shoved him aside as she tossed a jacket in the backseat. "I was in the wrong places at the wrong times, that's all."

Betsy sighed long, heavy, and loud from across the top of the vehicle. "You two gonna argue all day, or are we going shopping?"

"I could drive you girls around. Wait in the truck," JB said.

"No!" the two women answered in unison.

Marcy opened the driver's side door and leaned in, taking her time as she searched for something in the console. When she stood, she slid her sunglasses on, nice and easy and slow. "I'm sure you have something better to do than play nursemaid to two women. Get going."

JB closed the distance to her, leaning downward as she stretched upward.

"Marcy?" His lips were only a whisper away as he brushed her hair behind her ear.

"Uh-huh."

She closed her eyes and tipped her face up to his. For a moment, she almost looked like the first time he kissed her. Wanting? Yes. Willing? Maybe. Afraid? Probably. He'd been a little scared and unsure himself back then. In fact, he'd made her wait over a week for his kiss. Each day teasing her more and more, just to make sure she didn't turn him down when he made his move. He'd been young with an ego that needed to stay intact.

She still hadn't moved away, so he leaned downward.

"Are we shopping or what?" Betsy flung her arms up.

The two of them turned simultaneously in her direction. He'd forgotten Marcy's sister was even there, and evidently, so had she.

He glanced back at her. "Sorry. I didn't mean to lead you on. I just got carried away with the way I used to send you off for a day of shopping."

"We both got carried away for a moment. That's all. Forget it." She stop-signed him with her hand as she turned back to her sister. "Shopping. We're going shopping."

He scrubbed a palm down his face. Damn it, the next time he got half a chance, he'd kiss her. Slow and easy. Hard and fast. Didn't matter. He'd damn well kiss the hell out of her. Not gonna happen right now, though. And he had no one to blame but himself for that crash and burn.

"Be careful out there on the road. And call if you see anything suspicious." He planned to be keeping an eye on them from afar, but closer would be better.

She pushed past him. "Almost forgot. I left my phone on the counter, charging."

The moment she walked out of earshot, he turned to Betsy. "She had any trouble while I've been away?"

Betsy crossed her arms in defiance. "Now's a heck of a time to worry about how she survived."

"Don't fight me. Answer the question." He heard his tone and couldn't stop the harshness. He shook his head. "Sorry. Let's start again. Has anyone made any threats against Marcy? Given her a hard time for any reason?"

Glancing at the door, Betsy dropped her arms, concern etched her face. "What's going on?"

"Nothing maybe, but I don't like coincidences." He watched the doorway, ready to change the subject the moment his ex-wife pushed through. "Is there anything, anyone you can think of?"

She walked around the car, watching the same doorway. "The jeweler's wife over in the next county was none too happy about how their divorce turned out. Blamed Marcy for telling the husband he should stop giving in to the wife's money demands."

From the evidence so far, and his previous cases, the scene didn't speak of something so simple being cause for this kind of retaliation. "Go on. Anybody else?"

"Representative Benson and his wife were clients of Marcy's. He didn't like the fact they ended up in a nasty divorce." Betsy's words looped together with speed to get them out before her sister reappeared. "Wife ended up with a big chunk of their property in the settlement. He served Marcy papers for being a fraudulent counselor."

JB straightened. How dare anyone call her a fraud? She was one of the truest, most caring people he'd ever seen. Plus professional. "What happened?"

"His campaign chairman told him to let it go. Wouldn't want to bring up the divorce on the campaign trail." Betsy smiled. "He'd have lost every woman's vote in the district."

"Why?"

"Most people figured his wife's bruises and her broken arm were from her klutziness. No telling what might have come to light in a trial."

"Get hold of Deputy Evans and tell him what you told me about these people. Okay?"

Betsy nodded.

"Got it." Marcy rushed out the back door, waving the phone overhead.

"About time." He glanced back at her sister and lowered his voice so Marcy wouldn't hear as she approached. "For the record, I'm going to make sure nobody hurts her." He braced his arms on top of the driver's side.

"Never said you wouldn't." Betsy caught JB's gaze when she looked across the car. "By the way, why are you back in Crayton?"

"Just tying up some loose ends of dad's estate."

"That all?"

"That's all." He hadn't even bothered to think before he'd answered, yet hearing the words made him realize how much he'd shoved Marcy into the back of his mind and had moved on with his life. That really was the only reason he'd come back to town. Now that he'd seen her, however...

"Why?"

Betsy fiddled with the zipper on her coat. "No reason. Just being friendly."

He held the driver's door for Marcy. She slid in and buckled up, then he bent and kissed her cheek. That didn't make up for his come-on, shut-down a while ago, but it was at least a start. "I meant what I said. Be careful. What time will you be home?"

A pale, reddish fluster showed in her cheeks. "Well, it's about 10:30 now. I'd say by 5:00."

"I'll bring a pizza from Joanie's. Okay?" Keys in hand, he headed to his truck. His surveillance techniques were about to come in handy. He'd give them space, and they'd never know he was anywhere around.

"Sure. Sounds good." Marcy shifted into gear. "No—"

He grinned. "Onions."

"I was gonna say black olives." She sped away.

He'd give them a head start, or she'd pull off the road and give him an earful. The woman knew how to make a scene when she wanted to. He pressed speed dial on his phone for the police station and waited by his truck, giving her time to think he didn't plan to follow.

"Deputy Evans."

"This is JB. I talked to Betsy about anyone who's given Marcy a hard time in the past few years."

"You need to stay out of this and let us do our investigation."

Evans sounded irritated.

JB didn't care if the man was or wasn't. "I told her to call you with the same information."

"That all?"

This conversation wasn't making his day any better. "Yeah, that's all. Thought you might like the help."

"Thanks for the information. Sorry for my tone. I got the sheriff calling in every hour on the hour. Leads coming in that mean nothing except for when the owner of the tattoo parlor called. Said they've gotten a couple of pieces of hate mail, but nothing to write home about." Evans exhaled heavy. "Then there's Landon."

JB tensed. "What's he done now?"

"For one thing, it's a job keeping him out of my evidence and paperwork. Was he like that when you two were partners?"

"I only worked with him on one case." JB's shoulder's tensed. "Since you mention it, I've heard he's an in-your-face type of guy. Want me to talk to him?"

Evans thought a good, long time. "No. Keep me informed if you hear anything, though. You, I know. You, I trust."

"Sure thing."

"And try to keep an open mind about the idea that Marcy isn't a target, JB. I still say there are coincidences in the world."

JB ended the call, started the truck, and sped down the road, catching up to Marcy's car. As usual, she drove five miles below the speed limit. He gave her a few car-lengths.

Coincidence...maybe, maybe not. Didn't matter. Marcy was his main concern, and he'd watch out for her whether any of them liked it or not—Evans or Landon.

...

Marcy glanced out the corner of her eye at Betsy. "What were you and JB talking about?"

"Trying to be civil to one another." Betsy lip glossed, then blotted a leftover napkin she'd found in the console.

"Did you tell him?" Marcy doubted she had. Otherwise, she and JB would be at home having an entirely different conversation.

"No, I didn't tell him. Did you, little sister?" Betsy rolled her window down and let her long, red hair blow free in the wind. "He's bound to find out sooner or later. Better if it comes from you."

Marcy checked her speed. Her shoulder still hurt, and

these hills weren't something she wanted to miss a curve on. "What makes you say that?"

"You could explain to him why you asked for a divorce in the first place." Betsy motioned to JB trailing behind them. "I'm sure he'd have a few questions."

Marcy gripped the steering wheel. "If he hadn't wanted a divorce, then why did he sign the papers?"

"Did it ever occur to you that a man doesn't take kindly to being served divorce papers from a wife that kicked him out for no reason?"

"I had a reason."

"What?" Betsy mocked her sister. "What reason? And don't say because he wanted to be an FBI agent. JB's been wanting that since he knew what they did. So tell me what he did that day that pushed you over the line."

"I forget." Marcy bit her lip. Lie. That was a lie. She remembered exactly what happened.

He had Thursdays off from the Crayton Police Department back then. The day before had been when he'd returned from the two-day undercover op that had upset her. They had had words, and she'd gone to a different bedroom to sleep. Didn't matter… he'd slept on the sofa. Thursday morning, from right after breakfast until lunch, he'd spent his time online, researching everything he could find about being an FBI agent. Even made phone calls to the agency and talked to someone about careers. After lunch, he'd researched living in Washington, DC. Asked her what she thought about moving. Would she be able to start a marriage counseling practice there?

She'd balked. Refused to talk about a move. Then he'd asked her to give it a try. JB had never before asked for anything for himself. Never. She'd told him no. Get over it. Crayton was enough excitement for the two of them.

He'd looked up at her from the computer and asked one more time. She'd seen the look on his face. Knew how much he wanted to be an agent. So she'd set her no-way expression and shook her head. Then he'd turned off the computer and said "I love you." When he walked outside to mow the yard, she saw the slump of his shoulders. The defeated gait.

In that moment, she'd realized she was the one too weak to go, but he deserved the chance to follow his dream. She had no doubt about him being a good agent, so she'd packed his bag and set it on the front porch. Otherwise, he'd have never left her. She had to admit, though, that she'd hoped he would simply appreciate the sacrifice she was making and come back inside.

Looking back, that had been the worst mistake of her life. Some things you couldn't change, though, and their separation was one of them. Not then. Not now. They didn't even really know each other anymore.

"Don't think I'm defending JB." Betsy hung her arm outside and fought the breeze with her hand. "But you asked for a divorce when you sent the papers. What if he's remarried?"

"He didn't."

"Did he tell you that?"

"Not in so many words. But I know I'm why he came back to town."

She knew his walk and the way he steered his truck and how his eyes looked right before he reached for her. Since his dad died, he didn't have any other family around town but her. So why else would he have made the trip? He could have settled the paperwork long distance…

"Making a lot of assumptions aren't you?" Betsy straightened in her seat, tugging her seatbelt into place. "He told me he came to settle his dad's estate. That and nothing else."

Marcy didn't bother to answer. In fact, she was a little worried. He'd been nothing but the perfect gentleman since he got to town. And that kiss on the cheek before they drove away…what was that? Nothing but a simple little peck a person would give to a friend. Maybe that was all she was to him now. A friend. Someone you watch out for. Someone you give a peck on the cheek.

Heck, he hadn't even tried anything when they were in bed together last night.

"Hey, slow down." Betsy grabbed her arm rest as they rounded a curve.

"The speedometer says I'm doing forty-five. That can't be right." Marcy'd been so intent on rationalizing herself and JB, she hadn't noticed the gaining momentum of the car. She clenched the wheel as she pressed on the brake. The car didn't slow. Pressed again, and the pedal went to the floor bed. "Oh, my gosh. No brakes."

"Down shift. Down shift." Betsy gripped the window brace.

"I did. Nothing's happening."

The road ahead ran the rim of the lake, beautiful and breathtaking…except not now. Marcy visualized the steep hill interrupted only by twists and turns as it snaked down to a four-way stop at the bottom. Blind side-road entrances. Blind curves. She cringed. The dilly-dip of a couple of small hills. And finally what the kids called "dead-man's curve" loomed on the final stretch. If she couldn't slow down, they'd careen off the side of the hill. Best case scenario, they'd end up in the water. Worst case, they'd smash in to the boulders alongside the lake. Explode and burst into flames.

Marcy gripped the wheel tighter. "Call JB."

Betsy reached for her sister's phone, but his ringtone cut

through the air before she could dial. She pressed speaker.

"What the hell are you trying to do? Slow down." JB growled.

The urgency in his voice somehow calmed Marcy. He was nearby. "No brakes. We don't have brakes."

"Down shift." She glanced in her rearview mirror, saw him pull up right behind her.

"Nothing happens!" She'd never get to tell him how much she— "JB!"

. . .

JB watched an oncoming vehicle hug the edge of the road to stay out of Marcy's way. Her tires spit gravel as she veered onto the right shoulder. One wrong skid, and she'd be over the side of the drop-off. He gripped his steering wheel and synced with her on the swerves.

"I keep hitting the brakes, but nothing happens." Marcy sounded lost. "What should I do?"

"Pull the emergency brake."

"Nothing."

Someone must have tampered with her car. Might be suicide on his part to venture into the oncoming lane, but better his than hers. "Try to stay in the right lane so I can come up alongside you."

"What about traffic? You could get hit."

"I'll be okay. They got the other shoulder to run off on." At least he hoped like hell they would.

"What about semis?"

The road was usually loaded with trucks this time of day. If one of them came around a blind corner, it would roll over JB's vehicle like a bump in the road. "Do what I said, Marcy."

"I'm having a hard time staying in my lane."

Why had he let her drive? Her shoulder wasn't healed enough to handle these curves at high speed. Her car had already passed seventy miles per hour. "Concentrate on steering. Stay as much in your lane as you can."

If he lived through this, whoever was after her would wish they'd never heard of JB and Marcy Bradley. He pulled into the passing lane. "I'm coming around."

He floored the accelerator and slipped around her car like she was sitting still. Settling about a car length in front of her, JB tried to think one step ahead. Didn't take long to feel her driving rhythm. He chanced a quick look in the rearview mirror. The steel resolve on her face didn't fool him one bit. Betsy didn't look so good, either.

"I'm going to slow down till you're only a few inches off my bumper. If I can jolt us right, your fender may hook on my hitch," JB said.

"What should I do?"

"Stay on the road. If you feel us lock together, then follow my lead on steering." He lowered his speed in increments. "Hang up, and call the police."

"Already did from my phone," Betsy said. "Cops have traffic stopped at the bottom of the hill. They'll head up the minute they see us stop or...stop."

"Good. Hold on." Their bumpers brushed, jolted, jimmied. He increased his speed and tried the slow down again. Once more their bumpers rubbed like two stock cars on an oval race track. Still no hook up. "Stay calm. I'll try again."

He sped up, inched back within a foot, then slammed on his brakes. His hitch grazed over her bumper. Charged into her grill and the radiator. The two vehicles locked together as steam from the radiator poured from beneath the hood.

As fast as he'd stopped, he laid tread as he sped up enough to ease the collision. A few seconds later, he slowed to a halt in the middle of the road.

Slamming out of his truck, he heard the scream of sirens as the police made the climb up the hill. "Pull the hood release, Marcy." As soon as he heard the telltale click, he lifted the hood of her car. Yanked the battery cables free. The car shut down as radiator water gushed out on the road.

As he pulled the driver's door open, he prayed she was okay. Her air-bag-scraped face was the most wonderful thing he'd ever seen.

"Are we stopped?" she whispered.

"Yes, sugar. We're stopped." He released her seat belt and guided her out. "You okay, Betsy?"

"Yeah. I think so. But I can't get the door open." Betsy's muffled voice laced with pain.

"I'll be back as soon as I get her to the side of the road." JB carried Marcy to the grass and laid her down.

A passing downhill motorcyclist ground to a stop. "I got this one," he called.

The man power-pulled the passenger door open and lifted Betsy out. She vehemently yelled that she could walk as he carried her over to the grass and deposited her next to her sister.

JB nodded and held out his hand. "Thanks."

"Sure thing." The man accepted the gesture, then jumped back on his bike and disappeared around the curve as the first police cruiser lurched to a stop.

Deputy Evans piled out of his car, resting his forearm on the top of the doorframe. "Paramedics are two cars back."

"Good. Betsy needs one." Marcy's voice shook with her words.

JB stood, squared his shoulders, and directed his anger

at the deputy. "You got the guts to tell me this is another coincidence?"

Evans shook his head, seating his cap as he walked in the direction of the survivors. "No. This was no accident."

"You're right." JB knelt, leaning against Marcy as she bent over Betsy. "Damn right."

Chapter Eleven

Twenty minutes later, Marcy'd been cleared by the paramedics. She walked over to JB and laid her hand on his back as he crouched by her car looking for evidence. He'd been inside the car, under the car, in the driver's seat, the passenger seat, rear seat, and even on top of the car. She figured his next adventure would be in the trunk and under the hood.

Evans and Kennett worked the same sites, making notes as they went. Making more notes every time JB hollered out a comment. His under-the-breath mutterings went ignored by the police. Then Landon showed up.

"Heard there'd been an accident. Thought I'd see what I can do to help." He reached to take the report from Evans, but the deputy jerked his notes from the man's grasp.

JB stepped between the two men. "Back off, Landon. This isn't your case."

"Wilson assigned me to Crayton. I'd hate to have to arrest you for interfering with an FBI investigation." Landon reared back and smirked with an air of authority.

Marcy watched JB's veins bulge on his forearms and his jaw work its way into a set as he inhaled loud and deep. She took a few steps back. Her husband walked slow and easy in the man's direction. Stopped face-to-face, toe-to-toe with the other agent. Not an inch separated the two men.

"If you know what's good for you, don't ever threaten me again." JB pulled out his phone and pressed some numbers.

"Who are you calling?" Landon asked.

"Wilson."

"You can't. He's got a new phone, and you don't have access."

"Yeah. Well, he texted me the number as soon as he got it."

The agent looked perplexed and pursed his mouth to the side.

JB focused on the mouthpiece. "Wilson...you better get your man out of here before I send him to you special delivery... I mean, there's been an attempt to kill my ex-wife today, and Landon's overstepped his boundaries with the local police. He's got no authority in Crayton except the robbery, and thanks to him, Leon's out on bail."

Landon grabbed at the phone. "Let me talk to Wilson."

JB shoved his hand away. When the man reached again, her husband wrapped his fingers around the invading hand, then squeezed as he forced the man aside. "You got a phone. Use it."

The man backed off, flexing his fingers to get blood flow.

"Wilson," JB turned his back to the man. "Ends up the shooting, the bombing, today's attempt... They've all been directed at Marcy. The local police will get to the bottom of this. And, since I'm no longer with the FBI, I'm staying in town 'til this is settled. So, they don't need Landon. Get him out of here."

Landon pointed his finger at him. "Too far, JB. I've tried to overlook your almighty, I'm-right attitude. No more. You've gone too far this time."

JB pointed right back at him. "We'll talk about that later. For the moment, get the heck out of here."

The other man left in a frightening huff, although no one seemed to care.

Like a switch had been thrown, JB dropped his anger and went right back to his investigation. She loved to watch his mind work, along with the force of his body, as he studied the crime scene.

After a bit, she returned to Betsy. The paramedics would head to the hospital with her sister soon. She'd probably request the sirens even though they weren't needed. After motioning she'd be right back to her sister, Marcy walked over to the car.

A leave-me-alone look flashed as JB turned. The expression disappeared as he stood, replaced by one of concern. Deep-seated concern. Marcy was a little worried herself. What had she done to deserve these attacks?

He wiped what was likely a mascara smudge from beneath her eye, another stain from her cheek. "How you doing?"

"Okay." She loved the way he kept touching her every time she got within arm's reach.

"How's your sister?"

"I'll tell you how I am." Betsy's voice carried loud and clear across the roadway. "I'm bruised. I'm hungry. And they think I've got a broken arm."

JB's hand pressed against Marcy's back as he guided her over to the ambulance where an Insta-Splint encircled her sister's arm.

"Sorry about the break. Could have been worse." He looked back at the conjoined vehicles. "A lot worse."

Betsy motioned for the paramedic to incline the stretcher, then motioned the guy away once he complied. Waving JB over as if to share a secret, she flinched with the effort. "I'm not a fool. I know where Marcy and I were headed. Mama'd be missing two of her daughters if it wasn't for you."

He grimaced. "Sadie'd make my life a living hell if I let anything happen to one of you."

"Thank you, JB." Betsy hugged his neck as her voice broke. "Thank you."

Nodding, he patted her shoulder.

She leaned back. "You ever tell anyone I hugged you, I'll call you a liar to your face."

He grinned and stepped aside. This was one for the record books.

The driver headed to the front cab while the paramedic hopped in the rear with Betsy.

Marcy stepped on the fender to get inside, too.

JB braced the door open. "I thought you were okay."

"I am. I'm going with Betsy."

"No." He reached up and lowered her to stand on the ground.

"What do you mean no? You're not going to tell me what to do." She sidestepped him, trying to maneuver her way inside the ambulance.

JB grabbed hold of her arm. "I can't protect you if you're not where I am. That means you stay here until I finish looking this scene over."

She pushed him in the chest. "Get out of my way. I'm going with my sister to the hospital."

"Afraid I have to agree with JB on this one." The deep,

gravelly voice of Sheriff Davis, her uncle, entered the conversation.

"You're back." Marcy hugged the older man who'd put his life on the line for the past thirty-five years to get the riff-raff off the streets of Crayton. The same man who gave hugs and horseback rides to his sons and daughters, nieces and nephew, and now grandchildren through those same years. She bit her lip to control the quiver of pent-up tension. "Sorry you had to come home early from your vacation."

"Saw enough sights. Need to work." He hugged her back, then climbed into the ambulance and did the same with Betsy. Hopping back outside, he turned to JB and offered his hand. "Glad you got to town when you did."

Sounded like her uncle had been expecting JB. She glanced back and forth between the two men. Seemed like what she didn't know could fill a bucket.

"Good to be here, sir." As he looked the sheriff in the eye, JB's expression reflected the respect he felt for his mentor.

"What do you know about this FBI guy? Landon, I think it is." Sheriff Davis pointed in the other agent's direction where he'd taken up residence by his car for the moment. "Evans says he's been getting in his way."

Her husband looked at his one-time partner standing at the perimeter of the scene and narrowed his eyes. "The only case we ever worked together went bad. Funny thing though, he made sure he wasn't there the day it came down. You watch out for him. I don't know what he's up to, but he doesn't need to see the evidence."

The sheriff nodded.

Evans waved to get the group's attention. "We're gonna load these vehicles up. Get 'em back to the impound lot where we can get a better look."

"I'm not finished with the car yet." JB seemed torn between staying within arm's length of her or finishing his inspection. He chose the car. "Marcy, don't you dare get in that ambulance."

Who did he think he was? She'd go where she wanted, and right now she wanted to be there for Betsy. Surely riding in an ambulance to the hospital couldn't be dangerous.

Smiling, she nodded to JB as he waited for her acknowledgment. Once he raised the hood on the car and leaned across the fender to get a better look, she inched backward toward the open, rear door to the medic's van. As she turned, she was met by the sheriff as he slammed the doors closed before she could jump inside. He pounded the side of the ambulance twice with a fist before they pulled away.

"I need to go with Betsy." Marcy reached into the air as if trying to catch the accelerating ambulance.

Her uncle ignored the statement as he walked across the roadway. "Call Sadie. Tell her to get to the hospital."

"I'm a grown woman who doesn't have to listen to you. Sure as heck won't listen to JB." She tromped behind the shoulders she'd been hoisted on to get a better view of the Labor Day parade when she was nine. "I can take care of myself without you two."

Whipping around, her uncle gave her one of his serious-as-heck sheriff looks. She stopped wide-eyed and edged back a step.

"You are a woman who came mighty close to meeting your Maker today, young lady." He pointed at JB. "From what I gather, if it weren't for that man right there, I suspect you would have. So until we get this all figured out, you do what he says."

He didn't wait for her answer, just stalked toward the

entangled truck and car.

Marcy sighed. "You and JB are stubborn, bullheaded males."

Without breaking stride, the sheriff glanced back at her. "Call Sadie."

Everything her uncle said was true. Everything JB told her to do was for her protection. Everything about the past few days had ripped control of her life right out of her hands. She hated depending on others. Especially JB. If she wasn't careful, he'd get the idea she needed him.

She watched him climb under the car one more time. A succession of Sheriff Davis, Deputy Evans, and Patrolman Kennett joined him one at a time. When he finally rolled from underneath and stood, JB clutched his arm against his side. She could tell yesterday's injuries had been forgotten in today's craziness, but his body still remembered. After examining the bag of evidence in his hand, he handed it to the sheriff.

JB's gaze briefly locked with her own then he started toward her. She met him halfway.

"The sheriff's going back to town so he can keep an eye on the vehicles." He tucked a windblown strand of hair behind her ear. "I've still got some work to do up the road a ways, so why don't you go along with him?"

Trust and tenderness surrounded her. "I'll wait here. For you."

His expression conveyed worry, tiredness. "Okay, but I want you to sit in Evans's cruiser. Or at least stand beside it where you can jump in if anyone or anything doesn't feel right. Understand?"

"I will. I promise I will."

She longed to feel his arms around her while he told her everything would be okay. As if reading her mind, he pulled her against his chest and bent to kiss the top of her head. Her arms circled him, and even though he flinched as she brushed the big bruise on his side, he held her close.

For a moment, it was like old times. Marcy and JB Bradley, full in love. Where nothing mattered but them being together, even if the world around collapsed.

"We're ready, JB," Evans shouted as the tow truck pulled away with its load.

Releasing his hold on her, JB nodded to the men, and the hardcore set of his jaw returned. "You be careful of anyone you're not really, really sure about, Marcy. That includes clients or anyone you get a bad vibe from. Anyone."

She grabbed his arm. "Surely, my clients wouldn't hate me this much."

Chapter Twelve

Hours later, Marcy sat in her uncle's office at the police station. JB sat in the main room, scouring the evidence from the accident. No, "accident" wasn't the right word—attempted murder. Every police officer around used those words. Evidently, she'd skyrocketed to number-one priority for the Crayton Police Department.

JB, Uncle Cal, and Evans joined her, each nonchalantly taking a chair in a very friendly cop mode. Did they think she was stupid? They were there to pick her brain. Try to unlock leads she wouldn't even know existed in her thoughts. Of course, she'd play the game.

"Where's my food?" she asked. Hunger had long since made itself known.

"Kennett's gone to pick up the food from Joanie's." JB leaned his straight-back chair against the wall. He flinched when he slid his hands behind his head.

"How's your side?"

"Fine." The look he shot her meant, *Don't ask in front of*

other people. "Now, we need to figure out who might have a reason to target you."

"No one." She straightened and interwove her fingers. Flexed them like the rhythm of breaths, in and out, in and out, faster and faster.

JB reached over and covered her hands, squeezing in his gentle way. "It's okay, sugar. There's nothing to be nervous about."

Bobbing her head, she unlinked her fingers and placed her hands on the desk in front of her. "I know you need my help, so I've been trying to think of anything I've done to make someone mad. And I can't come up with anything."

Her uncle moved a notepad in front of him. "What say we ask you some questions?"

"Okay." That would be better. She could answer questions.

"Let's start with the robbery…Leon…his wife."

The sheriff might have been the one to ask the question, but Evans and JB watched her intently as she replied. Jotted their own notes.

JB plopped his chair down on its four legs, bracing his elbows on his knees. "Tell me about the papers Representative Benson served you."

"How did you know that?" She hadn't said a word concerning the almost lawsuit to anyone but her sister. "Betsy…Betsy shouldn't have told you."

"Don't blame her. I asked if anybody had bothered you while I was gone."

Marcy jumped to her feet. "Why should you care? You sure didn't when you walked out the door."

He stood. "Got that a little wrong, don't you?" Nose to nose, he stared right back and never blinked. "You're the one who packed my duffle and parked it on the front porch that night. Locked yourself in the bedroom after you stuck a sign on the door saying you didn't need my attention anymore."

She looked up into the eyes she could barely stand to look away from. The ones she'd let leave because he wanted the world, and she only wanted Crayton…and him. If the times were reversed right now, she'd toss both their suitcases in the back of his truck. Escape to wherever he wanted to go.

He palmed his fingers through his hair and squinted. "What the hell did that mean? Didn't need my attention. For what? Sometimes, Marcy Bradley, you need to be a little more specific."

The sheriff cleared his throat. "Could we get back to the case at hand?"

Kennett pecked on the office glass, his hands filled to the brim with food and a tray of drinks, which he deposited on a side table. The sheriff excused himself to go check for incoming faxes. JB retrieved a couple burgers from the sack along with a canned soda and retook his chair, thunking back against the wall with more force than necessary.

Others wouldn't notice that he practically growled as he bit into the food. Wouldn't notice the hard sigh as his body released its tension. Wouldn't notice the flash of sadness in his eyes. She noticed. She noticed more than she had in a long time. She'd hurt him more than she ever realized.

Shaken by the memories, Marcy inched back in her chair.

The sheriff rejoined them empty-handed and grabbed his meal before sitting down behind the desk. "Let's take a little breather. Been a long day."

Evans placed a Styrofoam container on the desk in front of her and the two shakes she'd ordered, then took his own food and walked into the adjoining room. Said he needed to check in at home.

She smiled at the heart and flower designs floating

around her name on the top of the Styrofoam. Cute. That was a first because Joanie had never been one to be flowery. Nice to know her friend was thinking about her. Marcy sipped her shake and opened the lid of her sandwich box.

The smell of beef, tomatoes, lettuce, and onion triggered her stomach as she reached in for the usual, white-wrapped burger. Her fingers touched a folded piece of paper underneath the sandwich. A note…how nice. Burger in one hand, Marcy was poised to take a bite of the soft bun and makings as she unfolded the note.

She choked on her gasp of inhaled shock. Dropped her food as she stood. Backed away from the terrifying words.

• • •

JB shot out of his chair, engulfing Marcy in his arms as she turned to him. A quick glance showed a paper on the desk next to her food. Kennett reached over and picked up the note.

"Don't touch it." JB grabbed the rookie's arm.

Kennett jerked his head in a self-imposed sigh and grimace as he released the sheet of paper. "Sorry, man. I wasn't thinking."

"Nobody else touch it." The sheriff motioned to close the door, then nodded to Kennett. "Read what it says."

"Dear Ms. Lucky, three times is usually the charm. You must have nine lives." Kennett glanced at Sheriff Davis.

JB felt Marcy tremble in his arms, and he pulled her closer to his chest, one hand rubbing circles on her back. The other pressed into her hair as he held her close. This wasn't a time to think in terms of boundaries in their relationship. This was about keeping her calm.

"Read the rest," he said. She deserved to know exactly

what they were up against.

Kennett nodded. "...must have nine lives. If you keep being so lucky, I'll finish off your hot-shot ex-husband instead. Your choice. Your life? Or, his?"

The four men exchanged looks of definable anger. Sheriff Davis motioned for Evans and Kennett to collect the food bags from Joanie's as evidence.

When JB looked down at Marcy, he'd never seen her so quiet, so pale. He seemed to be the only thing holding her up. After leading her to the low, leather sofa at the back of the sheriff's office, he sat with her cuddled in his arms. Minutes on minutes passed. The police work wrapped up, and the sheriff closed the door behind himself and the officers as they departed the room.

"Someone really hates me, don't they?" she said.

"Don't worry. We'll get to the bottom of this."

JB felt himself swaying back and forth from side to side, hoping Marcy would walk through her shock and come out stronger. His mind raced with whys, what-ifs, whens, and hows—as well as plans for survival. He never let himself imagine otherwise when put into a life-or-death situation. Attacks called for justice. Attacks against his ex-wife called for survival. Whoever sent the message would feel JB's attack mode before this ended.

"What have I done?" she whispered.

"Not a thing." He kissed the top of her head. "Someone sick enough to write that note doesn't need you to have done one single thing. Sick people imagine what they want. Wreak havoc from there."

She sat, cupping his face in her hand. "If you'd been out there on the road by yourself today, and your brakes went out, you'd have gone over the edge. Crashed into the water."

"Nope. Might have gone over the edge, but you know

me…" Trying to lighten the mood, he poked the side of his head with his finger in an always-thinking motion. "Halfway down, I'd have opened the door and did a half-pike into the water. Swam across the lake and back again, then grabbed a couple of fish and backstroked to shore."

Marcy fake-smiled, and a smidge of color returned to her cheeks. "What kind of fish?"

Good. She was trying. He also knew she hated the water. Ever since the day their fishing boat capsized, and he'd jumped in to save her. Yeah, she'd gone in the water after that, but only if he was around.

"Bass. Super-big bass." He widened his arms in exaggeration. "Of course, I'd make you clean them."

She scrunched her nose and sweet-grimaced.

"Then I'd hose you down to get the scales and gunk off before we…" He tweaked her nose as visions of their hot afternoon exploits from the past flooded his mind. From her smile, she remembered, too, "…jumped in the lake to cool off before we…"

Marcy pressed her fingers against his lips. "Before we fried up those fish in a cast-iron skillet so big and heavy only you could lift it from the stove. And, you'd make hushpuppies and fried potatoes and your special wash-it-down concoction."

He'd have rather talked about what came between the cooling off and the frying fish. But that was a long time ago. Before signatures on a divorce decree changed their status. He forced a grin to keep the conversation light, keep her calm. "That brew tasted like medicine, but it got the job done, didn't it?"

"Got the job done."

They shared a small, breathy laugh that spoke volumes. He squeezed her close for a moment, kissing her forehead.

"To the good times we had, sugar."

"To the good times." She slid down on the sofa next to him and rested her head in his lap. Before long, her breathing slowed, her body eased, and her eyelashes fluttered, fighting sleep.

It had been a long, exhausting day. They all needed some rest. Thankfully, she could get some while everyone else worked through the evidence.

He stroked her hair as he did a chronological lineup of the day. Joanie should have a clue about who might have been around the food. Sheriff Davis would do his investigation. JB'd do his.

Marcy's breathing calmed into sleep, and her body relaxed against him. A shudder raced through his mind and his shoulders, and he clenched his jaw. Today, he'd almost lost her again. True, she wasn't his to lose anymore, but that didn't matter. He'd watch out for her just like he had in school. He rested his head back against the sofa. Much as he needed to check on what was happening outside the room, he'd stay with her in case she needed him.

The door opened with a click, slow and gentle. Sheriff Davis pushed it open further, and in stepped Marcy's mama. She looked tired. Didn't matter. Two of her girls were in danger, and no one would be able to keep her away. Sadie nodded, then tilted her head to look at her sleeping daughter. Slipping over to the sofa, she motioned she'd take JB's place.

When he shook his head, she pointed to the door. The sheriff waved him over, indicating that he needed to talk. JB slowly eased out from under Marcy as Sadie moved in. His ex-wife barely stirred, though she clutched at his hand as he let go. Her mama took hold of the grasping fingers.

Marcy's stepfather Truman entered the room and sat in the chair by the desk. He crossed his arms and leaned the chair back against the wall, mouthing his silent intent to watch out for the two women. JB nodded a thank you and headed to the door, then stopped in front of Truman, making sure to keep his body between him and the women.

Truman and him had never worked a case together for the Bureau, but they each knew what the other did. Where they went. What went down. They'd formed an unspoken bond as special agents in the field, never mind the family connection.

JB pulled a leather case from his pocket, flipped it open, and rubbed his thumb across the FBI shield he'd worn for the past few years. There was a time he thought that shield and what it meant was the world. The law was his job. Just not this time.

Closing the case, he held it out to Truman. "I know I've already given my resignation to Wilson, but I wouldn't want to tarnish the badge by even keeping it in my pocket. What needs to be done in the next few days may not exactly fall under the letter of the law, 'cause I plan to do whatever it takes to keep Marcy alive."

Truman closed his hands around the case. "You sure you want to do this?"

"You'd do the same for Sadie."

The man clenched his jaw and nodded. "Difference is Sadie's my wife."

JB fixed his gaze on the door, kept his voice low. "Just because I signed the divorce papers doesn't mean I want anything to happen to Marcy. We had some good times. Trouble is we're like two engines pulling in opposite directions. Ultimately, one of us had to let go before we both burned out."

He remembered the quiet in the house that last night before she'd set the duffle bag on the front porch. Even then he'd known the end of their marriage was near. Known there was nothing he could do but watch the end play out. Too stubborn to be the one to admit defeat, he'd waited for her to make the final break. One part of him had hoped she wouldn't. One part had known she would.

"Marcy might have been the one to push me out the door, but in the end, I was the one who let go. Stayed away and let go because…" JB glanced back at the leather case and nodded. "I figure you'll get my badge where it needs to go if something happens to me."

"Watch your back out there." Truman shook his hand.

"JB." Marcy's mother called out softly. "Before you go, there's something I need to—"

"No, Sadie." Truman shook his head at his wife. "Let it be."

"But, I told you last night about—"

"I understand, but just let it be." Truman stuffed JB's leather and shield in to his pocket.

JB glanced at the two of them, then at Marcy still sleeping quietly on the couch. His core tripped at the beauty of her parted lips, her fluttering eyelashes, her gentle fingers tucked lightly beneath her cheek. How could he ever think any less of her than the day they were married? She'd stayed with him as long as she could. Worrying about when he'd be home from the job, tending the wounds he'd returned with.

Sure, he'd been right to stay away once they'd parted. And he'd go again as soon as there was no more danger to her. He couldn't be the safe nine-to-five man she longed for, whose biggest excitement was scratching off a lottery ticket. That kind of life would kill him one second at a time. So he'd let go again, leave town, and never come back to Crayton.

She deserved better than him. All these years, he'd wondered if he was the best choice for her. Was he good enough? Had his dad been right that he wasn't worth the price of a ticket? Gazing at her right now as she slept, he didn't believe anyone was good enough for her. But he'd do anything within his power to keep her alive.

Anything.

He closed the door behind him as survival mode kicked into gear. Survival for him and Marcy meant using his skills and keeping a clear head. He knew how to stay in control. To do what he'd been trained to do in evaluating a case. In protecting the victim. In taking the criminal down. He had to think of this like every other case he'd ever had. Look for clues and meet the objective.

Only one thing hadn't been in the manual. How to handle your emotions when someone you cared about was the target.

Chapter Thirteen

JB joined Sheriff Davis and Kennett as they walked out the front door of the police station, each with their own look of determination.

"No one goes in my office," the sheriff shouted over his shoulder to the patrolman guarding his office doorway. "And I mean. No. One."

"Where we headed?" JB jogged around to the passenger side of the sheriff's patrol car. Kennett slid into his own cruiser and shadowed along behind.

Sheriff Davis' hand rested firmly on the wheel. "Joanie's. Evans will catch us up with his findings before he heads home."

"I've got a few questions for the restaurant workers myself." JB had more than a few, and there'd better be answers. His brain shouted for him to respect the position he was in. This wasn't his case, his turf, or even his town anymore. Technically, he wasn't even a lawman at the moment. What he needed to do was follow the lead of the man who trained him years ago. "That is, if you don't mind, sir."

"Figured as much. Don't overstep your non-position though." The sheriff grinned as he pulled to a stop in front of Joanie's Pizza, Pub, and Pool Hall. "Ever sorry you left town? Joined the FBI?"

"In case you hadn't heard, I quit the FBI the day Marcy got shot. Turned in my service revolver to the deputy. And just handed my shield to Truman." He eased out the passenger door before he had to answer the real question. "He'll get it to the right person if something happens."

The sheriff nodded. He knew Truman's connection to the FBI. Then he glanced at the gun holstered on JB's shoulder. "You got a permit to carry that one?"

"Yep. I've got a permit for everything I'm carrying." Of course, improvisation didn't need a permit. And he'd learned the art of making do with what you've got when your life was in the balance.

As his and the sheriff's breath fogged in the air, JB surveyed everything along the street, mentally shucking the unnecessary back out into the air. When he first started out, the sheriff had taught him the look-and-discard routine on this same street years ago. The system served him well through his undercover work.

Something was there. Something he was missing. Something to start a trail. What? He drew in a deep breath. Where? He looked again.

Joanie's sat on the end of the 500 block of Main Street, right next door to a family-owned furniture store and across the street from Dee's Morning Diner. Not much help there. The diner closed at 2 p.m., but maybe the insurance office on the right held an answer. Used to be a receptionist at the front desk by the window. He'd check them later.

Kennett parked his patrol car and sighted in on the same

surroundings.

"Well, what do you men see?" Sheriff Davis donned his hat and rested his hand for a brief moment on the butt of his gun holstered at his waist, an assurance check the man was known for, before heading to the front door of Joanie's restaurant.

JB's shoulder-holstered Glock was in plain view today. Putting on a Crayton Police jacket would have been misleading, and he'd left his own jacket in his truck at the impound lot. His backup, a .38 Special, was holstered on his inner, left ankle. Hidden under his jeans on the outside of his right calf was a quick-release knife and holder. "Depends on what the workers say?"

The rookie nodded, following behind the sheriff and JB as they entered Joanie's. Evans met them at the rear of the restaurant, his expression serious and frustrated. The report covered the happenings—food cooked, food bagged, food waiting by register. There had to be more.

Sheriff Davis pulled out his pen and notepad. "Evans. Kennett. One of you check the alley trash cans."

"Trash cans?" the deputy asked.

"See if our artist dumped the markers in the trash on his way out." The sheriff glared at the men. "And, one of you get out front. See what you can find out from the customers."

The two policemen lowered their eyes and scattered in opposite directions.

JB forced a casual tone to his voice. "Evans seems the same as before I left."

Sheriff Davis glanced at the swinging doorway. "Yep. Still questions anything he hasn't thought of. Otherwise, he's one hell of a good deputy. Good man, too."

"What about Kennett? How long's he been here?" JB remembered to slip into his conversational stance.

"Rookie's been here close to a year."

"Appears to have a good grasp on the community."

"Came with good references from a sheriff up in Illinois."

"Why'd he choose here?"

The sheriff shook his head. "Smooth, JB. But you asked one question too many to be passing time."

JB didn't care if he was smooth or not. Anybody could be focused on Marcy. "I'm not ruling anyone out I don't know."

"It's not one of my men." Davis's tone held authority, conviction, and understanding. "Trust me. I'd know."

JB scanned the restaurant as the lowering sun glared through from the outside. "Sorry. Next thing you know, I'll be interrogating dust specks in the air."

Starting at the front door and working his sight-field around section-by-section, he visually and mentally scrutinized everything. Top to bottom, bottom to top, stool to stool, table to table, booth to booth. He tensed. Coincidences topped the list of things he didn't like. Convenient details were number two.

Why was the guy in the second booth still in town? Why here? Was he really having pie? Or, rather, conveniently nursing a cup of coffee while he pushed uneaten pieces of crust around a plate?

JB made no pretense of friendliness as he walked to the booth. "Who are you?"

The broad-shouldered man who'd pulled up on his motorcycle and had carried Betsy from the car earlier in the day didn't bother to look up. He motioned the waitress for a coffee refill. "Didn't say."

Pushing himself where he shouldn't go was a technique JB had mastered. Right now, he didn't give a damn if he used tact or not. In fact, a good knock-down fight might clear his mind. He braced his arms on the table then leaned into the man's space. "I want an answer. What are you doing in Crayton?"

The man's jaw worked, and his expression said "back off" when he raised his head, but he kept his cool. "I don't believe you've showed me your badge, officer. If you are an officer."

JB reached for his FBI credentials, but Sheriff Davis' firm and gentle hand clamped down on his shoulder from behind. Finally, JB blew out a sigh and leaned against a stool at the counter behind him. Hell. He had no credentials. And he'd pushed too far.

Realizing he needed to let the police focus on the case, he glanced out the plate glass window. Wilson had been right, he was too emotionally involved. But, then again, how could he stay out of the way?

Sheriff Davis slid into the conversation as he sat on the cushion on the opposite side of the stranger's booth, popping his finger on the table...*tap, pause, tap, tap*. That used to be the code the sheriff used to mean *watch what you say*. "My friend here didn't mean anything by his questions. We're working a case right now, and he's just a little over imaginative."

The man sat his cup down, glanced at the sheriff, then grinned. "Once I heard about the trouble going on around town, I figured you'd be looking for me. Seeing as I helped at the scene this afternoon." Hands splayed in a don't-get-excited attitude, he stood, then held out his hand to JB. "You probably don't remember me. I'm Cain Connery."

JB grasped the man's hand and didn't let go. "Cain... Cain Connery. Seventh grade, I pummeled you for swiping my lunch."

The men stepped apart, eyeing each other with memories.

"A guy'll do what he has to when his belly's empty." Cain eased back into the booth. "Besides, I prefer to remember junior high when I crushed you into the ground every chance I got on the football field. Of course, Marcy was so infatuated with you, she still never gave me a second glance."

The sheriff shuffled his pen and notepad to one hand, and shook Cain's with the other. "As I recall, by the time you two got to high school, you'd both learned how to communicate. Good thing, 'cause I'm not sure which one of you'd have whooped the other."

JB grabbed a chair from the closest table, crossed his leg over the seat, and folded his forearms on the back. Yeah, he remembered Cain from years ago, but the man still hadn't said what he was doing in town. Last JB heard, Cain and his dad had been in some trouble down in the Gulf area. Maybe somewhere along the line he'd decided to hire his gun out to the highest bidder.

Sheriff Davis leaned back as if comfortable with the whole situation at hand. "Sorry to hear your dad has gone and moved to Alaska for good. I always loved hearing his stories on hunting."

Cain tensed, then eased. "Yeah, well...he's got some new stories now. Like the one where the polar bear didn't back down."

"What made him go to Alaska?" JB remembered Cain's old man. He hadn't been much, but at least the guy had stuck around until his son had joined the Army and shipped out. Had never made him a punching bag, either.

"After my discharge, it seemed like every place I landed, he showed up a few months later." Cain took a gulp of coffee. "When my job got relocated to the Anchorage office, I actually thought he wouldn't follow me that far north. Of course, I hadn't expected him to show up when I worked on the oil rigs in the Gulf, either."

Kennett returned with Joanie.

"Some of the staff needs to clock out," Joanie said. "Okay to send them home?"

"Not yet," Sheriff Davis and JB spoke in unison.

"Looks like I'd better get out of your way." Cain laid a ten on the table and stood.

JB stood also. He still didn't have his answer. "If you're gonna be in town for a while, maybe we can get together for a beer sometime."

Cain grinned. "A beer sounds good. But don't waste your money if you just want to know why I'm in town."

"Which is?" the sheriff asked.

"The old man signed over the house and cabin to me. Figure I'll remodel the house and make a few bucks when spring comes. That is if I can pick up a job for the winter." Cain opened the front door. "Hope you guys find your man."

Sheriff Davis, JB, Kennett, and Joanie headed to the kitchen.

"Hey, JB." Cain stood in the half-closed doorway, motioning him over. "I asked some questions of my own when I got to town. I know you were FBI, but right now I figure you'll do what you gotta do to protect your ex-wife. Let me know if I can help."

"Thanks, I appreciate the offer." JB wasn't quite sure what the man could do to help though. "What line of work are you in nowadays?"

Cain set his jaw, then slid his hand in his pocket returning with a small leather case. He made sure to keep it concealed between the two of them as he showed his DEA badge. "A little of this. A little that."

Suddenly the idea of him as an ally sat real good in JB's gut. "You just may be hearing from me."

"Hey, that woman I pulled out of the car okay?" Cain slid the badge back in his jacket.

"Hairline fracture in her arm."

"Not that it matters, but who is she?"

JB laughed. "Talk about wanting to know something. That's Marcy's older sister. Betsy."

"Betsy? From tenth grade history class? Umm, might need to give her a call." Cain stepped to the side as customers piled through the door. "She still appeared to be one feisty, little hellcat." He stepped outside and pulled the door closed.

Sheriff Davis looked on from the kitchen doorway. "I ain't telling Betsy what he said."

"Me, neither. She barely tolerates me as it is." JB led the charge into the kitchen. Time to move on to the next interrogation.

Thirty minutes later, the workers were clocking out, and Joanie looked as deflated as JB felt. Evans had been right—there wasn't anything of value to be learned. Didn't make sense. The note hadn't magically appeared in Marcy's sandwich box, but no one had seen anything.

Burt the cook punched his card and patted JB on the arm as he passed by, heading out the back door. "Maybe the new guy Joanie just hired'll be able to shed some light."

Joanie straightened. "What new guy?"

Chapter Fourteen

JB's gut tightened. Icy prickles crawled beneath his skin as he felt his muscles tighten. The missing link hovered in the air.

"You know. The new waiter who started this afternoon." Burt walked back to the group.

"I didn't hire anyone," Joanie said.

The men tightened their semi-circle around the cook as Joanie stepped out of the way.

JB realized his place in this questioning was nil unless the sheriff gave him leeway to ask. On the other hand, he could listen, make his own notes. He focused like his life depended on the words. No—like Marcy's life depended on the words.

Sheriff Davis hung his hat on a pot hook in the corner before he took a seat at the small table. He motioned to Burt. "Take your time, and tell us what happened."

The aging cook emitted a nervous squeak, his eyes slumped like his tired shoulders, and his hands brushed against his pants legs. He'd been a fixture in the restaurant for over twenty years. Today would be one of the man's most important days at work.

"Don't be nervous." Joanie handed him a glass of water. "Take your time."

JB sensed the unease wrestling its way through the cook. "Would you like to sit down?"

"No." Burt wrung his hands. "I mean I'd rather not sit, sir. But, I will if I have to. Whatever you want."

JB slouched against the counter behind him. He needed to put the cook at ease. Glancing at the canned goods stacked on the kitchen shelves, he wished all the foods hadn't been bought in bulk. One can could feed a dozen or more. "You've got a lot of food stockpiled back here." He walked over and grabbed the smallest can of pineapple he could find. "Mind if I open this?"

Joanie shook her head. "Fine with me. Put it on your next bill."

He jabbed the can under the opener, then fumbled on purpose. "Never could get the hang of these. Can you give me a hand, Burt?"

The cook took the can and hooked it into the opener, then reached for a bowl to dump the slices in. Joanie moved forward to finish the job herself, but the sheriff raised his finger and barely shook his head. She stepped back and then perched on a stool she pulled from under the counter.

JB accepted the bowl of fruit and forked some into his mouth, smiled. "Good stuff." He took another bite. "Now Burt, all we want you to do is tell us what happened. Can you remember? Can you help us nail this guy?"

The cook nodded, gulped his water down, then swiped his sleeve across his mouth before placing the glass in the dishwasher. When he turned to the group again, he looked composed. Ready. "Was about two or two-thirty. I'd just finished up the order Evans called in. A big one, and I wanted everything to be done 'bout the same time. If everything's hot when it's put in the bag, then it's hot for the customer when they get home. Or to the police station in this case.

"Anyhow, I had it all wrapped and piled, ready to go in the bags when this new man walked over with a Styrofoam container. Had flowers drawn on top. Said Joanie decorated it special for Marcy's sandwich. He grabbed one of the sandwiches, plopped it in the container, closed the lid, and stuck it in the bag. Packed the whole damn order for me."

Joanie cleared her throat. "I never hired anyone new. And I didn't have time to be decorating any special box what with the special delivery down the street."

The sheriff leaned on the table. "What special delivery?"

"One of the men at the lumber yard called in at 2:10 for a whole apple pie and a gallon of ice cream if I'd bring it down by 2:15," Joanie grumped. "Except when I got down there, no one 'fessed up to placing the order."

"I'll check on where the call came from." Kennett made a note.

"Probably a disposable phone." JB forked another chunk of pineapple into his mouth.

Joanie flushed. "You think the guy called to get me out of the way, so he could have access to the kitchen?"

Sheriff Davis turned his focus back to Burt. "What happened next?"

"Not much. I mentioned he must be new. Didn't think much of it. Joanie's always giving somebody down on their luck a chance." The cook glanced at his boss. "Told him my name. He never told me his, though."

"Wouldn't matter, he'd have lied anyhow. What else?"

Burt fiddled with his ear lobe. "Had a big skull earring

with swords hanging off it. I mentioned he needed to get it under the hair cover. Told him Joanie's a stickler for cleanliness and proper attire. Fact is, I pointed him in the direction of the storeroom to get a clean apron 'cause the one he had on looked like it had been through the mill and back."

"What'd he say?"

"Said he grabbed the first one he saw and went to clearing tables. Seemed kind of nervous. In a hurry. Kept looking at the clock over the sink," Burt said. "When he walked out the back door, I told him unauthorized breaks didn't happen around here. Said he forgot his insulin shot and would be right back."

"Did he come back?"

"Not yet." The cook's body eased, like the air in a balloon being released.

"You did good, Burt. Real good." JB walked over to the dishwasher, deposited his fork and bowl, then turned to Burt. "Don't suppose you could give us a description of the man?"

"Sure thing." The cook walked next to Kennett, looked up. "Yep, 'bout his height. Slim in the pants. Walked with a bad limp. You know, the kind with a hip stuck out and a draggy foot."

JB kept a straight face, but details on this description were a little too specific. A little too exact. A disguise meant to distract.

"Dark brown eyes." The cook's voice strengthened. "His bushy, black beard made me wonder why Joanie hadn't made him shave. Then I saw the scar at the edge of the hairline." He stroked his finger from his temple, across his cheek, and into the beard area. "Figured that's why she let him pass."

The sheriff stood, held out his hand. "Thanks. You've

been a lot of help. We may need to ask some more questions later, but I think we've got what we need for now."

Kennett and JB shook the older man's hand, too. And Joanie gave him a hug before he stepped out the back door.

Burt turned around. "Almost forgot the tattoo. Had half a heart on his forearm with ragged edges. You know...like one of them cutting strips on a box of waxed paper. And some numbers in it."

JB focused on what might be an identifying mark. "Could you make out the numbers?"

"Not all of them, but there was a 3 and an 8, I know for sure."

"Thanks, Burt. Thanks a lot."

After the cook left, Joanie closed the restaurant early and then headed to the pub area through the adjoining doorway.

Five minutes later, Sheriff Davis, JB, and Kennett stepped out onto Main Street.

"Nothing but one big masquerade. At least we know his height," the rookie said. "And the color of his eyes."

"Even those could have been contacts." JB's insides rumbled with fearsome thoughts. "The tattoo might mean something. But the scar might have just been the paste at the edge of the whiskers."

Kennett started down the street. "I'll check on any surveillance cameras in the area. See you guys at the office."

The sheriff and JB climbed in the patrol car and headed to the police department.

"What do you think?" Sheriff Davis asked.

JB clenched his hand then released. "I think this looks damn professional. The guy didn't miss a trick. Got Joanie out so there'd be no questions. Wore everything to make a witness not really see him. Knew Marcy's whereabouts." He ground his fist against the door.

"So where does that leave us?" The sheriff angled into his parking spot, and the two men got out and braced their forearms on the top of the cruiser.

JB assessed what he knew of the attacker.

Somebody with experience in disguises. At the restaurant for sure. Maybe other places.

Somebody with knowledge in explosives, because no matter what the gas company said, he knew in his gut the blast at her office had been professionally set.

Somebody skilled in automotives and weapons. Very skilled in marksmanship to have inched closer to the target in front of the bank, yet only wounded the victim instead of shot-to-kill. Because looking back, this had all started right then and there.

Why then? What had been different in the everyday life of Marcy that day?

Then there was what the note on the burger had said. Something about finishing off her hot-shot ex-husband.

Where did that leave him?

JB's heart pounded with adrenaline, pierced with pain at the only conclusion. He'd come home. He'd brought this with him. He'd dragged Marcy into his life of danger. Just like she'd said—danger followed him. This time it had followed him home. Right to her doorstep.

"It's me. Whoever's doing this is after me through Marcy. The guy knows everything. Almost like he knows me personally. Almost like..." JB couldn't say the words.

"One of yours? FBI or something close?" From the look on Davis's face, he'd already reached the same deduction.

"Maybe. Then again, I've had some rough cases lately. Locked a lot of people up who didn't go easy. Some of them had mighty big-time friends."

Sheriff Davis straightened. "One of those the case where you felt like you'd been ratted out?"

JB nodded. He'd always wondered if it had been someone from a previous case who'd recognized him undercover on the second one. Turned him in for a price. In fact, he hoped that was what happened, because otherwise, it meant someone in the Bureau had busted his cover. Either way, someone was out to get him. Why?

"You know the Crayton Police will follow procedure. Cover every possible scenario from our end until something shakes out one way or the other. That's all we can do." The sheriff heaved a deep sigh. "What are you gonna do?"

JB knew the drill. Get the victim, the witness, into hiding. Rotate backup watches on the safe house. Keep the victim safe at all costs to yourself. This case was different. Marcy was the victim. Survival would be key in his mind. "I'm taking her into hiding until you and your police figure this out."

Sheriff Davis leaned away from the car. "We can protect her just as good here in Crayton."

"The hell you say." JB hated to get in the man's business, but Marcy was his to save. "I'll protect her any way I have to. Got that? Any way I have to."

"I know it's hard to hear, but you've got to get your emotions under control. Otherwise, you'll get both of you killed. Be careful you don't overstep your—"

"Overstep?" JB raised one finger from his fist. "There's only one person who better be careful about my overstepping. And he better be damn afraid, because he's targeted the wrong person this time. He's target Marcy. Nobody does that…nobody."

Chapter Fifteen

Marcy felt like she'd slept for days, when in truth, she'd nodded on and off for the past couple of hours on the sofa in the sheriff's office. Every noise she heard outside the room put her on edge. JB and the sheriff must have been gone for a while, because the first time she heard their voices had been about twenty minutes ago.

She swung her legs over the side and sat up on the cushion. Time to face the world. Shuffling her fingers through her hair and accepting the lip gloss her mother offered were the extent of any attempts she made to improve her appearance.

Truman led the way out the door, then Sadie, then Marcy. She glanced around the room until she recognized JB's shoulders. Her insides relaxed with the thought that he would be the one taking her home. She didn't have to be afraid with JB around. Even if she had made somebody angry…very, very angry. She needed JB closer, so she stepped in his direction, but, intent on his conversation, he didn't turn to face her.

"Wilson, if you call my cell phone, you'll reach the Crayton Police Department, 'cause I've got a new one." Voices echoed through the speaker phone.

"Damn it." His boss gritted out the words. "Give me the number."

"No. Technically, I don't work for you or anyone else right now. I only called to keep you in the loop." JB swept his right hand to the Glock in his shoulder holster as the front door opened. "You want to get a message to me, talk to Sheriff Davis or Deputy Evans."

The rookie walked in with a couple surveillance disks dangling from his hand.

"Or Patrolman Kennett. Don't leave information with anyone else. Got that?"

"If you tell me your plans, I can cut my vacation short and give you a hand." Wilson's tone sounded attentive. "I assume you'll be heading to some type of safe house there in the area."

"Crayton doesn't have a safe house, but I've got a place lined up."

"Tell me where, and I'll get some coordinates on the place. Who knows, you may need the Bureau's help at keeping your ex-wife safe."

"I appreciate the offer, but I'm good with the few people in the area knowing where we're headed." JB stood, cricking his neck from side to side. "Besides, it could take a while getting this mess straightened."

Wilson grunted. "I thought you were already divorced."

"Yeah. But as far as I'm concerned, she's still my responsibility. If I make it out alive, I'll get in touch with you."

She rubbed the pads of her fingers from the bridge of

her nose across her eyelids and stopped. What was he talking about? Safe house? Hiding? Sounded like some kind of plan had been put into play while she slept. Shouldn't she have been involved?

JB's touch brought her back to the present.

"What's wrong?" he asked, shoving the phone in his pocket.

"Nothing." She shook his hand free. Fought the threatening tears. Make it out alive didn't sound good. Didn't sound like something she wanted him to take on out of responsibility for her.

Responsibility…responsibility…

A flood of memories rushed her emotions.

The last time her dad left on an assignment, she'd begged him to stay home for her kindergarten play. She had a leading role. He'd said he couldn't. Said he had responsibilities. Her mother would record it, and they'd all watch the video when he got back. She'd cried, explaining it wouldn't sound the same, wouldn't look real. He'd hugged her and told her he was sorry, but he had to go. Some responsibilities couldn't be pushed aside. She'd needed him…needed him there—then. Instead, he'd rejected her for his job. For a case that cost him his life.

Now here was JB, feeling responsible for her. Either he'd end up dead because of her. Or reject her once everything was settled. Reject her and leave for another case. She couldn't face either of those. She wouldn't be an obligation to hold him back, but she also wouldn't let losing him break her heart. Somehow she'd push him away like she had before. She just needed time to figure out how to do it before he got himself killed.

"My eyes were watering from the dry air in here. You know how contacts make your eyes feel funny after sleeping in them."

JB frowned. "You don't wear contacts, Marcy."

"So?" Babbling was the best she could do for the moment. A plan to get her defenses back in place would take a little time. For the past few days, she actually thought about telling him how much she wanted him to stay. To admit she'd pushed him away. To tell him the truth about... no, she'd been right to hold onto her secret. Ultimately, she was nothing but an inconvenient responsibility.

Sheriff Davis motioned JB over to his phone. "It's the call you were expecting."

JB palmed her cheek. "You're just tired. You need to eat. Get some carbs in your body. Protein." He closed his fingers around hers and pulled her along behind him, then sat her in the chair closest to him when he picked up the receiver from the desk phone. "Someone get her a soda and some peanut butter crackers from the vending machine."

"Chocolate." Marcy folded her arms on the desk. If she had to be part of this, then she needed caffeine, calories, and chocolate. "I want three chocolate candy bars." She glanced at JB "And two Paydays."

"Thanks." A grin lightened his face as he shot her a wink, then he turned back to his phone call. "Cain, if you're still willing to help, I've got a plan...thanks... This is what I'm thinking..."

Marcy zoned out from the conversation. What had happened to her life in the past couple weeks? For some reason, the thought of being dead before morning didn't compare to the feeling that would come when JB left again. No, when she forced him to leave again. Otherwise, he'd never leave...too damn principled.

He'd stay to complete every project, unless someone told him to leave sooner. The moment she had him alone, she'd tell him to go. Let the Crayton Police take care of her. She could handle pushing him away a lot better than waiting for him to reject her later. Suddenly, it dawned on her. She hadn't shoved him away for his sake years ago. She'd done it for her own peace of mind. Done it so she wouldn't have to feel the pain if he chose the FBI over her.

Her mother sat a soda in front of her and pressed an opened candy bar in her hands. Marcy went on automation. Bite, chew, swallow, drink…bite, chew, swallow, drink.

Glancing around, she realized everybody in the room had stayed for her. They'd been there through the years. And had put themselves on the front line for her now. Was she the only one who had enveloped her emotions in a cocoon since she was a child? Faced anything but her own emotional peril?

The front door pushed open a second before the scent of pepperoni and sausage and onion and green peppers filled the space. Joanie plunked three large pizza boxes on the front desk, then detoured in Marcy's direction. "Figured you might be hungry."

Second through the door, Burt set down another three boxes. "Me and the boss made these ourselves. Haven't let them out of our sight. So chow down."

Marcy hugged her friend, then the cook. "You guys are the best."

"Okay." JB walked up beside her, took her hand in his free one while the other still held the phone. "Let me know as soon as things are lined up on your end." He punched a button on his mobile, ending the call.

"Are you hungry?" Joanie asked, giving him a hug.

"Starving, but we gotta go." JB tugged Marcy behind him.

She resisted until he stopped at the doorway. "What do

you think you're doing?"

"You and me are gone." He took her by the elbow. "That's the only way I can protect you until we get this figured out."

"I'm not going anywhere. Uncle Cal will watch out for me." She yanked away. "Besides, this is my mess. Not yours. I made someone mad. Not you."

Oxygen seemed to be sucked out of the air as the room quieted.

"I don't think this is about you, Marcy." The pained expression on JB's face tore at her heart for a second. He sighed heavy before clenching his jaw. "In my opinion, whoever's doing this is angry at me. Followed me to Crayton. To you."

"How do you know?" She swayed for a second then steadied herself against the bookcase.

"That's just one possibility, JB," Sheriff Davis said. "You could be wrong."

"No… I can feel it in my gut. I brought this guy to Marcy's doorstep the minute I stepped foot in town." JB moved in front of her. "If walking outside and letting him shoot me would end this, I'd do it in a heartbeat."

She inhaled, deep and loud. When he brushed the back of his fingers against her cheek, she tilted into his warmth.

"Only this jerk wants to kill you." JB's voice broke for an instant. "Wants to make me live without you forever. You were right about danger following me. This time it followed me right to you. And there's no easy way out for either of us."

Leaning against his chest, she let the impact of his words sink in as his arms folded around her. She knew JB would fight to his last breath before he let anything happen to her. Each other…their lives depended on each other. No one else could save them.

"Will you trust me, Marcy? Go where I can keep you safe?" He eased his arms away.

"Wouldn't we be safer here in town?"

Shaking his head, he puffed a loud sigh. "There are too many people in Crayton. Too many possible suspects. We've got to narrow the trail so the police can track him down."

Her mind followed his words. Grasped his meaning. "You mean lure him to us?"

"Yes. We can't just sit around waiting for his next attack." He zeroed his look on hers. "I'll do whatever is needed to keep you safe. But, first, I need you to trust me enough to go along with the plan. Can you do that? Will you let me get us some place safe while the police do their job?"

She nodded, then nodded again. A deep sigh purged her nerves as JB walked back to the doorway. She made her round of hugs to Truman, Uncle Cal, and her mother. Sadie's hold tightened, but Marcy pushed away. She had to go with JB. She'd put his shove up against anybody's in the world.

He held out his hand to her, and she reached for it as she walked toward him. The two of them stepped outside, the door closing behind. Parked at the curb right in front of the station was JB's truck. A police officer stationed on each side meant the truck had been swept for security.

JB and Marcy eased into the cab and pulled away as she looked out the rear window. His hand closed over hers, squeezed. She turned back around. One or both of them could be killed before this ended. The thought coated her with apprehension and fear. As long as they were together, she could face her death. His? Never.

She might as well face the truth. She still loved JB more than life itself. From the moment he bumped in to her during seventh grade math to a few moments ago when she made sure to get him the Payday's he liked so much, she loved him. If she had to, she'd step in front of a bullet for him. Didn't mean they'd stay together once this was over, but for now, they were each other's rock.

She leaned against his shoulder to absorb some of his strength. Suddenly, calmness ebbed through her.

"I got you, sugar." His hand squeezed again. "I'm not gonna let anything happen to you."

Straightening, she forced a weak smile and nodded. "I know."

But what about him? He reached for one of the candy bars she still clutched in her hand, and she ripped the wrapping open for him.

Would he step in front of the bullet for her? Yes. Would he give up his life for hers? Yes. Would he take her some place safe, then leave? No. He'd stay. Stay until the end.

Even his own.

Chapter Sixteen

"You're awfully quiet." JB reached for the second candy bar Marcy held ready for him. "Did you eat anything?"

She nodded. "We should have brought one of the pizzas."

"Pizza would leave a scent the worst tracker on earth could follow. We'll eat later." He sped up, checking the mirror for headlights. None. Good. Rounding a blind curve, he slowed and checked the mirror again for anyone who might have sped up to catch them. Nothing. Good. Every minute they gained meant one more point for him and Marcy.

She flipped the heat on to low.

"You cold?" he said.

Nodding, she reached for one of his jackets. Once she snuggled inside the oversized coat and zipped it, she looked like a child playing dress-up. Her safe, little world here in Crayton had been shattered. Shattered by him. He should have stayed away. Trouble was, he didn't want to stay away. He checked the rearview mirror one more time.

The FBI agent in him clued her in on the escape scenario.

Just like any witness he'd protected, she didn't need to know the particulars, just bits and pieces. She was smart and self-reliant, but they were playing in his ballpark now. He knew she could pull this off. She didn't need to know how bad the situation might get. He knew, though. He knew they faced a crazed killer who'd stop at nothing to seek his revenge.

JB accepted the fact that the creep was from his past. Coupled with the job he just finished, there could be only one conclusion. Had to be the same psycho who'd ratted him out, landing him in the hospital with scars to last a lifetime. Only this torture was on a whole different level. A personal level.

"Looks like we're headed home. How's that going into hiding?" She shivered.

He turned the heat dial to high. "We'll only stay long enough to set the plan the sheriff and I devised into play."

"What do you mean?"

"When we get to the house, I want you to throw a toothbrush, change of clothes, and whatever else you need in a backpack. Don't make it heavier than you can carry." After jerking his head to catch the driver's profile in a passing car of the oncoming lane, he turned back to the road ahead. Slowed as they neared their street. "Don't turn the light on in the bedroom while we're there."

She scooted closer to him. "What about you?"

"I'll toss a few things in another pack." He pulled up to the house. Turned the key off. "With luck, whoever's watching our house will think we're here for the night. No matter what, we have to set the lure and reel the creep in. Hopefully, that will be all the sheriff needs to catch him. If not, then you and I will take off through the woods once I get a call from Davis."

"Where to after that?"

"We'll sneak out the back and hike to the other truck I told you about."

"Why can't we just stay here at the house? You can protect me no matter where we are."

"Whoever's doing this is a pro. If we just sit here surrounded by police, he could go into hiding for years before he strikes us again. We're not going to live like that. Right now's the time to make him mad enough to make a mistake." He grinned. "And chasing us through the woods I know like the back of my hand may prove so damn frustrating to him that he tips over the little edge of sanity he still has. Very few people know these woods like me. Very few."

JB stuffed ammo from the hidden side door compartment into his pockets. Grabbed his extra Glock, knife, and leg strap from the headliner. "Remember Cain Connery?"

She nodded.

"He's back in town and offered to help."

"Do you trust him?"

"I did a little checking. Ends up he's with DEA."

She blew out a sigh. "So where are we going?"

"I'll take you to his old man's fishing cabin over by the lake. Cain and I used to hang out around there. He's been staying there while he gets his dad's house in shape, but he'll stay in town." JB loaded the extra Glock and handed it to Marcy. "You remember how to use one of these?"

She nodded, again.

"Want a holster?"

"No, I'll use my coat pocket."

The Marcy he remembered had a more than healthy respect for guns but knew how to load, aim, and shoot. The gun didn't scare her. Shooting a person? She could. Worst case scenario, she would. Living with the guilt would come later.

"By the way, this guy may have audio equipment targeted on the house, but we've set up a block until I click the detection equipment into action. Ready?"

She blew a long, slow breath through her lips. "Let's go."

"Okay. Curtain up. Act one. Time to play the game. Pretend it's any normal day." He grinned as he slid from the truck. "You know...like last night when you tried to kill me with that damn soup."

She opened the passenger door. "Can I help it if you don't know how to say you're sick?" She dropped to her feet. "See if I ever make minestrone again. In fact, I've decided to go on strike when it comes to cooking." She clutched his jacket tight around her.

He slung his arm across her shoulder, and they walked inside. Set the lock and closed the shutters at the kitchen window. He used to hate those wooden-sun-blockers as he always called them. Tonight, they were invaluable.

Still doing their chit-chat thing, he sat a listening device on the counter, nodded to her, and clicked the button. They walked to the living room and turned on the lights, closed the blinds. If the perp tried to listen in on them, the device on the counter would alert them. Until then, they could talk normally.

She picked up her horticulture book and headed down the hallway.

"What are you gonna do with that?" He turned on the kitchen light and pulled her against him to whisper in her ear.

"Take it with me."

"No. Too heavy."

She shot him one of her looks that could get him to agreeing with anything. Not this time. "Marcy, I've got my own backpack. Guns and ammo. And, if push comes to shove, I've got to be able to react on a breath." He hovered over her as she did her patiently listening routine. "No. No book."

"Okay." She walked into the bedroom to pack with the book still in her hand.

Who did she think she was fooling with that compliance routine? He knew she'd put the damn thing in her backpack then shuck it halfway to the cabin when even an ounce of extra weight felt like a hundred pounds.

Clicking on the radio, he slipped down the hall, packed his bag, and stashed it beneath the window in the guest bedroom. They'd make their getaway from there. He returned to the living room and hoped she'd be ready when the sheriff's call came.

By his estimate, the replacement truck should already be in place out on Oak Hill Road, so there was nothing left to do but wait for one of two things to happen. Either, the perp would activate the listening device, or the police hidden in the neighborhood would pick up his movement in the direction of their house. With luck, the police might even nab him. Luck had been with them the past few days. Maybe there'd be a little left in the tank.

He settled back on the sofa and waited. Still no Marcy. Where was she? How long could it take to shove a few things in a backpack? He headed down the hallway and found her leaning against the wall. A backpack on one side of her feet, a duffle on the other side. How much stuff did she think he'd let her take?

Grabbing the backpack, he walked over to the window in the guest bedroom and dropped it next to his on the floor. The thud as the thing landed told him the book was inside. Aw, hell. He moved the book to his backpack.

But, for damn sure the other bag she had in the hallway wasn't going.

"Marcy?"

"I'm in the living room."

He walked to the sound of her voice, turned the corner, and caught a glimpse of the other duffle sitting by the front door. Looked like his big bag. Looked like the bag she packed years ago. The one he'd returned to Crayton with.

"I've decided I'm not going." She sat on the arm of the sofa. "I've decided I don't want you around here anymore." She motioned to the bag. "I've packed your stuff, so it's time for you to go." She stood, defiant as hell, pointing to the door. "You promised you'd leave when this is over. Well, I don't want you getting hurt for me, so go now."

"No." He narrowed his eyes on hers. "We don't have time for this right now."

She stormed to the adjoining dining room, pulled open a drawer in the china cabinet, and rummaged to the bottom. Returning, she slapped a big, white envelope on the coffee table. "Know what this is? This is the divorce papers you signed."

He glanced down fast enough to see the attorney's name and return address on the label. "Yeah. I know all about us being divorced. You sent. I signed. I get it."

"But I never signed them."

"We're wasting time here." He turned to walk to the kitchen. Stopped. Something in her words jabbed him like a knife and twisted. He pivoted back to face her. "What the hell did you say?"

"I never signed the papers." Her face flushed, her chin issued an occasional quiver, and she blinked. "Never filed them. So we're…we're—"

"Still married?"

Biting on her bottom lip, she nodded.

Sonofabitch. Damittohell. And every other curse word he'd ever used struggled not to come out of his mouth. "Me? You and me are still married?"

"Yes, JB. We're still married." She dumped the envelope's contents on the corner desk, then rummaged in the drawer and came up empty-handed. "Don't worry. I'll file the papers tomorrow."

What? What did she mean don't worry? His whole world had just stopped with a magnitude eight earthquake hitting his epicenter. They were still married. Him. Her. This wasn't good. Not good on so many levels. So worry was exactly what he intended to do.

"Maybe I'm being a little slow on the uptake, but how did this happen?" He raked his hand through his hair. "Did you get busy with a hair appointment? Or shopping? Or maybe you just forgot where you put the envelope."

"Trust me, I didn't forget." She raised her chin in defiant rebuttal. "Like I said, I'll file the papers tomorrow."

File them tomorrow? She'd file them tomorrow. Hell, by this time tomorrow, they'd probably be dead or fighting for their lives. He started to laugh. Couldn't stop himself. Laughed louder. She was going to file the divorce papers tomorrow…then what? Have a pedicure?

"Don't you think that's a little late, Marcy?"

"Stop laughing. This is serious."

"Damn right this is serious." He grabbed her shoulders, turning her toward him. "Why the hell didn't you finalize the divorce when I sent the paperwork back?"

"I don't know."

"Not good enough. Why?"

"Because I couldn't believe you signed the papers." She wiggled out of his hold. "Why did you sign them?"

"You sent them. I signed them."

She shoved her hands against his chest. "As you said a while ago, not good enough."

Covering her hands with his own, realization of this situation began to set in. "Because that's what you wanted, Marcy. I always gave you what you wanted. You wouldn't have sent the papers if you hadn't really wanted the divorce."

She jerked her hands away. "Not fair. That's not fair."

"Fair? You want to talk about fair?" He kicked the tote bag across the living room. Sure he'd never received the final divorce decree, but he'd figured those papers were waiting for him somewhere. "For over a year, I've believed I'm a divorced man. Single. With all the rights and privileges that word implies. What if I'd remarried?"

Gripping her fingers in the front of his shirt, she shook the fabric with all her might, as her fisted hands bounced off his chest. "Did you? Did you get remarried?"

"No. No, I'm not married. Except to you, that is."

Her fingers loosened, and she stepped aside.

He focused on what to say next. What not to say.

His marriage vows had been sacred to him. But once she sent the divorce papers, and he signed… Well, he hadn't been a saint for damn sure. There'd been a lot of nights he'd searched for someone to take her place. None ever worked out in the light of day, though. Most hadn't even worked out in a room's darkness.

"I can't believe I've been in town all this time and not so much as a hint at us still being married. Who else knows about this?"

That had to be what Sadie wanted to tell him back at the police station when Truman stopped her. The man would have realized that by JB knowing they were still married, it put another level of pressure on the whole survival gig.

Anger he'd had from her divorcing him was null and void now. Didn't mean they'd get back together, just meant they'd have time to talk in a civilized tone and walk away friends.

"Doesn't matter." Again, she rummaged through the desk drawer.

"What are you looking for?"

"A damn pen." She slammed the drawer closed. "I need a pen to sign the papers. That way, you'll have to go before you get hurt because of me."

What made her bring this up now? He sure as heck didn't know, but now wasn't the time to argue. Plus, he damn sure didn't intend to leave the house without her. So divorced or not was a moot point at the moment.

He walked over, picked up the divorce papers, flipped to the signature page, and carefully ripped out the area with his signature. Looked at her blank line and ripped it out, too. "Now you don't need a pen."

"What the heck do you think you're doing?" Marcy's voice raised at least an octave as he placed her signature section in her hand.

He tore the divorce papers in half, then half again before placing them back in the envelope. "If you want a divorce, looks like you'll have to process the papers again." He ripped his signature into shreds before wadding it in a ball and shoving it in his coin pocket where Marcy's ring had permanent residence.

She stomped down the hall. "I'm not going with you."

JB followed. "Yes you are."

"Why? Why do you want me to go?" She leaned back against the wall. "You don't even want to be here."

"What gave you that idea?"

"On the phone. At the sheriff's office." Disappointment and anger filled her voice. "I heard you say you had to stay here until you got the mess with me figured out."

"Is that what this is all about? What I said to Wilson?" He grinned, tilted her chin up. "Are you my wife?"

She nodded.

"Do you agree the shooting, the bomb, your brakes, and everything else is a mess?"

She nodded again. "What about the staying until it's settled? When this is over, you'll leave…I don't want to…feel like that again." Hiccups jerked her head like an animated bobble-head.

His insides warmed with the thought she still loved him. Might not be enough to keep them together, but she at least cared what happened to him.

He sighed heavily. They should be concentrating on surviving the night, not rehashing the past. He wouldn't lie. He hadn't come back to Crayton for her. He also wouldn't lie to himself. He still cared. Might even care more than he wanted to admit. But, this wasn't the time or the place to rationalize what that might mean.

Hooking his thumbs in his jean pockets, he tried to say what needed to be said without making any long-term commitments. "Doesn't matter if we stay here or if we go someplace else, I plan to protect you to the end. Not because you're an obligation. Or because you're just another assignment, so to say. I'm here because I want to be. Because I care about you. I care a lot."

"No. No." She shook her head. "If that were true, you wouldn't be treating me like I'm nothing but a friend."

"Now, what does that mean?" Raking his fingers through his hair, he tried to keep up with her assumptions. And listen for the beep if the audio detection device sounded.

Her body seemed to sink into the wall instead of against it. She wouldn't meet his eyes with hers. "You know."

That was the problem, he didn't know. Had no idea. First, they were still married. Now, they were supposed to be friends. What the—? "Help me out, Marcy. What am I supposed to know?"

She straightened away from the wall and marched to the kitchen, arms braced on her hips. "You haven't kissed me once."

"Yes, I have."

Sure, they hadn't been the kisses he ached to give her, because he'd promised himself he'd stay on good behavior. Keep his lips and his hands to himself. Much more of this, though, and his good behavior could go rot in hell. No, this wasn't the time. The phone might ring and they'd have to go. Of course, they were all packed. And the sheriff still hadn't called.

"You call kissing me on the top of my head a real kiss?" She pointed to the spot, then regained her previous posture. "Or that peck on my cheek, my forehead? Those aren't the kisses I remember. That's how you'd kiss a sister...if you had one."

She was about to come undone, and his insides reacted with anticipation. Even in her agitated moods, the woman could take him places his willpower couldn't block. Been a long time since she'd come undone in his arms. He relished the thought of holding her as she gave him her emotions, body, and soul. Everything.

He stepped forward, and she stepped back, landing against the counter. His next step pressed them jeans to jeans, body to body. Then he leaned in, bracing his arms on each side of her. His hardness to her softness. "Does that feel like I think you're my sister?"

Her intake of breath answered his question even before she shook her head. He couldn't stop himself from tilting into her even more. His mind had no control over his hands as they slid around to her backside and pressed her against him. Closer and closer. He groaned when she squirmed into him. She blushed, bit her lip, and then something flamed in her gaze.

"For the record, I've wanted to kiss you ever since you walked out of that bank the day I got to town." He brushed his fingers across the parted lips in front of him.

"That still doesn't account for the way you acted last night." She whispered, moistened her lips.

"What do you mean?" Sooner or later, he'd figure this out or the phone would ring or the perp would barge through the door or he'd give up and let her stay here. Which meant he'd stay, too. For now, he enjoyed the fact she was mad because she loved him.

She wiggled her fingers, but her hands stayed on her hips. "I laid there all night, and you didn't try one little thing. No nudging or coaxing. No hands. No fingers. Nooooo…well you get my drift. All you did was go to sleep and ignore me."

"I was sick."

"And this morning?"

Should he tell her he almost crawled back under the covers to be with her? "I went to get donuts."

"Donuts." She shook her head. "See, that's what I mean. All you wanted was donuts."

He narrowed his eyes on her. Best not say what he'd really wanted. "What can I say? I was hungry, and donuts sounded good about then."

Damn, he thought he really did something wrong. Had him worried for a second. If she knew how hard ignoring her had been, she wouldn't be worked up right now. The sense of rejection she felt flooded her expression. She thought he didn't want her any more.

He kissed her lips, soft and tender and slow. She nipped at his lower lip, and his tongue eased between hers as she invited him, teased him.

"We should talk before we…" He brushed his hands from her shoulders down her arms to her fingers. Slid his arms through the looped stance of her own. "You're the counselor here. Shouldn't we take this slow, Marcy? Talk and…" The sensible side of his brain nodded yes, but the rest of his brain fought the idiotic, levelheaded idea.

Her hand slid to the back of his neck and eased into a caress. The pressure he liked. The rhythm he liked. He moaned. His no-make-out plan was quickly going down the drain. Gripping her hair in his fingers, his kiss deepened. He grazed against her mouth, her ear, her neck. Hunger for her flooded his body, right along with any willpower he might still have left. Sensibility lost all meaning. Her head fell back, and she sighed, Marcy's sign of yes.

Control, he needed to regain control. Her thumb stroked up and down the side of his neck in lazy circles. Without thinking, he dropped his hands to her breasts, stroking and circling, as his mouth found hers again. Her firmness pressed against his fingers, against him, pushed him to the edge even before she slid her hand beneath the bottom of his T-shirt. Warmth from her palm grazed his skin, twitched his nerves all the way to his core. Broke what little resolve he had left.

His breaths were heavy. Hers fast. He lifted her to sit on the counter as she tugged her top upward and off. Definitely not what he planned.

"Aw, hell." He ripped his shirt over his head and flung it to the corner. "Talking is highly overrated anyhow."

"Highly…" Her fingers fumbled with the clasp on her bra. "…overrated."

She fell loose in his hands, and his thumbs made their

own stroking rhythms as he took his fill. He'd forgotten how beautiful his wife was. Her moans increased with the touch of his mouth, his tongue. She gripped him to her, her nails biting into his shoulders. He slid her closer to the counter's edge, and she slipped her legs around him.

Damn. They were still dressed from the waist down. Her thighs gripped against his sides as he fumbled with the top of his jeans. Buttons, zippers, he couldn't get his mind to think. He realized how long it had been since he tasted her skin, and he couldn't seem to get his fill. She arched and sagged against him, panting.

Bed. He needed to get her to the damn bed. Get their jeans off. His hands slid beneath her bottom and lifted. She looped her arms around him as he carried her toward the kitchen door, her fingers tight in his hair as she tilted his head back to receive the deluge of kisses she planted on his face.

"Oh, Marcy…Marcy."

"Yes, JB." She sucked his ear, nipped. "Yes. You're back. Nothing's changed."

Nothing's changed blared across his mind. He stopped. Eased her to the floor and unhooked her hands from behind his neck.

Her breathing came in ragged pants as she reached to pull him back. He gently pushed away, took a step backwards. They needed space. Room to feel what was real. What wasn't.

"What? What did I say?" She grabbed her top from the counter, shimmied it over her head. "What's wrong?"

"You said nothing's changed, and you're right. We're about to fall right back into each other's arms." His own breaths were heavy and deep. "Don't you see? We can't do that again. Pretend nothing's wrong? This time we need to talk."

She crossed her arms over her sweater. "So talk."

He recognized her stance. Her tone. She'd already shut down to anything he might say. "Things can wait till you're in a better mood." He stepped to reach for his shirt.

"No. Now." She blocked his path. "You make it sound like it's all my fault we never talk. How about the times I asked you questions about your childhood? How your day went? How it felt to arrest someone? You evaded every one of those questions."

She was right. There were things he kept so deep inside himself that they would never see the light of day again. Didn't mean there weren't things they needed to face as two people who cared about each other.

"Forget I mentioned it," he said.

"No. Either we have a conversation right now, or I'll be damned if I walk out that door with you."

"Okay. What do you want to talk about?" He'd give her a conversation she wouldn't soon forget.

She didn't flinch, just reached out and pressed her fingers against the brand on his chest. "This. I want you to trust me enough to tell me about this and the marks across your stomach."

That whole topic was off limits. Way off limits. He might not be able to hide the scar, but reliving it was one of those things hidden in a compartment in his mind. "You couldn't handle it, Marcy."

"Try me." She leaned back against the counter. "Or maybe it's you who can't handle it."

Over the line. She'd stepped over his personal line. No one, not even her, said he couldn't handle something. But there'd be no sugar-coating. This would be a telling point in any relationship they might ever have in the future. He sucked in air and blew it out.

"Jennings, my partner from a couple years ago, was killed while on assignment. Once leads stopped trickling in, the homicide got turned into a cold case. Then, not long after I worked the meth case with Landon, I got a lead. A good lead from a trusted informant. Wilson even agreed I should do a follow up. So I went to meet the guy where he wanted. Waited an hour. He never showed." JB filled a glass under the kitchen faucet, then chugged it down. Filled it again.

"When I got back to the car, three men with masks were waiting for me. Shoved me in the trunk, right alongside my informant that they'd already killed. They'd took my guns and my phone, but I wasn't worried. Might take a while, but I figured once I didn't show up back at the office, the FBI would zero in on whoever was carrying the phone and follow them to my location through the GPS."

His gut steeled with a double-clutch at the thought of just how damn long it had actually taken. "They found me dumped in an alley, a couple days and a lot of beatings later."

She'd started to fidget. Grabbed a soda from the fridge. Took a few sips before she sat it on the counter and turned back to face him. "Go on."

He gulped his second glass of water down. Filled it again. Rechecked to make sure the listening device on the counter was working.

How far should he go with this story? He'd always tried to protect her from the bad things in life. Never wanted to hurt her more than her father's death and his career choice had already done.

Everyone had said she was fragile. To work around her childhood trauma. But he knew she could be strong when she needed to be. Otherwise, she'd never have made it through the case studies in college to become a counselor.

Maybe he'd been wrong to not at least give her a chance to prove how strong she was to herself. Time to give her that chance.

She rolled her hands at him. "I said go on. Don't worry, I'm okay."

He braced his hands on either side of her as she once again leaned back against the counter. Stared her in her eyes. "They tossed me in a dark closet and brought me out every few hours to pelt me some more. I fought back. They didn't like that, so they smashed my hand with a two-by-four. Tossed me back in the closet. I fought back again, so they smashed the other hand."

She cringed.

He managed a light laugh. "No big wup."

Gulping down the third glass of water, he realized the toll this telling was taking on him. "The next time I fought back, they started with the knife across my belly until one of them reminded the others that their boss didn't want me killed."

She'd pulled her eyes away from his stare. He should stop, but he couldn't. She'd been right about this being hard for him, so they needed to walk through this together.

He tugged her into his arms and held her tight. "Every time things got bad, I thought of you, sugar. Of the good times we used to have."

"Really?"

"Really." Truth was she'd been what made him keep getting up off the floor to throw one more punch. Take one more breath in the cold darkness. Her. He'd have been hard-pressed to come out alive without their memories. "Made it easier thinking about you. The way you look first thing in the morning. Those mewy little sounds you make while you sleep. And your jasmine-scented hair."

Twining his fingers in the soft strands, he nuzzled his nose against her ear. Lowered his lips to hers and kissed. One long, tender kiss.

She kissed back. Soft and light and sure. Then stared him in his eyes once again. "And the brand?"

He cricked his neck, lifted his eyes to the ceiling, and sucked in a deep breath. That had been bad. A breaking point. "The last time they opened the closet door, they said I'd be happy to know they had their final orders. Come on out, I was going for a ride. I tried to get to my feet, but stumbled getting up. They pulled me out. Held me down on a table. The jerk whose nose I'd broke the day before kept tossing my badge in the air. Then he snapped it into some pliers and held it over a candle flame."

Feeling in his gut what had been about to happen, he'd focused on a water stain in the ceiling. Focused and focused and focused till he passed out from the pain of the brand. "And the rest is history, as they say."

She kissed the mark, then eased her hands back around his neck. Caressed the tension from his shoulders. Trailed her finger back down his chest. God, he loved the feel of that. Back to where they'd started, he slipped his hands up under her sweater. She felt good and warm and—

The phone rang.

The listening device on the counter beeped. The bright red light flashed.

The world grabbed them back.

Chapter Seventeen

Marcy slumped against JB as he lowered her to her feet. He pointed to the device and put a finger in front of his lips, then reached for the phone. She knew to stay quiet as he played the phone call con that had been planned.

"Yeah, we plan on being at the party tomorrow afternoon." JB pointed to the shirt he tossed in the corner, then covered the receiver as if it were a normal conversation. "Hey, Marcy, what are we taking to the barbeque?"

"Deviled eggs?" She could barely get the words out without her voice trembling. Setup routines might come easy to law enforcement folks, but she was a novice. Lying seemed ten times more difficult than telling the truth.

Especially when her mind was still trying to wrap itself around the torture he'd endured. She'd tried to listen as his wife, but then there was the moment when the pain had become too much to handle. Was then that she'd almost switched to her counselor mode, put up her shield of protection. But, she hadn't...she hadn't. She swiped her hand across her cheek. She would not cry. Would not let him know she might not be able to handle them being together for the long haul.

She tugged on the bottom of her sweater. Stuffed her bra in the pocket of her jeans. The implication of the past few minutes flew from her core to her brain and back again. He wanted her. They might be dead before morning, but skimming her fingers across the tanned hardness of JB's chest had been ecstasy. Pure need, want, and lust ecstasy. That she wanted to finish.

Instead, she picked up his shirt and stood quietly beside him in the kitchen.

"…yeah, she said deviled eggs. I'll bring a cooler of beer, too. What time?" JB pulled her against him and encircled his arm around her shoulders. "Two sounds great."

How would she ever get through this? A shiver took her, and he squeezed her tighter.

"Yeah, it's been a long day. Think we're gonna turn in early tonight." His cheek rested on the top of her head. "We'll be there. See you tomorrow."

He locked the key pad, powered off the phone, and shoved it in his pocket. They clung to each other for a brief moment, which ended in one long kiss before they broke apart. After pulling his black, thermal shirt back on, he strapped the Kevlar vest in place. He double-tied his boots, checked the back-up gun on his inner, left ankle, and strapped the knife holster on the upper part of his inner, right calf. The knife thingy was new, like the scars on his chest and the brand.

Where had he been the past few years? What had he done? She wanted to know, yet part of her didn't. She figured he's share what he wanted, when he wanted. Following his advice to be his wife, not his counselor, was exactly what she planned to do. She'd listen with love whenever he decided to talk...even if it was years from now. No more counseling techniques would float between the two of them.

She watched as if a moviegoer at the cinema. The film an action-adventure flick. The hero hot and dangerous. The woman in trouble and willing. Together, they'd run the gamut and come out in each other's arms by the time the credits rolled. Only two things wrong. This wasn't a movie. And the credits might be their obituaries.

He cupped her face in his palms as he kissed her one more time. Her fingertips stroked his cheeks. Tender and deep, their kiss sealed their commitment to stay alive.

Holding her hand, he walked to the hallway. "You about ready for bed, sugar?"

She nodded. He pointed to his mouth for her to talk.

Stretching, she stepped into the bedroom, then crossed to the bathroom. "I'll be there in a sec."

"Good. I'll lock up and get the lights. Meet you in bed." JB headed to the living room to make the round of typical get-ready-for-bed sounds.

Thinking to the upcoming run and the cold weather, Marcy scurried to the toilet. Once finished, she opened the door, and the nightlight's soft glow illuminated enough for her to see what looked like two people snuggled in bed. She jerked on an intake of fearful breath before JB pulled her to the side and covered her mouth with his hand. Pillows...he'd scrunched pillows in bed.

Next, he bundled her in his down-filled parka she kept in their closet. After she pulled a pair of ear warmers on, he topped them with a ski hat, and finally, she tugged on her wool gloves. She realized the temperature would have dropped outside since the sun went down. Plus, the weather forecast had been for a cold front to move through sometime in the next few days. After JB pushed thermal gloves over her wool ones, she figured he planned on a blizzard overnight.

Back in the truck, before they came inside, when she asked him why they couldn't stay at the house and wait for the creep to make his move, JB said this looked like a highly professional job. Staying at the house to see what might happen was a risk he wouldn't take with her life. Hopefully, the police would nab the guy, and they'd be back by noon tomorrow. If not, they'd be safe somewhere else.

She'd understood. For the first time, she also understood that if it wasn't for him protecting her, he'd be hell-bent on finishing the job himself. Maybe her needing protection meant safety for him. She planned to keep that thought until a better one popped into her mind.

"Snuggle on over here, Marcy. Get yourself warm." The rehearsed dialogue rolled off his tongue.

"No. I'm fine on my side." Her mind raced to remember what came next.

"Well, I do mind. Now snuggle up, I'm cold. Good night, Marcy."

She fake-giggled. "Good night, JB."

He tugged her down the hallway, their footsteps quiet on the carpet. Role play finished at the guest room window as he donned a pair of night-vision goggles. Then he fitted her with a pair right before he lifted their backpacks, opened the window, and dropped them to the ground. He lowered himself out the window.

Leaves crunched to the back of the house. He plastered himself to the wall like a sticker on a notebook, then dropped to the ground. Flat on his belly against the dirt, legs spread, boots dug in, gun drawn and aimed, he was in combat mode. Ready to shoot, run, or fend off attack.

All she could do was wait inside, peek over the window sill, and listen. She knelt, leaving her gloved hand on the sill. After a few more crunches that sounded more like a scampering possum, his hand covered hers and tugged. She climbed out into his waiting arms. He positioned her backpack and locked it in place, then tweaked her nose with his finger, grinning as he settled his own pack in place.

For having her bundled for extreme cold, he looked casual in his clothes, except she knew the Glock and holster were strapped over his shoulder out of view. Knew they both had on Kevlar vests. Once she touched him, though, she felt the softness of layers of sweaters beneath the light jacket, coupled with the thermal wear she'd seen when he raised his jeans to position the knife on his calf. He'd stay warm.

He'd mentioned he needed to be able to react hard and fast. Fingerless gloves and lack of a hat caught her attention. The gloves she understood for the gun, the knife, but he should wear his hat. She pointed to her own then him. He shook his head, pointed to his ears and the surroundings. She got it…he needed to hear.

Again, the crunch of leaves. This time from the front of the house. He tensed and spun in that direction, gun raised, finger on the trigger.

Her heart rate notched up as fear grazed her senses. She'd heard people in counseling talk about the taste of fear. Until now, she hadn't known what such a thing would taste like. Now she did. Not so good. Wouldn't be easy to forget. Her breathing jumped into overdrive as she tried to ignore the vile taste permeating her senses. She had to get her control back. The last thing he needed was for her to hyperventilate.

JB pushed her back and stepped in front of her. Held his hand for her not to move. The rocker on the front porch squeaked with movement. Wind? Was there enough to move the chair? More crisp, brittle sounds of breaking, dried leaves littering the ground.

He tugged her close behind him and edged to the corner of the house. Flattening herself to the siding, she tried to blend in with her dark coat and gloves. He'd made sure neither of them had any light color clothing on. He inched a small corner mirror out in front of him. She glanced over his arm to see the reflection. Nothing.

Turning back to her, he holstered the gun. Evidently, he thought it was nothing more than the wind.

She looped her thumbs under the backpack straps across her chest. That had been their I'm-ready-to-go signal years ago when she'd gone hunting with him. He did the same with his, then turned and headed in a low crouch to the tree line. She followed close behind.

Her vision focused, cleared, and she stumbled, crashing into him. He turned, catching her with one arm, then jerked his eyes to the left. The semi-automatic strapped to his thigh was in his hand before she realized JB had moved. The one she thought of as his SWAT gun. Her heart raced, pounding fast and heavy. He never wore that unless the situation was wild. Unpredictable. Dangerous beyond dangerous.

And, she'd never seen him pull it…until now.

He pushed her in front of him, then turned and walked backwards behind her.

The taste in her mouth deepened. What the hell had he seen?

Patting her coat pocket to make sure her own gun was still there, the enormity of their situation bombarded her. After about twenty steps, he motioned her to stop. She steadied herself and stood beside him. Ready and waiting to follow his order. He nodded and hooked his thumbs under his straps—she did the same.

They moved forward as one as the woods closed in behind them.

Chapter Eighteen

JB flipped the image through his mind as he shortened his strides so Marcy could keep up. What had zipped around the back of their house as he turned to catch her? A fat raccoon? A wolf? Or something more ominous? Maybe a shadow, nothing else. A shadow. His gut instinct warned otherwise. As professional as the hits had been so far, the perp wouldn't chance entering the house before the people inside had a chance to fall asleep. He would wait. Wait until they were sound asleep, then charge in to wreak his chaos.

The couple trekked through the trees and brush, downed limbs tangled in mud from tiny hillside rivulets. A slight mist of rain helped cushion the sound of their footsteps on the fallen leaves. The hike stayed uneventful. He stopped, pointed to a few deer making their way through the night, trying to stay warm. For an instant, it seemed like old times. He heard her breathing lessen just a bit. A shared moment, fingertips, and a memory. Then the moment passed, and they trudged on through the darkness of the forest.

The sound of a truck revving its engine signaled him they were close to the next leg of their journey. He tucked her close behind him until glimpses of the road ahead flickered through the brush. They crept to the edge of the tree line. The truck idled close to a hundred feet down the gravel road. Inching through the cover of trees and darkness, he positioned them straight across from their ride. His mind, eyes, and instincts sharpened to the surroundings. Was this the right truck? The right driver? Or, had someone else come? Figured everything out?

A lighter flickered in the driver's area. First time got his attention. Second time, he got enough of a look at the man behind the wheel to risk their lives. Marcy leaned into JB as he pointed to the open, passenger door on the rear cab of the truck. Interior lights dark, only a small, directed, pin-sized glow of light beamed from the floor bed.

"When we break the trees, all you have to do is get in the back seat. I'll be right behind you." He tightened his fingers around the sleeve of her coat. "Understand?"

She nodded. "Are you sure it's Cain?"

"Yeah." At least he hoped the driver was Cain. If JB's instincts had been wrong in trusting the man, then it wouldn't matter, because their lives wouldn't be worth the price of a bullet.

"Are you sure?" She glanced at the truck and back to him, her eyes wide with fear.

Ignoring her question, he eased his Glock from the shoulder holster, and then hung his arm back down his side, finger on the trigger. "Get ready."

Grasping the straps, she hefted her backpack further up on her shoulders, the look on her face focused and intent. He looked behind them one last time and scanned right, front, left.

Up the road, headlights beamed in the distance, growing in size. The man in the truck jumped out, ran around the back side, a shadow of a pistol in his hand. JB shoved Marcy to the ground and crouched beside her. Looked like Cain's build. Who was behind the wheel of the approaching car, though?

JB handed Marcy the Glock and released the semi-automatic from his thigh. If he was wrong, they'd need everything he had. There'd be no time to run. No time to disappear. No time to think. Reaction meant everything. Would his timing be better than the perp's?

The man stopped by the back fender. Headlights closed on the scene. Marcy shivered as she braced on her elbows, gun focused straight ahead and tight in her grip. JB locked the semi-automatic's handle into place, ready to fire. Didn't matter who heard the click. Too late for stealth.

"Hold where you are." Cain's voice rasped. "I got this covered."

The car pulled to a stop along the truck. "Car trouble?"

Cain wandered back around the rear fender, zipping, readjusting his pants, his coat. "No. That last beer made a beeline straight through. Had to stop for a nature call."

A man's laugh floated through the air. "Been there."

"Thanks for stopping, though."

The car drove away, the taillights disappearing around a bend in the road. Cain jumped in the driver's seat and started the truck.

"Now." JB tugged Marcy upward.

She ran to the open doorway and launched inside. He braced himself as he landed on her a second later. The truck was moving before he got the door slammed.

Settling to the passenger side floor bed, JB motioned Marcy to the other side. "Who was that?"

"Old man Parson and his wife. From the looks of them, they must have been coming home from Joanie's." Cain turned onto the main road which smoothed out the bumps in the ride.

"Anybody else been by?"

"Not that I saw." Cain handed back a thermos and cups. "I been driving a two-mile loop and some of the side roads for the past hour. Came back when I figured you'd be close."

JB poured a cup of coffee and handed it to Marcy after she tugged off her hat and gloves.

"There's a couple blankets on the seat back there if you're cold." Cain kept his focus on the road ahead except for the frequent glances in the rear and driver's side mirrors.

"Thanks." She sat quiet, sipping the heat into her body.

Cain's phone rang. "Yeah, I got them."

"If that's the sheriff, I need to talk to him." JB reached out to take the phone, then put it to his ear. "Anything happen there?"

"Nope. Everything's quiet on this end. Looks like the plan worked," Sheriff Davis replied.

"Go in the house now." Trying to muffle his words from Marcy, JB ran his hand across his face. "I thought I saw something as we left."

"You sure 'bout this? We'll blow the stakeout if we go in."

Adrenaline pulsed through JB's body. "Yes. Go inside now. Call back as soon as you check it out."

The call ended, and when he glanced across the floor bed, he looked into Marcy's brown eyes. "Probably nothing," he said.

She nodded, sipped more warmth from the cup.

A few minutes later, the phone rang, and he turned to muffle the words. The less Marcy knew the better off she'd be. "Yeah?"

Sheriff Davis cleared his throat. "You were right. He's been in and out. Looks like he came up through the crawlspace under the house. None of my guys saw or heard anything."

"How's that possible?"

"Kennett said it looked like the floor around the register in the utility room had already been cut out. Repositioned on some blocks under the house." Davis sighed deep. "No telling how long he's been planning this."

JB leaned his head back against the door, cricking his neck from side to side. The breath he took in expanded until the force of the Kevlar vest clinched tight against his body before he blew every bit of air out. He could feel her stare but didn't look over.

The sheriff cleared his throat. "He left you a couple of notes. One on the pillows in your bed. Along with ten 38-caliber bullets on the other pillow."

"Repeat the last." Inside, JB churned with heat, chaos, premonition.

"Ten 38-caliber bullets," Sheriff Davis replied.

JB tensed with rage. The creep had walked their floors, stood by their bed, touched their pillows. Who had he angered this much? Was it actually someone in the Bureau? Or someone who'd been sent to settle the score for a busted drug runner? Terrorism? No, none of his cases had come close on that count.

Maybe this was tied to Jennings' death in some way. Maybe there had actually been a child slavery ring, and the girl who'd lured Jennings to his death had been an innocent victim guiding him to the wrong place at the wrong time. Those involved could want to silence everyone involved before starting up again.

But in that case, why hadn't Landon been targeted? Wouldn't they think JB'd tell his new sometimes-partner his concerns from past cases? None of this made sense.

Why make it so personal? Why hadn't they finished him off right away, instead of torturing him for days and risking the FBI coming to his rescue, as they had? Why toy with them now, instead of just shooting to kill? He raised his shoulder and stretched his side enough to loosen the kink grabbing the bruise from the building blast. "What did the note say?"

"The one in the living room looked like it had been scribbled fast. Said he heard you say you knew the woods like the back of your hand. That he'd like a good chase. Go for it." The sheriff stopped. "That's all on that one."

JB thought back. Exactly when had he said that? "What does— Wait, I said that in the truck. That means he's really got some heavy-powered listening device somewhere in that yard."

Also meant this was a game to the guy. A hunt. Somewhere behind them was a killer. Right now, they were ahead, because JB had expertly crisscrossed his and Marcy's path in the woods. The man was probably lost about now. Lost and mad. Getting madder by the minute.

"We'll check."

"Also, means he knows this was a set-up. Read the other note."

"Is Marcy listening?" the sheriff asked.

"No." He braced for bad…real bad. "Go ahead. Read it word for word."

"To the lovely couple. Sorry I missed you. Hope she didn't hurt herself when she stumbled. See you soon." Sheriff Davis sucked in a breath. "Would have loved to hear the ending to what you started in the kitchen. Marcy sounded hot. I like my women hot."

JB's eyelids flew open, and he ground his fist into the seat beside him. He stilled, then rested his hand on the knife strapped to his thigh. The sonofabitch was gonna pay. Fast or slow, didn't matter. He pulled himself back from where he'd mentally gone. He needed to focus.

Reactively, he reached for Marcy, and she scrambled across the floor bed into his arms. His arm engulfed her as she huddled against him, her fingers unconsciously stroking his jaw line. Even though she didn't know what was wrong, she was scared. Scared because he'd let his anger rage. He willed himself to relax enough so she wouldn't be afraid.

"You okay?" Sheriff Davis asked.

"Yeah. We're okay." He clutched his wife against him. "We'll keep the plan in place. Let me know if you get anything else."

"Sure thing."

"I'm gonna hand the phone over to Cain. Read him the notes before you hang up." JB passed the phone forward to the driver.

Marcy's hand found his. "Did they catch him?"

"No, he was already gone when the sheriff went in."

"You said something about a note. What did it say?"

"Just something about hearing us inside the house earlier. He thinks he can outsmart the rest of us." He eased her away, patting the seat. No way would he tell her what the second note said, but she needed to know the guy was hunting them. "Marcy, whoever is after us is sadistic. I think he may be involved with the hit men who branded me with my shield. This is all a game for him. Back at the house, he left a note saying he'd enjoy chasing us through the woods."

Her eyes narrowed with righteous indignation. "Means that was him outside the house. He watched us leave."

JB nodded. He heard Cain click the phone off and knew he was taking everything in from the front seat. Maybe he'd have some suggestions once she dozed off.

"We made it to the get-away truck, so that means we lost him."

"For the moment." How should he word what he wanted to say next? Straight and to the point. "I gave you the gun for a reason. Promise me you'll pull the trigger if our lives depend on it." What a thing to tell his wife to promise. But better prepared than surprised.

She nodded. "I promise. He won't take either one of us if I can help it."

Good. He knew he could count on her. "For now, I want you to lie down and get some sleep. We need to get some rest before the next leg of the plan."

She stretched out on the leather as he covered her with the blanket. "Will he?"

"Will who what?" He knew damn well what she meant.

Scrunching her hat and gloves under her head for a pillow, her cheek rested gently on the softness, her eyes boring into his. "Will the man outsmart all of you?"

"No, Marcy. He won't. I told you before, I'm not gonna let anything happen to you." Stroking her hair, he kissed her lips, then leaned back, gave her a smile. Her eyes closed along with her small return smile. "Get some sleep."

She snuggled under the blanket. "You know, from a purely psychological reasoning, I think the guy's trying to make you suffer. Sure, he wants to take me out, but mainly he's in it to make you feel a pain he's felt. You know…like you hurt his woman or daughter or mother, someone like that, and he'll hurt yours."

"I've already thought of that." He leaned his head against hers.

"And when the time comes to settle the score, he needs to see your reaction as I die. Then he can live the rest of his life at peace knowing his revenge was complete."

See his reaction? His reaction would be to kill the damn sonofabitch.

Still, what she'd said was an interesting deduction. One he could use. That might be what the jerk wanted, but he'd use the plan against him when the time came.

"Thanks, sugar."

"For what?"

"An idea." He needed to think on a decoy to be the final lure when the time came. "Guess you were right, danger follows where ever I go. I should never have come back."

She brushed a kiss across his lips. "I'm glad you did, though."

Cain kept the truck moving down the road, his eyes never looking back. Never a hint that he could hear everything that had been said.

JB tried to think what they might have missed. Too much at stake for him to overlook any clue. If the clues were there, they were hidden like a man covering more than his tracks. Like someone covering from a trained background.

"Here's something else. He's reacting to a perceived wrong. One you may not even know happened." She elbowed up just a bit, looked him in the eye. "Yes, he wants you to be there when I die. He won't decide whether to let you live or not until then, either."

He knew what she meant. Seeing her die, knowing he hadn't been able to stop it, would be the ultimate suffering. And to live with that would be even worse than dying.

"Of course, that all depends on how far he's gone over the edge of reason by the time he finds us." Sighing, she laid back down. "Bottom line…who knows I'm your wife?"

"Not just that. They'd need to know where you live and that I'd be here."

How would anyone have known he'd head back to Crayton at this exact time? Sure, he'd thought about heading home after Jennings was killed, but he'd shaken it off. There'd even been the meth lab bust that went bad when he worked with Landon for the first time. Still he'd decided to stay with the FBI. Wasn't until after he'd been hurt on the last case that the idea—go home, see his ex-wife, make amends—kept flashing in his mind. Then the reprimand for nothing from Wilson had been the tipping point.

None of this fell together. At least, none he could see right now. Maybe he'd think better after a little sleep himself. Otherwise, the only rationale was that they followed him and chanced on the perfect setting to make him suffer. Not likely.

Sliding her hand from under the cover just enough to touch his body, she closed her eyes. A few miles later, her soft sleep sounds pulsed in his ear.

JB flipped the attacks through his mind, piecing them together with what she'd said about the thug chasing them to see if anything shook out. Could the would-be killer have seen his reaction each time? Been getting off on the rage and misery he saw JB experience in each desperate moment?

The bank shooting. Had the shooter actually tried to kill Marcy or just wound her? The office building explosion. He'd got her phone call to pick her up. Had there been a listening device in her office? After all, he'd only been half a block away when the blast ricocheted through the air.

If this guy were that sophisticated in his techniques, then there'd be no way to trace the bullets or the note back at the house. There'd be no evidence from the crawl space underneath the place. There'd be no prints. No DNA.

Nothing that didn't belong there.

JB'd done the same in his undercover work. Having all the procedures thrown back in his face was either a blessing—because he knew what to look for—or a trail to the end, because the person had figured out his modus operandi. In which case, that meant every reaction he made would be calculated into the creep's plan.

Who knew him that well? Who knew how much Marcy meant to him? Or was that just a guess?

Cain glanced over the seat. "She asleep?"

"Yeah. What did you get from the notes?"

"Cat and mouse."

"Exactly." JB leaned his head back. "Cat and mouse. In fact, she may be right about him trying to make me feel his pain. Maybe leaving me alive as more punishment."

"You've riled somebody mighty crazy out there." Cain shook his head. "This isn't about some gang retaliation or a hit being put on you. This is flat out personal. I bet there's a link between this and your past couple cases."

JB's thoughts flashed to the last case. The thugs beat him within an inch of his life, slashed the knife across his chest until one of the guy's stopped the others. Said their orders were to keep him alive. So they burned his shield into his chest and threw him in the gutter. Now this. "That's my thinking, too. You been with the DEA long?"

"Long enough to know you follow the roadmap back to whoever's out to get you. Check off the players in your past jobs. Don't leave anybody out as a suspect. Nobody."

"Yeah." JB learned in training, no one was above suspicion. Who, though? Who'd he missed? He couldn't think any more, his brain was tired. His body ached from the past few days of blows and bruises. A fog settled around his thoughts… There was a clue…there had to be…one clue was all he needed. Tired, so tired…there was always a clue…someplace…where was the damn clue?

"Get some sleep, buddy. No telling when you'll be able to rest again." Cain turned the radio on low. "I'll drive up to Jefferson City. Nurse a beer in one of the bars for an hour or so. You two can sleep back there. With the tinted windows on this truck, no one will be able to see you. Should still give us time to get you where you're going."

"Appreciate it." JB angled his head as close to Marcy as he could, holding her hand. "You know, right before we left the house, she told me she never signed the divorce papers. Never filed them."

"That's some mighty heavy news to have dropped." Cain paused, clearing his throat. "How you feel about that? About still being married?"

"I don't know…I honestly don't know." He'd think about that later. Right now, staying alive was top priority. His eyes drifted shut.

Ten .38 bullets. Why thirty-eights? Why ten? Why…?

Chapter Nineteen

She was awake, but Marcy didn't want to open her eyes. Instead, she wanted to lay there with JB just a touch away and pretend they were home in their own bed. Tucked beneath a nice, warm blanket with a shared glass of wine on the night table. They'd have nothing to do but make sure each other was happy.

"Wake up, sugar." JB nudged her shoulder.

She stretched, smiled, then elbowed up on one arm and caressed his cheek. Reality slammed full force as the past twenty-four hours flashed through her mind. She jerked to sit up.

His hand pulled her back down. "Be careful. Someone might be following."

"Where are we?" Her insides felt fueled by fear. Her outsides hurt and ached from the bulldoze effect of brush and trees slamming against her as they ran through the woods earlier. "How long have I been asleep?"

"About four hours. Cain's been taking us on a road trip

around the county." He shared his cup of coffee with her. Handed her a sack. "Even bought us a couple of sandwiches at the bar in Jefferson City."

Famished, she scrounged inside and came up with a hamburger. "You don't know how much I need this."

Cain kept his eyes glued to the road ahead. "My pleasure. By the way, I swung by the cabin and upped the heat. Plus there's plenty of food stocked up."

"Thanks." Marcy swallowed a bite of burger. "And thanks for helping us. I doubt you ever planned on being part of a good-guy-bad-guy scenario."

"You're right about that. I'm just a nice, peaceful kind of guy." Cain glanced at JB, and the two men shared a like-hell expression.

Someday, she'd ask what that was about, but for now, she was content to know she and JB had a friend willing to help.

Every so often, Cain glanced in his mirrors. "About twenty more minutes to drop off."

"Eat up, Marcy." JB straightened. Checked his gun. Reached under his sweater, readjusting the Kevlar vest. "As soon as you're finished, I want you to start stretching your arms and legs. You need to be able to run the minute we hit the ground."

She swallowed the last bite before finishing off the coffee. "Did you sleep? Eat?"

He nodded. "Always thinking about how I am, aren't you? How'd I get so lucky?"

"You were the best-looking jock in high school." She longed to feel his arms around her like the times they parked at Crayton's lookout point, cuddling to the sound of soft music. They'd even gone there a couple times after they were married.

Cain cleared his throat in mock gruffness. "I beg to

disagree about him being the best jock in school."

"Well, you were always a really close second."

For a moment, the three of them laughed at memories. Then the quiet consumed them.

"Get your gloves and hat on, Marcy." JB worked his legs in a pedaling motion, stretched his arms forward, and bent his back.

She followed his lead and gradually got into her own rhythm. "What time is it?"

"About three. We should be to the cabin by four, four-thirty, at the latest."

"Won't it be light by then?" Her hand checked to make sure the gun still rode in her pocket.

"This time of year, probably won't be light until five-thirty, six, maybe later."

"Getting close." Cain turned the truck onto what had to be a rutted, gravel road from the bounce and jog motions. "Just so you know, I've got a guy waiting alongside the road where we're gonna stop."

JB's jaw clenched. "Who?"

"Don't worry. He's okay." Cain glanced back. "I wouldn't bring him in otherwise."

She could see the look on her husband's face. He wasn't convinced. Wasn't happy about the change. His hand hadn't left the Glock in his shoulder holster since the guy was mentioned. She tensed right along with him.

"Why?" JB asked.

"Figured we need a diversion in case we are being followed." Cain flashed his lights. "Me and him will do a deal out here in the middle of nowhere. And, of course, first I'll want a sample. Should give you enough cover time to get a good ways into the woods."

"Does he know we're in here?"

"He knows someone's here."

JB eased the gun from his holster, motioned her to the far side of the floor bed. She moved quick and silent. Her insides churned with nerves and nausea and nagging stomach cramps. She shouldn't have eaten the burger. Scared didn't even begin to describe what she felt, except that underneath it all was the knowledge that her husband would do what had to be done. And she'd do the same.

Cain stopped the truck, backed up, and angled the truck bed toward what must be the woods, front end to the pavement. Someone coming down the road wouldn't see them get out. The engine purred into a parked rumble, the slight illumination from the headlights clicked to blackness.

"Keep your finger off the trigger. The man's okay." Cain said. "If I wanted to take you two out, you'd already be dead."

"You might have tried. Let's get this done." JB turned onto his knees, holstered the Glock, and then rested his hand on the door handle. "Cain?"

"Yeah?"

"Thanks, man. I owe you one."

Cain nodded, opened the driver's side door, and then jumped out.

JB clicked the rear, passenger door open at the same time. Marcy crawled behind him as he slid from the truck, then he held out his hand to her. He crouched, Glock back in his hand, and pointed at the rear of the truck bed. She knew to wait until he motioned, but she hitched the backpack into place, then patted her pocketed gun one more time.

"Hey, there." Cain's words came from behind them now. Evidently, someone else had pulled up. "I hear you're the man with the good stuff around here."

"Where'd you hear that?" The other man's voice held a

heavy Texas twang.

JB motioned her to get out of the truck, stand behind him. She did exactly as he said, as fast as she could, as quietly as she could. She wouldn't let him down.

"Some guy back at the bar said this road held pure gold." Cain's voice had taken on a friendly, down-home country drawl. "Figured I'd stop by. See what you got."

"What you looking for?" the other man asked.

"Maybe a little…"

JB jerked Marcy forward. Crouching, they ran into the woods. Further and further. Trees and more trees blocked their path. He tried to keep the limbs from flying back to hit her once he passed. Some didn't, some did. A trickle of warm blood oozed down her cheek after one blindsided her like a whip. Bushes and thorns grabbed at her jeans. Large, low-lying rocks seized her footing. She tripped. Fell. Knocked her chin on the ground. JB grabbed her and lifted her straight to her feet.

She looped her thumbs under the straps. He turned back to his trail-finding mode and surged ahead. She followed. One foot in front of the other. Her lungs burned. Leg muscles tensed. She needed water, needed rest. How long had it been since they left the warmth of the truck at the edge of the woods? Still she followed. Her right calf cramped, and she grimaced with a reactive groan.

JB turned. The set of his jaw conveyed his anger at the unexpected sound, then his expression shifted to concern. He laid her on the ground, massaged her calves, grabbed a bottle of what looked like water from his backpack, and motioned her to drink. The taste screamed of electrolytes. She took half and gave him the rest. He massaged her legs until she motioned to stand.

On her feet again, she looped her thumbs under the

straps one more time.

He leaned in, placed his cheek against hers. "Not much further, sugar."

Her mind shouted how much, but she didn't ask.

He forged ahead.

She followed.

. . .

JB slowed his pace once Marcy's leg cramped, amazed she'd been able to keep up for that long given having surgery a couple weeks ago. If they could have driven instead of hiked to the safe house, the trip would have been easier. But the more twists and turns, detours, and unexpecteds they could throw in the perp's way, the more time they bought for the sheriff's department to search for clues. The more clues, the better chance of tracking him down.

The pinkish glow of dawn on the horizon urged him forward. His one goal was to reach the cabin before daylight. Ten minutes ago, they'd approached the wrong cabin. They'd turned away in time when the sound of a dog's bark from inside signaled their approach. He heard the owners tell the pet to lie down.

Soft pine boughs swept aside as JB walked through the trees. He stopped. The cabin visible through the tree line called up memories he forgot even existed. The flagstone steps leading down a more than slight incline to the dock. A porch wrapped around three sides of the house. The black, cast-iron bell on one of the end posts of the railing. This was the right place.

Motioning Marcy to stay behind him, he crept to the back side of the house, gun drawn. He gave a quick look through the lower pane of glass on the only window along the back wall. Nothing but closed, louvered shutters greeted him. On the south side, he found the same at the next two windows. Made sense. As he recalled, the two bedrooms were on the south side of the house.

They reversed their steps to the north wall as his mind played the inside set up from fifteen years ago. Back corner... kitchen...one window...curtained. Through the crack of the two yellow panels, he managed a good view of the room plus part of the bedrooms across the way. A nightlight shown from the bathroom nestled between the two open doorways, just like Cain said he'd left the place. He also said the heat would be on. They could use some heat.

JB felt more than saw Marcy shiver. She was cold, tired, and way past her limit for survival, but still she did everything he told her to do. Someday, he'd tell her how proud she made him the past few hours. Hell, the past few years.

The front side was the tricky part. He had no intention of letting her out of his sight, but at the same time, he needed to get a look in the living room and unlock the door with the key Cain had given him. He needed to sweep the interior for possible lurkers, stomp on all the damn floors, and climb into the attic, too. Interior sweeps were routines he prided himself on for saving lives in unknown situations.

Stomping on floors had been added tonight after the conversation with the sheriff.

So much for routine. Surprise would have to do this time. He motioned her to follow on the count of three. Yelling, he jumped on the porch, quick-glanced through the window on his way to the front door, shoved the key in the lock, and turned.

"Watch my back." Glock tight in his grip and aimed, he charged inside.

She already had her gun drawn and aimed in the

opposite direction.

He did a visual sweep of the living room-kitchen. Opened the entry closet. Coats, shotgun, ammo, tackle box, fishing poles, cooler. Next, he swept the front bedroom... bathroom...second bedroom...a bigger bath...closets... under sinks...pantry...utility room. Every room he went to, he stomped from the perimeter inward, even shoved the bed out of the way to find the floor beneath. Last, he hoisted himself up into the attic, along with the powerful flash light Cain had left on the table.

Nothing. Good...good. He motioned Marcy inside, then slammed the door and set the lock. His gut told him the perp didn't know where they were. To have gotten this far with no sign of the coward felt like a once-in-a-lifetime feat of luck. A feat that wouldn't have been possible without a lot of good people risking their lives. He'd pay them back one day.

After one more quick look out the windows, he holstered his Glock. "We made it, Marcy. The place may not look like much, but it's clean. We're safe."

She stepped further into the living room. Her weary eyes took in the bare-bones surrounding of a man's cabin. "Looks like a castle to me."

He grinned as she shed her hat, gloves, coat, and boots. She held up the gun he'd given her, shrugging her shoulders as she looked at her jeans pockets. No room there.

"Keep it within reach whichever room you're in." JB pulled the refrigerator door open. "Hungry?"

"Is it okay if I take a shower first?" The frailness of her tone spoke volumes. "I can wait if I have to, though. Maybe I should wait. That's what I'll do, I'll wait." Her eyes twitched from wall to wall, nervousness wobbled in her voice. "I'm so tired, I can't think anymore. Just tell me what to do."

He grabbed her in his arms. Kissed her hard and deep

until she kissed back with the same depth and passion. Until their mouths and hands followed the roadmap of the other's body, hungry for touch, for hope. Until her body eased to a soft sag against his chest. She pushed away enough to kiss his chin then smiled.

"I think I'll take a shower now." Heading toward the front bedroom, she picked up her backpack from the sofa.

"We'll use the back bedroom. It's bigger. Easier to defend." JB also figured it might be easier to escape from if need be. "Looks like a brand new bathroom's been put in."

She walked to his requested room, then popped her head back out the door. "What were you stomping around the house for?"

"When?" He knew damn well when.

"While I covered you from the doorway." She tugged off one of her sweaters. "Sounded like you were marching in the half-time band."

"Beats me. I didn't even notice." He grinned. "Why don't you go take a shower while I cook us up some breakfast?"

She cocked her head, narrowing her eyes. Guess she didn't believe everything he said. "Ummmmm...is that right?"

"Okay. The sheriff said he thought the guy had hidden under our house last night. Satisfied?"

She nodded, then as the implication sank in, she clenched her hands against her jeans. "That means he heard you and me... Got his fix from listening to us. Oh, that's sick. Really, really sick."

He avoided her look. "Go take your shower. Warm up while I fix us something to eat."

Mumbling, she walked into the bedroom. "That creep needs some serious medication."

He laughed. Listened for the click of the bathroom door,

then the sound of running water in the shower. Again he checked the entire floor, plus the walls this time, doubtful the man would use the same technique twice, but it didn't hurt to be sure. Taking the broom with him, he climbed into the attic again, walked the rafters, and pounded the roof for any sign of tampering. Nothing.

When JB climbed back down, the sound of running water still filled the air. Without much thought, he sat bread and bacon and eggs on the counter and started a pot of coffee. The smell of the fresh brew eased his mind. Still, the ten .38s troubled his thoughts.

Who'd used a .38 in his last few jobs? Had there been ten people taken down on a case? Or arrested? Crazies always focused on perceived wrongs. And this guy was crazy for sure. Psycho…to have crawled under their house. Listened. Let them get away. The jerk felt invincible.

Not for long.

He dropped the bacon into a skillet. Sizzling grease splattered his arms as he pushed the slices around with a fork. He stared at the spots, absorbed the pain, and kept thinking.

Maybe he'd arrested this guy's relative. If Marcy was right that she was secondary, that he was the one the man wanted to torture with fear for her life, then this had to revolve around a woman being hurt during a case. What women had been in his last few jobs? A mother or sister? Wife? Girlfriend? Arrested? Death was a strong retaliation for an arrest, even prison. One thing he knew for sure, he'd never killed a woman on any of his cases. Never even shot one.

In fact, the only time there'd been a woman killed had been two jobs ago. The meth bust. The one where part of the lab blew sky-high. The one that cost one woman's life in the explosion and another shot as she fired on the incoming agents and police. One cop and two agents took hard hits that day. One died, one disabled, and one scarred for life. But JB had nothing to do with the shooting or the explosion.

He'd been logistics that day. The liaison between the teams. The man who gave the order to go in once everyone had settled into place. Landon was supposed to have been in charge, but he'd failed to show up until later. Overslept or something. Of course even with that on his record, Landon had managed to keep his position with the FBI. No. This couldn't be tied to that job. JB hadn't even pulled his gun the entire day.

The bedroom door clicked open, drawing his attention away from the eggs he'd dumped in the pan with the bacon a few second ago. Standing center in the doorframe, the vision of Marcy shot straight to his core. His gaze traveled from her fresh, clean face, along with her smile, to her still-wet hair combed straight to her shoulders, to those long legs. Legs silky and smooth and sexy...visible from beneath an oversized, almost-white shirt. He longed to run his hands from her toes to her thighs to her—

His insides jerked and twisted like a knife. A man's shirt. Why did she have on a man's shirt? Cain's? Maybe she found it in the bedroom. If not, that meant she brought it with her. And, in that case, who did the shirt belong to? He felt his hand grip the handle of the spatula. His jealous, male ego jumped into gear. Stupid, stupid reaction.

Who was he to say she couldn't see other men? He'd been the one to stay gone for three years. Him and the other side of his damn ego. But, the idea that she's been with another man, while knowing they were still married, stung. Stung to his core. His heart felt on fire, pounding faster than a ten-mile run would create. Until he signed those divorce papers, he hadn't even looked at another woman. And, she'd...she...

Exasperated because he couldn't stop the pain he felt. Jealous he'd let her give herself to someone else. Angry his ego had kept him from coming back sooner. He flung the spatula into the pan, and it bounced from the heat to the stove to the counter.

He had no right, he shouldn't, but he had to know. "Who's shirt have you got on?"

Chapter Twenty

Marcy caught the spatula as it slid from the counter headed to the floor, then watched as JB stormed out the front door to the porch. He raked his fingers through his hair before glancing back through the screen at her. She opened her mouth to speak, but he held up his hand not to.

"Never mind. Not my business." Shaking his head, he stomped down the steps.

"Where are you going?"

"To the lake to cool off."

Cool off? They didn't need cool. If anything, they needed a fire in the fireplace. "What if the man chasing us shows up?"

"Shoot him."

The sizzle of the pan pulled her back. She turned the burner off and slid a lid in place. She'd never seen JB like this. What did he mean, whose shirt was she wearing?

After pouring herself a cup of coffee, she walked to the front door and focused on him as he stood at the far end of the dock. Shoulders straight, legs braced apart, hands on his waist, kind of like he was getting ready for a battle.

He yanked his black insulated shirt up over his head after dropping his Kevlar vest to the dock, then tucked his shoulder holster and Glock in the bait box on the dock. His fingers worked the laces on his boots, shucked them and his socks. Next, he shed his pants and thermals. She smiled at the view of his backside. She loved to watch JB's muscles and body. Her hands tightened around the warm mug.

Whose shirt did he think she was wearing?

His dive into the maybe-forty-degree water surprised her. Was he crazy? She dropped her cup and grabbed a wool throw cover before barging out the screen door. He was swimming across the small cove. Yes, he was crazy. Definitely crazy.

"JB, stop. Get out of the water. Get. Out. Of. The water." She ran down the hill toward the dock, dragging the throw. Her feet tangled in the wool, and she fell forward. Rolling like a mummy being wrapped, she caught herself on a sapling and came to an abrupt stop. At least the material protected her legs from scrapes. Her feet were a different story. Who in their right mind would run outside without shoes on? And where was she headed? Water and her were not going to mix. Not today. Not ever again.

Stuck with her back to the dock, she fought to untangle her legs from the cover and hold onto the tree at the same time. A dripping splash of water, then footsteps on the dock assured her he'd made it out of the lake. "Help me."

"Hold on," he said.

She gripped the sapling with both hands as her weight worked with gravity on her downhill slide. "What's taking so long?"

"Getting dressed."

"I don't care if you're dressed or not. I need some help up here."

Sounds of movement from the dock area at least meant he was on the way. His jean-clad legs appeared as he planted his boot-clad feet next to her. Dropping the black thermal bottoms from his hands, he crouched to her level. "How did you get in this predicament?"

"I was coming to save you." Her fingers were fast slipping from the tree.

"Save me? Really? From what?"

"From the lake. From the fish. From whatever the heck reason you jumped in." Marcy looked up, then grabbed onto the sapling with both hands again. She wasn't about to chance sliding into the water. "Now are you going to help me or not?"

He pulled her to her feet in one smooth motion. "I don't need saving. I just decided to take a swim."

"Why?" She fidgeted from foot to foot. The ground was cold, plus pebbles ground into the soles of her feet.

A huge suck-it-in, blow-it-out sigh escaped his mouth. "Where are your shoes?"

"In the house." She shivered, scrunching the woolen throw around her.

"Sounds like a personal problem." He bent enough to lift her, tummy first, onto his right shoulder. He gripped his arm around her legs so she wouldn't slide over. Then bent enough to pick up his thermals before climbing up the slight incline to the cabin.

"I forgot them, okay? You can put me down anytime now." Balancing herself on her tummy atop his muscles, she actually enjoyed the view from where she was. She slapped him on his backside. "You know, I missed you."

"Did you now?" His hand popped onto her rear and

stayed. "I missed you, too."

Felt good. Good enough that she smiled to herself as he carried her to the cabin porch and sat her back on her feet. She blocked the doorway. He picked her up by the waist, set her aside, and walked on through. After quickly shaking out the throw, she followed him into the cabin's warmth and closed and locked the door behind her.

JB laid his Glock and holster on the table, then filled their plates and poured them each fresh coffee. "Let's eat."

She shook her head, then took her hip-cocked out, hands-on-hips stance. The one that meant she was prepared to wait however long it took. "Not until we get this settled. First you ask whose shirt I'm wearing. Then you go jump in the freezing lake. There has to be a reason."

"You want to know the reason?" His voice growled calmly. "Do you really want to know, Marcy?"

"Yes." Suddenly, she wished she hadn't pushed for an answer. Her throat tightened as she flattened her mouth in an attempt to convey strength. "Yes, I do."

"No man..." He looked her down and up, pointed, then caught himself and put his hands on his waist. "Aw, hell. Never mind." He grabbed his cup of coffee, took one long gulp, and sat it in the sink before starting to the front door again.

She ran in front of him and turned to face her crazy, bullheaded husband. The man who hadn't bothered to put a shirt on when he got dressed from his swim. Damn, he was making this hard to concentrate with all the tempting muscles staring her in the face. "No man what?"

He stopped and braced his arms above her and to the sides. Tilted his forehead to hers. "No man wants to see his woman in another man's shirt. Okay? Least of all me. I know I don't have much right to say—"

"You think this is another man's?" She picked at the almost white, long-sleeved shirt now covered with dirt and sticks from her fall. That's what this was about? All this because he couldn't admit he was jealous. If she hadn't been mad as hell, the scenario would almost be touching.

"Well, I sure as heck didn't have one in my duffle." He pulled his forehead back. "I don't want to know whose it is, Marcy. Just don't wear it in front of me again."

Son-of-a-gun, he was trying to play the martyr. Baloney on that. She wouldn't let him off that easy. She hadn't done anything wrong. Giant ego or not, this time he'd come face-to-face with the fact he wasn't always right.

"Get out of my way, you big lug." She laughed, pushed on his chest again and again and again. Tilting to get around him, he blocked her way with his body. She tried the other side. "Get. Out. Of. My. Way."

He moved, and she stomped across the floor to the bedroom door. On second thought, this wasn't over. She stomped back even quicker. Pushing him against the front door, she took her stance. Toe-to-toe, forehead-to-chin, you might say. She had him right where she wanted him.

...

JB had her right where he wanted her except for one thing. If she couldn't understand how he felt about the shirt, then they'd need to have a good, long talk. Not what he'd planned for the rest of the day.

Her hands gripped the collar of the shirt she had on and began to pull the material up over her head. She got stuck. "Dang it."

She undid a couple more of the top buttons. All sense of propriety disappeared when the shirt gapped, and the smooth roundness of her breast made him long to reach out. He kept his hands to himself. She was riled. And he was still none too happy about the man's shirt.

Again, she grabbed the collar and pulled upward, her head disappearing like a turtle hiding in its shell. What was she doing? The hem on the shirttail slid up her legs, all the way to her hipbones. Heaven help him. Staying mad was not going to be an option. Not at this rate. In fact, his groin had already made up his mind for him. He inhaled deep and blew out a long sigh.

She tugged one more iota, and the front of the shirt tail bottom exposed her soft mound. He placed one hand on her hip, easing her toward him. Shifting himself toward her. One hand shouldn't get him in too much trouble.

"Stop that." She swatted his hand away, then reached for the collar again.

Maybe it would. Or, maybe he just caught her by surprise. He reached out again. This time she didn't push him away, so he caressed her upper thighs, creeping higher in small increments. She felt good and warm and, in his Marcy-starved state of mind, almost-willing. He was for sure willing.

Her finger pointed in the general direction of the inside of the shirt collar. Where laundry marks are made. "What does that say on the collar?"

What did it say? At the moment, he didn't give a darn what happened to be on the collar. Still, he looked. Looked closer. Son-of-a-gun. Fool...that's what it said. "Says JBB."

His inter-looped initials, his trademark signature, stared back at him.

"And, what does it say on this side?" She pointed in the same general direction.

"Says NBD." Never back down.

These letters, along with his initials, were the way he'd

marked his belongings since he was old enough to go to the store and buy an indelible marker. His fingers inched higher on her body, and she pulled the shirt back into place. He didn't remove his hold, even made lazy palm circles on her lower, lower back. Her cute little derrière.

She shoved him away. "Now whose shirt is this?"

"I never had a lavender shirt in my life."

"This was white until I accidently washed it with my purple sweatshirt." She kept him at arm's length, tapping her foot. "Answer my question. Whose shirt?"

Sheepish, he glanced at the floor. "Mine."

He found his hands empty and shoved them in his pockets to keep from reaching for her. Dang, he wanted this woman. But, from her expression, the irritated look on her face, he wasn't sure where he stood at this point.

"I kept this shirt when I packed your duffle years ago. And I've slept in this shirt more nights than you can imagine." She wadded the material in her hand, blushed. "Imagined you there beside me more times than I want to remember."

As he stepped forward, she braced her hand against his chest, and for a moment, he thought she'd come to him. Let him hold her. Make everything right in their world. But, she didn't. Instead, she pulled her hand away and placed it on her heart.

"I know I'm the one who shoved you away, but I also waited for you, JB. I cried and I yelled and I crawled in our bed alone. Every single night…I slept alone. I woke up alone. I ate alone. I showered alone." She paused. "I curled up in the swing on our anniversary…alone."

The look on his wife's face was agony. He could see how he broke her heart by staying away so long.

She twined her fingers through his, then let them go. Her

heat stayed with him. "I called you. Time and again, I called. Why didn't you answer the phone?"

Yeah, he'd seen her number on his caller ID many times, but he'd only returned the call once. Right before an undercover assignment.

Looking back, he couldn't believe he'd put her through all those days. No. She'd said he wasn't good enough...or had she? Not those exact words, but that's what he heard. And when she set the bag on the front porch and locked the door, it was a blow that took him back to all the doubts he had as a child. Still, that hadn't been the worst.

The worst he remembered was her turning away from him at night every time he got hurt on the job. Not feeling her warmth against his side had come close to making him quit the force. And being a lawman was what kept him getting out of bed every stinking day. What made him know he meant something in this world. Of course, she was what made him lay down at night.

He stroked his palm through her hair, twisting his finger in the softness. "You sent me away, and I told myself that's what you wanted. Thought I was making you happy by being gone. Maybe you found someone else. Now I see it was my own damn male pride that kept me away."

The day he signed the divorce papers she sent had been the first time he felt the coldness of having a hole in his heart. Seeing her in anguish now was worse. Ten times worse.

"I don't want anybody else." Her fingertips brushed across his lips, then she closed the distance to his body. "Ever. And, I don't want to be alone any more. I just want to lay by your side every night. Be your wife." She laid her cheek against his chest. "I'm sorry, JB. I'm sorry I ever threw you out."

"I'm sorry, too, sugar. For everything."

His heart felt like it might burst. He scooped her up, nuzzling her neck as she looped her arms over his shoulders. All he wanted was her warmth surrounding him. Every last inch of him. Now and forever.

Pausing only long enough to grab his gun and holster from the table as they passed, he carried her to the bedroom and placed the Glock on the nightstand by the bed. After laying her down, he tangled his fingers through her hair. Spread it across the pillow like a blanket of temptation. A temptation he'd been drawn to since the day the soft, reddish-brown strands had first brushed his cheek as she'd leaned over to help him with an algebra equation.

She circled her palm around the back of his head, but before she could pull him to her, he rolled onto his back, taking her with him. His bare skin craved the feel of her heat. He slid his hand between them and searched for the buttons to set the shirt free. She sat up, her knees soft and tight against his sides, then she undid the rest of the buttons. Slow and sensual, one at a time, until the shirt fell open, stopped only by the fullness of her breasts.

He stroked his fingers across her skin until she arched, flinging her head back while her breaths came in tiny gasps. Pulling him to her, his mouth replaced his fingers. She opened her eyes and smiled, gliding her palms over his chest, his shoulders. He heard his own groan.

She blew her breath against his ear. "Now, JB. Now."

He shoved the shirt down her arms and off, then rolled her to her back. Covering every spot he knew she liked, he streaked a trail of kisses down her body. His hand caressed her inner thigh, then inched upward. She moaned as her body tensed. He gave her more, more until he felt her release, then clasped her to him as she trembled.

"Don't stop." Her voice softened, buffered by emotions

only she possessed, and only he could spark.

"Oh, Marcy. I'm never gonna stop." He walked to the bedroom door, closed and locked it. Then he shoved the chest of drawers in front of the door. The villain wasn't likely to try to break in during the middle of the day, but, if he did, the lock and chest would give JB a few seconds to grab the gun.

Smart enough to know danger lurked, she didn't ask any questions. She crawled to the end of the mattress and stood, her arms reaching for him as he walked into their hold. Her hands slid to the top of his jeans and undid the button a moment before she pushed them to the floor.

Her hands caressed the bruise on his side. There was no pain. Her lips kissed the brand on his chest. There was no pain. Her fingers traced the scars on his abdomen. There was no pain. He sighed heavily as he held her against him. Body to body, skin to skin, heat to heat.

Being in her arms felt good. Really, really good.

He was home.

Chapter Twenty-one

Marcy woke to the scent of her well-satisfied husband and cuddled closer against his chest. They'd spent the afternoon in bed, getting to know each other again and again. The clock on the nightstand read 4:00 p.m. "You awake?"

"Yep." He tilted her face up and tweaked her nose. "I thought you'd be too worn out to wake up anytime soon."

"I think I need some food." The cold eggs and biscuits they'd eaten a few hours ago had long since worn off. Her stomach rumbled for more now that her body was happy. Pleasured and happy. "I love you, JB Bradley."

"And I love you, too, sugar."

She'd never tire of those words. "How about I make some dinner?"

"Sounds good to me. I'll just lay here like a man of leisure." He grinned. "In fact, I'd like my meal served in bed."

She dressed, tossing his jeans at him. "You've been served in bed all day. Now get up and move the chest from in front of the door, so I can get to the kitchen."

Not bothering with the pants, he jumped up and shoved the chest aside. "Think I'll take a quick shower. Where's your gun?"

Oops. He would not like her answer. Even she didn't like her answer.

"I laid it by the front door when I went to save you." She scurried out the bedroom door.

His look said he wasn't happy with that answer. "Where?"

"Under the sofa cushion. Don't worry. I'm getting it right now." She pulled the Glock out and checked the load. Years ago, JB had drilled into her mind how to handle a gun. Right now, she was thankful he had. Ever since the sun came up, she'd felt safe. She could see anything headed her way. Night time would be different, and dusk was settling in.

JB glanced around the doorframe. "Don't go outside."

"I won't." She double-checked closing the curtains in the kitchen and the shutters in the living room before she pulled out the first pan. Her cooking skills in her own home weren't bad, but here might be a different story.

The sound of JB's cell phone echoed from the bedroom. Good news? Maybe it meant good news. Maybe she should answer. After all, he was in the shower. The ringing stopped, but no voice mail beep sounded. The sound of running water ended a couple minutes later. His phone rang again, and she walked to the open doorway to the bedroom. He slammed out of the bathroom, a towel wrapped around his hips.

"Yeah? Tell me you got him." The look on JB's face clenched with tension from the response on the other end. "Then why did you call?"

She heard the sizzle of the hamburger in the skillet and returned to the stove. Straining to hear the conversation, she couldn't make out anything but a few 'okay's before JB closed the bedroom door.

Willing the bedroom door to open, she stirred the meat till it browned. What was wrong? He wouldn't close the door unless something had happened. After flicking off the stove, she crept to the bedroom door, placed her ear against the wood. Nothing. Had he gone into the bathroom with the phone? Things would really be bad if he went to that extreme to keep her from hearing. She gripped the doorknob and turned—it didn't turn. She tried again, jiggled the handle. Locked.

A chill chased down her spine. But she mustn't panic. She leaned against the wall, hands clasped in front of her, eyes focused on the door. She swayed, bumping her hip on the wall to center her thoughts.

"Please open the door," she whispered. "Please let everything be okay."

Earlier had been wonderful. Love and sex and rekindling. That's what she wanted, how she wanted to live. No danger to him. No being so weak on her part that he had to shut her out in order for them to have a chance at being together. All she wanted was for them to close the door and live their life free of the outside world.

She felt the panic rising in her throat. The tightening of her chest. A sticky feeling lingered just below her skin. Breathe...exhale, breathe...exhale. She'd let herself believe everything had changed, that she could face whatever the future held as long as JB was part of that future. But what if she couldn't? What if the old insecurities came back?

Didn't matter. That would be then. This was now, and she needed to focus on keeping them alive. Her and JB's future would take care of itself. Right now he needed her to be strong.

"Breath," she said to herself. "Just breathe."

Even if they survived what was to come, this afternoon might be all they ever had.

• • •

JB tucked the towel around his body and raced for his phone. Caller ID showed Patrolman Kennett, and he flicked the button to on. "Yeah? Tell me you got him."

"Afraid not." The rookie sounded hoarse. Professional. Hard.

"Then why'd you call?" He searched his mind for what could possibly cause their non-communication plan to be broke. His mind's eye saw Marcy at the door. The moment she walked away, he closed the door and set the lock. Knowing her, she'd listen from the other side, so he stepped into the bathroom and closed the door behind him. His knees bent as he slid to the floor and settled, his back braced against the wood.

Kennett cleared his throat. "Sheriff Davis was following up on a lead this morning when Leon rammed him. Shoved him and his cruiser off the road."

Shoved? He braced for the worst. "Where?"

"Tourist lookout number one at the lake. A lead had been called in on a cell. Something about a suspicious hitchhiker."

He cringed. Once you went over the edge, that hill went straight down. What had he brought to this town? "How's the sheriff?"

"He's been airlifted to the medical center in Jefferson City." Kennett sucked in air and blew out hard. "They've got him in ICU. He's in bad shape. Probably gonna lose a leg. Lucky he's even alive."

Jumping to his feet, JB stared in the mirror and tried

to wrap his mind around the questions rattling through his mind. "Tell me everything you know."

"Leon's body was found in the dump truck that pushed the sheriff over the edge. Deputy Evans thinks he got all doped up, and once he realized what he'd done, he shot himself." Kennett paused. "I don't think so."

"Why not?"

"The cab of the truck looked like a scene from police 101. You know...gun angle, bullet casing, body position... everything seemed too perfect. And if you're about to do something that could land you in jail again, why would you settle up your bill at the hardware store yesterday? Tell the bank to get a payoff balance on your house ready for tomorrow? Wait. I need to take this other call." Kennett put JB on hold.

The sheriff must have been getting too close. Might not have even known how close. Leon was a perfect patsy for whoever was actually behind the Sheriff's accident. Stroke his ego. Give him a wad of money. The guy would do anything. Especially if you threw in some uppers. And maybe, just maybe, Leon had seen something the day of the bank robbery.

Kennett clicked back in. "You're not gonna like this."

"Tell me." He concentrated on the words, letting them fall into pockets of his mind like a sorting machine.

"One of the docs called from the medical center. Thought we should know Sheriff Davis is still incoherent but keeps rambling about his phone. Says he gets real agitated when he does. Seems to fight someone."

JB tensed as he peered out the small bathroom window. "See if Evans took the phone from the scene..."

"I just called. He didn't." Kennett's voice lowered. "In fact, he said the sheriff's coat pocket where he kept the private phone was ripped clean off. Hang up, and use the phone I gave you."

JB hung up. Jabbed the phone into the off position. Damnittohell. The perp had the phone. Could have a header on where they were from the few minutes of conversation he just had.

Wouldn't take the guy long to track down the secure number on the new phone. Simple elimination. The way the guy operated technically, he might have a trace on every number listed just waiting for the right voice to pick up. JB's voice.

Before they'd left Crayton, Sheriff Davis told him he'd nickname JB the Veterinarian in his contact list. Should slow the process. Maybe the creep wouldn't verify all the numbers. Even if he did, still might take the guy until morning to zone which number was which.

JB needed to stay off the secure phone, which sure as hell wasn't secure anymore. Or maybe he should us it…lure the guy right to them on their own terms. Either way wasn't good. Keep the phone, the perp would come for sure. At this point, he put nothing past the man, because no matter what, he would still find a way to come. This guy didn't plan on stopping.

Time to take a stand. JB'd keep the phone. Set his own trap. Wait for the man to show his face.

The disposable phone Kennett gave him before they left Crayton rang.

"I got lost in thought." JB said.

"What do you want me to do?" Kennett said.

"I'm formulating a way to lure the guy in. As soon as I do, I'll call you back on this line." JB figured the best trail right now would be the files at the police station. "Other than that, check the sheriff's office, and see what he's been reading. What's odd in the reports? Coincidental? Out of place?"

"Should I let Deputy Evans know what I'm doing?"

"I'd rather you didn't." JB realized he was asking the man to keep something from his own boss. "All I got right now are you and Cain. That's all I want."

Silence on the line meant Kennett was thinking about the request. "You know this could mean my job."

"Yep." If the rookie said no, then no it would be.

"Why?" Kennett said. "Why not tell Evans? Don't you trust him?"

"I trust him. He knows where I am. May even know the number if the sheriff gave it to him. But Evans has a family. He needs to walk in their door every night, not be lying at the bottom of a cliff like Sheriff Davis. Besides, it sounds like Crayton's gonna need him big time for a while." JB looked in the mirror again and shook his head. "We're facing a killer now. A pro."

"The sheriff had to be on to something big to nearly get him killed."

JB opened the bathroom door and checked outside the two shuttered bedroom windows. Marcy had to be livid on the other side of the locked door. "Makes sense. Why else would someone bother to run him over the cliff? Take his phone? Hire Leon to do the dirty work, then kill him?"

"Got it."

"The sheriff had to be real close." JB unlocked the bedroom door. "See what you can find out. Call me back."

• • •

Marcy stood at the counter buttering warmed-up biscuits when JB stepped out of the bedroom. He made the rounds of all the windows. Rechecked the locks.

"JB?" She tensed. The atmosphere had changed.

With a grunt for response, he braced the door on the second bedroom closed with a chair under the handle. The hardness in his expression said something was wrong. But as long as they were together, she felt safe. Secure in the cocoon of the cabin.

A Kevlar vest covered JB's cold-weather thermals again. Boots were full-laced and double knotted. Shoulder holster strapped in place. He carried the Glock in his hands as he made the rounds. When he turned, she saw a backup gun tucked in the waistband of his jeans. He was in FBI mode. Might not be part of the Bureau any more, but he was still tough—no-nonsense Special Agent Jean Bradley tough.

Her afternoon lover was nowhere to be found. Instead, her protector braced himself for battle. She couldn't stop the nerves making a race track of her body or the quiver of hair on the back of her neck. But she'd stay strong for him.

She sat two plates of hamburger hash and biscuits on the table, then touched his shoulder as he finished putting a metal cookie sheet behind the window curtains above the kitchen sink. The only other window minus louvered shutters was in the master bath.

"What's wrong, JB?"

He folded her in his arms. Held her close. She closed her eyes and braced for whatever he had to tell her.

"There's been an accident." His arms didn't let her move. "Your uncle's in ICU and Leon's dead."

A squeak of a cry caught in her throat a moment before she turned her face up to his. She jerked with the sobs caught in the same place. "Will he live?"

"They're not sure." He knew how close the nieces were to their uncle. Sheriff Davis had been their one constant in life besides Sadie and Truman. "I'm sorry, sugar. I'm sorry."

She laid her cheek against his chest. "What else?"

"I think the sheriff got close. Too close to whoever's after us."

"Leon?"

"No. He was just a cog in the wheel." JB smoothed her hair. Not the sexy tangle of before, but a heavy, protective slide of his fingers. "You might as well know the perp's got your uncle's phone."

She didn't understand phones and GPS and tracking, but her insides triggered a flash of warning. "He'll be able to find us, right?"

"If my phone's turned on, he can likely trace it. May have already." JB let her lean back, looking her in the eye. "You might as well know, I've decided to leave the phone on."

"Can't we run again?" There had to be another way. More time. She wasn't ready for this to end. She might not be able to face a life with him as a lawman, but she needed more time to make the memories she'd hold on to once this was over. "We could find another cabin and…and…"

"Could. But we won't." He scanned her face with his stare, as if making a photo negative for future use. "This ends here. On our terms. Okay?"

What would he say if she said no? Said she wanted to keep on running forever just to be with him? Said she'd give herself up for him to live another day? What would he say?

She straightened her back. Swallowed her fear. No, they weren't going to run any more. JB was right. Better to confront the attacker on your own ground. They wouldn't let the man chase them like they were the criminals. Like they were animals waiting for his pot-shot.

"Okay." People might think she was a flutter in the breeze, but she could stand her ground when push came to shove. JB needed her help, so he could work to keep them both alive. "Do you have a plan?"

Chapter Twenty-two

Thirty minutes later, JB laid out his plan to Marcy. "You'll get in the boat by the dock and set it adrift. You won't be able to turn the motor on, but you'll be able to use the oars if you're real quiet. Once you're out of the cove, you can start the trolling motor just like when we used to go fishing."

"I can't go out on the water by myself... I can't." She shook her head, eyes wide with stubbornness. "Change your plan. Come with me."

"You're a good, strong swimmer. You just hit your head on the side of the boat when it capsized that day. You got disoriented. Forgot to swim for the surface. That's all it was."

He swallowed the lump in his throat. He knew how hard this would be for her and doubted she'd gone fishing or swimming since he'd left town, but there was no way he could change the plan. "You can do this, sugar. I know you can."

Fear lacing her eyes, she shook her head.

"Trust me, Marcy. You. Can. Do this." He scoured his

mind for another way. There was none. "You asked about a plan, and I have one, but I need you out of harm's way to make it happen."

"No. I'm not leaving you here alone with the killer."

"Don't you see? If you're safe, then I don't have to worry about protecting you." JB covered her hands with his. "I'll keep him busy long enough for you to get in that boat and get the hell away. With you gone, he won't have anything to hold over me. It'll just be me and him. And trust me, I don't go down easy."

The look on her face said she'd go along with it. Her escape was his top priority. His personal to-do list—simple. Take the perp out. Or, if there was no other way, let the perp take him out. At least afterwards, the man would have no reason to pursue Marcy, and sooner or later, the local police would catch him.

Right now, everyone needed time. Good old-fashioned time.

"Why can't the police GPS the sheriff's phone? They should be able to do the same thing he's doing to us." She couldn't stand being immobile anymore, so she paced the perimeter of the room.

"This guy's a pro. Probably took him less than a minute to download the numbers. Then, all he had to do was toss the phone in the trash or the lake when he drove across the dam." He flipped through procedures in his mind. "I would have."

She stopped. "You still think it's the guy who ratted you out during the last job?"

"Yes."

"Why'd he do that?" She walked to the back of his chair and looped her arms around his shoulders. Placed her cheek next to his.

"If I figure that out, this could all be over." He grasped her hands, rubbing them in his fingers. "So, back to the question at hand… Can you force yourself to get in the boat and leave?"

Marcy slid her palm to his chest. She caressed the Kevlar covering his heart, over the spot where the thugs had branded him. "This must have hurt a lot. How did you stand the pain?"

"I imagined your lips coming to kiss me, not the hot metal." He pulled her down enough to brush his lips across hers. He'd never tell her the smell as the glowing shield seared into his flesh. How even the memory of their times together hadn't been enough to keep him from passing out.

"I'll do it. If you can stand up to that…" She pointed to the spot on his chest. "…then I can get in the boat." She rotated around and sat on his lap. "I'll pretend you're right beside me and we're out to catch Sunday dinner."

He knew how much effort that would take for her, but she'd work it out. Analyze her weakness and get it done. "Hey, you don't have your Kevlar on."

"I'll put it on when we have to leave."

Shucking her from his lap, he pointed to the bedroom. "Now. Get dressed as if you were going outside except for the coat. When the guy comes, he'll come hard and fast. We need to be ready."

She followed his instructions, returning with her boots as the last thing to put on.

"Once you get those laced and double-knotted, I want you to put your coat and gloves in the bedroom. Some place easy to grab."

His decoy phone rang. Caller ID showed Kennett.

"Tell me you got something." He said into the cell.

"Not much. In fact, some people might think it's a

coincidence." The rookie paused.

"I don't like coincidences."

"Me, neither. Hey, close the door. I'm on the phone." Kennett mumbled something under his breath.

JB raked his hands through his hair. "Who was that?"

"Evans." Silence came through the phone.

"He still in the office with you?"

"No, but he's gonna ask some questions." Kennett blew out a breath.

"Blame it on me. Now what'd you get?"

"Do the numbers 1-0-3-8 ring a bell with you?"

1038...1038. JB rolled the numbers around his mind. "No. Should they?"

The sound of papers being flipped echoed through the phone. Kennett cleared his throat. "Here goes. The shooting at the bank occurred at 10:38. From what the soda fountain clock that crashed to the floor read after the explosion, that blast occurred at 10:38. And, from what we got off the small timer on Marcy's brakes, it looked like she had her near-accident at10:30-something. I'm betting that last digit's an 8."

His mind reached for anything with a 1-0-3-8 in his past. For sure, the numbers meant something.

"We don't know what time the guy went in your house last night," Kennett said.

"Doesn't matter. He left a better calling card. Ten .38 bullets." He glanced at Marcy. "Has the sheriff come out of it yet?"

"No. He's in surgery right now." Kennett opened the door from the sound of the background noises on his end. "If I come up with anything else, I'll call. Just so you know," the rookie whispered, "Deputy Evans has his arms crossed over his chest and is staring straight at me. He's coming this way."

"I'm hanging up for now. Keep me informed." He paced the same route Marcy had minutes ago. "By the way, have you seen Cain around town today?"

"Once. He barely nodded then kept on walking." Kennett grunted. "This is a private phone call, Evans."

"JB?" Deputy Evans growled, obviously having strong-armed the phone from Kennett.

JB hated to keep him out of the loop. The man was good. "Yes, sir."

"If you and this rookie patrolman are finished with your conversation, I suggest you take a look at a clock and figure out 1038 fast." Evans muttered something in Kennett's direction, then turned his mouth back to the phone. "Me and the sheriff noticed the similarity in the timeframes late last night. He gave Landon a call to have him check through your office's FBI files for the numbers. Wanted to see if there's a link anywhere. Trouble is the numbers don't hold through on every incident, though."

"Like what?"

"Like the sandwich with the note to Marcy. That was nowhere close to that time."

JB floundered for a second. "Did the results on the food get back?"

"Yeah. Nothing. Just Joanie's food."

"Makes sense then. He didn't care about the time." JB said. "He only wanted to scare her. Show us he's in charge."

He could almost see the furrow on the deputy's forehead. The one the man always got when he calculated case points. "Hey, Evans. Don't think I'm trying to cut you out of this. I'm just—"

"Just what?" Evans' gravely-edged voice was blunt.

"You've got a lot on your plate since the sheriff's been

in the hospital. Plus, have you thought about the fact that whoever took out Leon and the sheriff may know you were part of the investigation?" He wondered how long it would take for the deputy to be a target. "I don't want to be the one standing on your doorstep telling your family how you went and got yourself hurt on my account."

"I'm a cop. I chose to be a cop. And my family chooses to be a cop's family. So thanks for the consideration, but let's put it this way… How would you like it if I kept you out of an investigation because you're married?" Deputy Evan's voice held strong and sure. "We're all in this together."

The deputy hit the nail on the head. They were all in this together. Ever since the last job and the hospital, JB had tried to accept help when someone offered. A hard thing to do when you made your own way most your life. He cricked his neck from side-to-side and faced the simple fact—these people were there to help him and Marcy. "You're right."

Evans chuckled. "I hope this phone's got a trace going, 'cause I want to play those words to the unit when this is over. Now hang up, so this cop can go do his job."

"Thanks. Let me know what Landon comes up with." JB paused. "By the way, if you see Cain, tell him thanks for the loan of his cabin. It's real nice."

He ended the phone call and glanced at his wife still tying her boots. This cabin was simple and welcoming with its sunrise picture above the knotty pine headboard. The lake stone fireplace, with heavy, black andirons and three-inch, oak mantle. Smells of fried fish and bacon that wafted from the vent over the stove every time it was turned on. If Marcy and he survived, maybe they'd see about buying the property.

She finished double-knotting her shoelaces and looked up. Smiled at him along with a ta-da of her hands.

"Real nice." He grinned at the woman he loved. "Real, real nice."

...

Sitting at the table for what seemed like hours, but was really only about fifteen minutes, Marcy concentrated on the map JB explained for the second time. He planned to hide one of his guns, the poker from the fireplace, and an extra clip for the Glock outside the cabin. The first time he went over the placements, she lost track halfway through.

After gauging the annoyance of his sigh before he started his spiel again, she listened. Focused. Steps and yards and meters jumbled in her head. North, south, east, and west meant nothing to her. Still she listened. Focused.

He glanced up at her own deep sigh. "What?"

She bit her lip. "Nothing."

"Then why the sigh?"

"What sigh?"

He turned the map over. "Where are the hiding spots?"

"Which one?"

With a tiny quirk of a snarl and deliberate narrowing of his eyes, he cocked his head to one side, breathed in deep, and blew out long. "For any of the weapons I just mentioned."

"Northwest from the corner of the front porch." Rote memory kicked in for her. "Seventy yards to the oversized, fallen branch." There, that should make him happy.

"What's hidden?" JB said.

"The...gun...no, wait a minute. The poker." She beamed with a correct answer. "Under some leaves."

"And?"

Should have known he'd expect more. He always wanted more, no matter if it were her, hot coffee, or answers. Her shoulders shrugged without trying. "I don't know what you want me to say."

He walked to the coffee pot and poured fresh brew into his mug, then returned to the table. "I want you to tell me where the other things are."

"I don't know." She shook her head. "And I don't even know which way is northwest."

"This is important, Marcy. Pay attention." He lifted his chin slightly before his eyes narrowed enough to look at her in firm rebuke this time. Rebuke she'd never seen in him before. He was worried. "Real important."

He flipped the map back over and started with the directions once again. North, south, east, and west. Steps, yards, meters. She listened. Focused.

"No, no, no, no, no!" She laid her hand over his. "I can't understand what you're saying."

"It's all right here on paper." His voice sounded like an impatient father trying to help his child with homework. "Right here. You just aren't paying attention."

"Yes, I am. I really am. But you're telling me your way. The lawman way. Precise and calculated." She rose from the chair, walked to the front door. "Come over here and tell me my way. Tell me in terms I can understand."

He grabbed the Glock from the table, shoved it into his shoulder holster, then came to stand beside her. Tension flashed in the air. Veins on his arms stood at attention as he rolled his fingers. Kept them moving. He was more than worried.

She nudged in front of him and took his hand. "Tell me where to find them as if we were out for a walk. Like you pointed to something you want me to see."

Straight, he stood perfectly straight, unyielding and professional. She snuggled against his chest. He tried to back away, but she looped his arm around her, snuggling more. She was trying to be what a lawman's wife should be, but he needed to help her learn the mechanics of his job. Her inner turmoil was her own to handle, and she was trying. She already knew seeing him hurt in person would be her tipping point one way or the other.

For now, she just needed to know where the weapons were hidden.

"Here." She pointed to her cheek. "Come here and tell me. Which way is northwest?"

From her periphery, she saw a tiny smile grab the corners of his mouth. From behind, he bent and placed his cheek next to hers, pointed to the right, then brought his arm back to the left a bit. "That way. Go off the porch and walk to the tree covered in big woodpecker holes."

She closed her eyes. Nodded.

His body relaxed against her. "There's a downed log along side."

"The one we saw the squirrel with a nut in his mouth run across?"

"Yep. The fireplace poker will be—"

"Lengthwise, under the leaves by the log. Next." She leaned into his hold. "Okay. Next."

His hold tightened around her, and he kissed her cheek, then nestled against her. "The gun. The gun will be loaded and ready to fire, so be careful. It'll be in the bait box on the dock."

"What if it gets wet?"

"It should still fire okay."

Hopefully, this would all play out without her being close to the water, so that weapon wouldn't do her much good. Besides, she had the gun he gave her tucked in her coat pocket. "And the extra clip?"

"Under a flat piece of shale by that sapling you grabbed when you were saving me."

After turning in his arms, she looped hers around his neck. "Now see, I know exactly where everything is."

"Don't forget. Don't ever forget how much I love you, either." He lowered his head, kissing her deep and long. For a moment, they clung to each other, his breath a whisper in her hair. "And always remember, I planned for every scenario possible today. No matter what happens, I walked through it in my mind and accepted the outcome. Remember that forever, Marcy. You will survive, I promise."

Her insides tripped. Something in his tone, his hold, his words. What had she missed? Those words sounded like goodbye. "What are you up to, JB?"

He grabbed the clip, gun, and poker, then headed for the door. "Lock up after I go out. Do not open this door unless it's me. Anyone else comes through that door without your say-so, shoot 'em."

She understood. Nodded. They dimmed the lights. Funny how quick darkness rolled in during the winter. Low and fast, he slipped outside. She set the lock and waited. Overcast, moonless nights in the woods meant complete, smothering darkness. Even though the dark wasn't something she relished, it didn't scare her. The water plan did.

Watching JB's brain work through the what-ifs of this situation made her see him as more than just her husband. Trained to the hilt, he possessed something else. Something she'd seen in him since the day he'd stopped Leon from taking her homework back in sixth grade. The bully never even landed a punch, because JB had turned to the right, faked to the left, and floored him.

She'd been impressed a seventh grader had stood up for her, especially the cutest boy in school. When he'd handed her the papers back, he'd grinned and told her to let him know if anyone ever bothered her again. The rest of that day had been a sheer loss of learning, because she thought of nothing but her champion, JB Bradley.

Now, like then, he knew how to anticipate the other guy's reaction before the movement. Once this was over, the FBI would ignore his resignation. Fight to get him back. She wanted him back, too.

Maybe that's what his words were about. He probably figured his career should be the top priority. There'd be no future for the two of them, because he planned to leave. What else could it be? Why else would he say those words in that tone? Why?

She reached for the horticulture book on the sofa. Flipped through the pages. Her husband had sneaked it into his backpack and carried the extra weight through the woods for her. Loving him was easy, so why did she always try to make things so difficult? Not this time. This time she'd never let him go…as long as he wanted to stay. She could handle him being a Crayton deputy. FBI agent? She didn't know. But he was one damn good agent; that much she did know.

Close to thirty minutes later, JB tapped on the window, then the door, then said her name. She unlocked the door, and he crept inside. They kept the lights off.

"What took so long?" she said.

"Did a little reconnaissance of my own. Listening. Watching." He gave one bear-shiver to shake off the cold. "The wind's picking up. Getting nasty out there."

"Is that good or bad?" She wanted something to be going their way. Anything.

"Neither. Is what it is."

"Want another pot of coffee?"

He nodded. "Want to play some checkers?"

She nodded in return. Could they shove a lifetime into the next few hours? They could try.

At ten o'clock, he explained the little they knew about the 1038 numbers and their role in the sequence of violent events from the last few days. Then he locked them both back in the bedroom, shoving the chest in front of the door. His theory was 10:38 might be a trigger for the killer. If he'd told her sooner, she'd have been worried all evening. Instead, she only had to worry for the short time.

They waited. 10:15 came and went. 10:30 came and went. He motioned her behind him, and she obeyed. Then he backed them up until they were in the furthest corner from the door, the window, the bathroom. If anyone came in, JB would take the blow. He might go down, but he'd take the shot for her.

Realization thundered through her entire body. Everything from earlier suddenly made sense. The placement of the weapons. How important she knew where they were. His words from before whooshed in her mind, taking root in her heart. To reach out, touch his back, would only be a distraction to him. Put him at risk. She wouldn't do that.

This might be the end, and all she could do was stand and watch. JB would take the blow destined for her. Go down. Maybe die in her arms. That was what the promise meant. And all he asked was for her to remember how much he loved her. She tightened the grip on her own gun. She'd never been so scared in her life.

The glow from the clock on the night table showed the minutes. 10:35. Was that the right time? Could it be off a minute or two? Was he watching the clock? No, he was tensed, every muscle cocked and ready. He glanced from place to place. Walked to the window and back. 10:36. Stepped to the bedroom door, listened, then backed up to her again. 10:37. He never looked at her. Never acknowledged her.

The minutes ticked by one by one by one.

She touched his back. "The clock says 10:50."

. . .

JB made sure Marcy was asleep before he dialed. Might be two-thirty in the morning, but he needed to check in with the Crayton Police.

The clang of a phone being dropped then picked up again reverberated through the receiver. "Patrolman Kennett here."

"Sorry to wake you."

"Don't worry about it. Sounds like you two made it through another 10:38." The rookie's voice cleared fast. Meant his brain woke on a dime.

JB scrubbed his palm over his face. He needed a shave. "Anything new?"

"Nothing. The sheriff came out of surgery good. Saved his leg. But he's still doped up. Not making much sense."

"Like what?"

"He'll be talking about Landon. How the man would check in with your boss on the numbers. Then he rambles about fighting the guy in the ski mask for the phone." Kennett's voice sounded tired. "Says the guy has brown eyes. Next minute he says they're blue. Doesn't make sense."

"Keep at it. Check with Landon to see if he ever got anything from headquarters." JB heard the soft sounds of Marcy mumbling to herself in her sleep. At least she could rest for a while.

The rookie cleared his throat. "When I called him this afternoon, it went to voice mail. He never called back. Went to voice mail a couple hours ago, too."

Maybe he should call Wilson instead. Why? His ex-boss was on vacation and couldn't do a damn thing to help him. "Try Landon again. Might be he can remember something about a case I haven't."

. . .

Except for light from the fireplace glow, the cabin sat in darkness when Marcy opened her eyes. Still half asleep, she stared as the digital numbers click forward on the bed side clock. 3:20 AM. So, far she'd watched seven minutes. Each click meant one minute closer to 10:38 again. The numbers seemed to mean something to someone angry enough to kill her and JB.

Last night, the two of them played checkers, popped popcorn over the fire in the fireplace, and racked their brains to find any connection to 1-0-3-8.

The only disruption during the night had been the gentle hoot of an owl. JB insisted they didn't turn any music on. He needed to listen, hear anything out of the ordinary. How could he hear anything through the closed door and windows? Finally, she realized he wasn't talking about the owl's hoot or the water's ripple or the wind through the trees. He meant he knew other sounds. The sounds of a stalker, a shooter. Still fully dressed, she fell asleep about midnight.

The faint glow from the fireplace and the smell of scorched coffee jogged her awake. She stumbled into the kitchen, spying the grungy coffeepot in the sink.

JB shuffled cards at the kitchen table, once again his Glock within easy reach. "I made a mess."

"Smells like it." She looped her arms over his shoulders, nibbling his ear. "Come to bed. Lay by me."

"We can't, sugar. Much as I'd like to, we can't." He kissed her palm.

"It's not even close to 10:38."

"But the psycho's been searching in the dark all night long. The dark can play with people's minds. Push them over the line. This guy's probably standing on the edge." JB pulled her onto his lap.

She liked sitting there. Safe and warm in his arms. "What makes you say that?"

His overhead stretch pulled his body closer to hers for an instant, and then he relaxed again. She watched his face as his arms loosely folded around her.

"He's missed you four times now. He lost us in the woods. And something tells me the phone didn't help him as quickly as he'd hoped, or he'd already be here. Trust me, he's furious. Furious at us. Furious at himself. That means his breaking point is close. Either the police will nab him or…"

"Or what?" Why had she asked? She knew the answer.

JB winked at her, then shuffled her off his lap and reached for the soaking coffee pot.

"No more coffee." She pulled on his hand. "Come back to bed."

He shook his head.

"Staring at the door isn't going to make the worst happen. Come to bed and wrap your arms around me. Get a couple hours sleep."

A heavy sigh followed his glance at the door before he followed her to the bedroom. After securing the room, he lay on the covers fully dressed as she snuggled against his side.

He glanced at the clock. Already 4:00 AM. He set the clock for 7:00 AM.

Chapter Twenty-three

JB didn't need the alarm clock to wake him. Howling wind muffled every sound except for the thunderous rain. He rolled out of bed, leaving Marcy and her warmth. Good sense should have kept him from stretching out on the bed in the first place, but the couple hours of sleep felt good. He clicked off the alarm. Let her sleep awhile longer.

Opening the living room shutters provided nothing but a view of the thick, spooky fog. This looked like the kind of day depicted in scary movies. The cabin in the woods. The fog rolling in. The man, the woman, the killer.

Shake it off, man. Shake it off. He closed the shutters.

All he thought about as he started a fresh pot of coffee was how to lure the shooter into their lair. This stalemate needed to end today. Otherwise, sloppiness might creep in. One sloppy moment could lead to one error. Sometimes, one error ended a successful agent's career.

Jennings had been a veteran lawman. During their brief time as partners, he'd taught JB everything he could. Would have been even more if the man hadn't taken the wrong call at the wrong time from the wrong person. He'd probably already have the case solved.

JB ranked the calls he needed to make on his decoy phone, then dialed.

"Deputy Evans here."

"Hope you got something for me." JB sat two cups on the table.

"Nothing. Let me shut the door." The deputy's footsteps echoed through the phone. "There that's better."

JB jogged the coffeepot out and poured. "Last night, Kennett said the sheriff seemed confused on what the guy looked like that attacked him."

"Maybe not. I got a call from the doc a few minutes ago. He said the sheriff's awake and talking fine. He still insists the man had brown eyes one second. Then one of his eyes was blue the next." Evans sighed. "And that partner of yours...Landon."

JB turned at the sound of Marcy's footsteps on the floor as she headed to the bathroom. "He's not my partner. I just worked with him one other time."

The slam of a folder on the desk rumbled through the phone. "Well, I don't care who or what he is. In my book, he's not worth the metal in his shield."

"Still not answering his calls?" Seemed odd, even for Landon.

"I checked with the phone company to make sure everything's okay with his line. They said his phone is sitting some place over in Jefferson City." Deputy Evans voice tensed. "Want me to call Wilson? Your boss? "

"Yeah. You got his number?"

Evans shuffled papers. "Sure thing. I knew I'd seen it in your file somewhere. I'll let you know as soon as I hear anything back."

"Thanks." JB lingered on the call. Thinking. Without the special contact lens he wore, Landon had one blue eye and one brown.

"You're awful quiet. What's wrong?"

Marcy walked into the kitchen fully dressed, including her boots. Hair brushed and smelling of toothpaste, she looked like a good morning wake-up. He hated to ruin her day, but she needed to know his thinking. He motioned her over and pointed her to the chair across the table from him.

"You still there?" the deputy said. "Kennett just walked in. I've got you on speaker phone."

"Yeah."

"What's up, JB?" Kennett asked.

"My cop instincts say everything comes to a head today." JB watched Marcy's face. Since he'd been old enough to remember, he could always feel a life-changing day the minute he woke up. Today, his instinct churned with fire and adrenaline. This day didn't feel good. "He's coming."

Her expression stayed strong, but her eyes held fear as he covered her hand with his.

"Hold on. Evans is trying to reach your boss." Kennett's said. "You got much fog out there?"

"Layers. Like pea-soup. Be mighty hard to come in by boat." JB glanced up as his wife walked to the front window and did a tiny peek outside. She palmed her hand upward a couple times. "Marcy just motioned that the fog is lifting. My bet is he'll still come in by road. Maybe walk a ways. You might want to alert anybody living in cabins out here."

Kennett chuckled. "Beat you to that one. Called everyone last night. Told them to leave the area, or else lock their doors and stay inside."

Evans mumbled in the background. Probably talking to

Wilson. "Okay. I'll tell him." The deputy cleared his throat. "JB, Wilson says for you to call him. Right now."

"Why?"

"He's checking things out. Landon never called him," Evans continued. "I'll let your boss give you the specifics."

There must be a clue to the 1038. Something so classified, it needed to be relayed agent to agent.

Evans and Kennett were talking over each other, and he refocused on their conversation. "What's going on?"

"Me, Kennett, and a couple other cruisers are headed your way." Evans said as a door creaked open and slammed closed in the background. "Kennett's headed out right now. Don't worry, we should be there ahead of 10:38."

JB glanced at Marcy. "The guy won't wait today. He'll get antsy. Nervous. Blow his routine."

"Call Wilson. Get your info. We're on our way."

"Hey, Evans, do me a favor before you head out. Request one of the Jeff City police narrow in on Landon's phone. Check out its location."

"You got it. Why?"

"Make sure he's actually where the phone shows." JB shook his head. He had a bad feeling. Real bad feeling about the person behind all of this. "Things in my life started to fall apart after I met Landon on that meth bust. As I said before, I don't like coincidences."

...

JB speed dialed his boss, and Wilson answered on the first ring. "Tell me you got something on 1038?" JB said abruptly.

"The guys in the office are still checking." Wilson's no-non-sense attitude carried through the phone. "We've put 1038 in as a random along with your name to see what comes up in the secure system. Nothing yet."

Marcy sat a refilled cup of coffee in front of JB and offered a scared smile before she walked back to the counter for her own cup. He fought the idea that he should have stayed away from her, away from Crayton. Recuperating in the hospital after the last job, the idea of getting back together with her had been the fuel to keep him going. His body might have been healed on its own, but the memories of her were what had healed his mind and emotions.

He knew then that he'd give up everything else to live the rest of his life with her. The past few days might be all they had. At least they'd been together.

The brush of her hand on his jerked him back from his thoughts. She sat in the chair beside him at the table, flipping through the horticulture book. Her eyes focused on each page as if taking in the colors and beauty of the scenes pushed the bluntness of the moment into the shadows. He noticed a tiny twitch right before she turned each page. She'd found her way to cope — one page at a time.

As for him, he needed to focus on the clues. "Come on, Wilson. My gut tells me we don't have many seconds on this end."

She twitched. Turned the page. Focused.

His boss cleared his throat. "Okay. Here's what we've got. One case came to a head at 10:38."

"Which one?" JB walked to the front window, then the side. Peeked through the louvers.

"Job before last. The meth bust. My guys are running the particulars right now." Shuffled papers sounded through the phone from Wilson's end. "Hey, before I forget. You were right about Landon. I never should have put him on the robbery case. Crayton Police says he's a loose cannon."

"Live and learn, I guess." JB's gut clenched tighter and

tighter. His bad feeling picked up speed. "I don't understand why he didn't call you with the 1038 when Sheriff Davis asked him to. He knew Marcy and I were in danger. Why not ask if you could run a check on the numbers? I'd have done that for my worst enemy if it meant their life."

"I don't know. Let's concentrate on you right now. Take care of him later." Wilson's to-the-point mode returned. "Here's what we've got. Date...not even close."

"What else you got?" he asked.

"Teams ramped into place by10:35 AM. You ordered 'go' to your men and broke through the door." Wilson quieted. "You know, I worked a long time getting that case together to have the glory go to a bunch of others in the Bureau."

Glory? What glory? JB felt no glory from that bust. People got killed that day. Some guilty. Some innocent. "Let's talk about that later."

"Later...yeah, we'll talk later." Wilson's voice kept fading in and out like someone panting as they ran.

What was that noise? A dog? Barking? Where?

"Did I just hear a dog on your end of the line?" JB asked.

"Yeah. The people in the room next door brought their dog on vacation. It's been a long night."

"I thought you were back in the office." He could have sworn Wilson had rattled papers on his desk. Maybe the staff just faxed him the info. Didn't matter. "What else you got?"

Wilson coughed. Gasped for air. "Explosion in the lab. Time...10:38. Gunfire from both sides. Four casualties in the room. Two men. Two women. Plus our own. Six taken to hospital. Fifteen arrests that day plus three higher-ups two days later."

"How do we know the exact time?"

Wilson paused, cleared his throat. "Notes say the watch on one of the women victims cracked and stopped at 10:38."

JB remembered that watch. He'd seen it being numbered for evidence, then a few days later, the watch was gone. He eased his Glock from his shoulder holster. The rest of his armor was in place, but he needed that gun in his hand right now. What had he heard? Sensed? Even with all the new information, why had the conversation made his cop instincts accelerate even higher?

A dog barked outside in the far distance...no, the bark was through the phone. Which? Damn, he couldn't afford to not be on top of sounds at this point. Had to be Landon.

"I'll call you right back. I've got another call coming in." JB snapped the phone closed, ignoring the second call from Deputy Evans for a moment. He needed to think. Landon would have already had time to target the cabin from the cell towers. He could be closing in even as JB spoke to Wilson. His insides tensed. "Marcy."

She stood, shuffled into her coat, and shoved her weapon into her pocket. She didn't hesitate. "I'm ready."

"If anything happens, when I tell you to move, don't stop to think. Just do what I say. Follow our plan."

"I will." She pulled her hat onto her head. "JB?"

"Yeah?" He couldn't take his eyes off her.

"Please be careful."

He grinned. "You sound like you care."

She raced into the crook of his arm, burying her head against him. "I love you, JB. Don't you dare get yourself killed before I can show you how much."

"I'm gonna hold you to that, sugar." He squeezed her against him with one arm and pushed the return call button on the phone.

"Deputy Evans here."

"You called me." JB knew Evans wouldn't have phoned again without a good reason.

"Jeff City tracked Landon's phone. Found him tied up in an abandoned house just outside of town. I'm patching you through to him now."

What the hell? Landon tied up?

The phone clicked a couple of times with connections and reroutes. Seconds drug like hours.

"JB, I'm not the one." Landon's voice sounded tense, a siren wailed close on his end. "Wilson set everything up to lay blame on me."

He tried to wrap his mind around those two sentences. Couldn't be. "How do you know?"

"Long story short. I called headquarters to check on some paperwork that I'd turned in to Wilson. They told me he'd been relieved. Arrested. Evidently, he'd been under investigation for some missing money. They believe Jennings got close, so he had him killed."

What the hell was going on?

"But I just got off the phone with him." JB pushed Marcy behind him and aimed his Glock at the door.

Landon grunted with pain. "The Bureau said he escaped before they got him to jail. He gave me a lead on your case last night, then ambushed me when I showed up."

That would explain Wilson's new phone number and so-called vacation. Never mind the strange exchange they'd had a few minutes ago. "But why would he be after you and me?"

"Something to do with that meth bust. Some woman that was killed. He said we'd ruined his life. Every time he punched me, he'd yell about how you and I would pay for what we did."

JB glanced up toward the roof. Had that been a footstep? A falling acorn? A squirrel taking a shortcut? "I didn't know either one of those women who were killed that day, did you?"

"No. But evidently, he knew one of them as more than an acquaintance." Landon coughed on an intake of breath. "He kept mentioning something about Oklahoma."

"The younger girl killed that day was from Oklahoma. I could swear her name was Carla."

"I don't know about that, but every time I asked who she was, he'd hit me again. Or get right in my face all crazy-eyed and say how I was getting my payback slow and steady. Seemed real proud of himself that he'd used blue and brown contacts to lay blame off on me when he killed Leon and ran the sheriff off the road." Landon paused. "Then he'd stomp around the room laughing. Crazy...like he'd gone mad. Once he calmed down, he became the cool professional again."

None of this made sense any more. Of course, when had it ever made sense? "There's got to be a reason."

"Don't try to figure out why. Focus on keeping your wife safe." The steady drone of the siren mingled with Landon's voice ramped the tension. "From what I gathered, he's after you by using her. Told me he didn't know which he'd enjoy more—my one-day-at-a-time agony, or the look on your face when he kills your wife right in front of you."

JB didn't know what a day-at-a-time agony for Landon meant, but he'd already figured the villain was after himself through Marcy. Now the missing link had fallen into place—Wilson. But who was Carla to him? That could be the key to tripping the man up. Carla? Oklahoma?

"You still there?" Landon asked.

"Yeah. Do you think he's targeted anyone else?"

"Don't know. He's got to be stopped at all costs."

JB didn't need anyone telling him what had to be done. He didn't need the badge to know the procedure. He also knew the unspoken procedures. Ones nobody talked about.

Ones that saved lives.

Glancing at his wife, he felt the ache of the hard clench of his jaw. God, he loved her.

Nothing she'd ever done or said had been to put him down. She'd only been protecting herself from her own insecurities. He'd done the same by believing the words from his childhood that he wasn't good enough. The hell with that. He was damn good. Good enough to fight to save her any way he had to. Whatever the situation called for today, Marcy would survive, or he'd die trying.

That simple. Raw and brutal. No regrets.

"Backup would sure be nice about now." He gripped the Glock tighter.

"I'm on my way, man. We're all on our way." Landon hung up.

Question was…would they get there in time?

...

JB dialed his ex-boss. He needed to know why the man had made him a target. He'd racked his memory for an answer. A reason. Knowing why would give him an edge. Allow him to turn the tables on the killer. Might even be enough to get out of this alive.

"What do you need, JB?" Wilson answered like a man in charge. Concerned. Willing to help. Like a man who actually cared.

For an instant, the thought crossed JB's mind that maybe Landon had played them all. But it passed. He'd concentrate on Wilson for the moment. "Tell me about the two women victims."

Papers shuffled again. Or was that the sound of dried leaves crunching beneath a boot? Slapping at clothing as someone ran through the bushes?

"No one ever came forward to claim the remains on one of them. You and Landon came up with the identification on the other woman. Twenty-six. A runaway who latched onto the city and stayed. You two tracked down the parents. Dad a farmer. Mom a gift shop manager. Landon arranged to ship her body back to Oklahoma. Only thing he did right on that job."

JB jogged his memory. "I never helped ID anybody on that case. Give me a minute to think."

He concentrated on the day of the bust. The going in. The blast. The wrap-up. The processing. The paperwork and sign-off. Nothing else. No Mom. No Dad. No Oklahoma. In fact, the only time he talked to Landon was an hour after the blast when he'd finally showed up. Said he'd overslept. Said a wreck on the highway had slowed him down. Said he'd forgotten his phone. From the little JB had seen Landon up until then, he'd always seemed like a rock-hard lean-over-the-edge protocol type of special agent. That day, he'd seemed off. Almost human. JB had found him standing in a corner at one point, staring at the floor.

JB forced himself to see the room in detail. Landon had squeezed the bridge of his nose. Face red as a stop light. Looked at the ceiling. Steadied against the wall. Squeezed the bridge of his nose again. JB had asked him if something was wrong. Landon had said he was just coming down with a cold.

Wilson had walked in about that time. The man had stared at the floor. Bent next to a young woman's body. Blond hair. Black, leather boots. Even touched her hand, her hair. Brushed the back of his fingers across her cheek. Strange behavior for an agent. Especially one who'd been in charge of the bust until that morning. Then he'd jumped up and walked out the door. Said he'd get out of the way.

Landon had said he would finish up his side of the paperwork at home. JB had never seen him again until he'd shown up in Marcy's hospital room.

JB blew out a sigh. Time to push. To antagonize. "Carla. The woman from Oklahoma was named Carla. Right?"

"Right. How did you know if you didn't help with the ID?" Wilson laced his voice with accusation.

"You mentioned her."

"I never mentioned Carla at work."

Quiet, quiet, quiet.

Had Wilson realized what he said?

"Maybe I'm wrong. Maybe it was someone else who knew a Carla."

"That's right. B...because I never knew...never... There are lot...lots of women named Carla in the world." Wilson seemed to choke on the words.

"Yeah, couldn't have been you. That guy always talked about his girlfriend. Some woman named Carla." JB had him dead to rights. Everything that had happened since he'd arrived in Crayton was revenge. Revenge for someone Wilson loved. JB loved Marcy. Everything fell into place. "The guy talked about how they were going to South America. A vacation. Might even find a place to buy. Wish I could remember who that was."

He knew exactly who it was. Wilson. At the time, JB had wondered how they could afford a vacation property on an FBI salary. He'd figured the woman must be rich. The way Wilson had talked about her, one would have thought she was the greatest thing he'd ever had in his life. Must have been to push him to this.

A bump on the side of the house jerked his attention in that direction. After walking to the window, he leaned his ear against the louvers. He could swear he heard a footstep on the porch. Not loud but still a footstep. JB's anger roiled. When you couldn't even trust your backup, you were on the devil's doorstep.

Wilson panted. "You never did say where you were hiding."

What the hell. The man had to be close anyhow. "We're at a friend's cabin on the lake."

"Bet you even got one of them green wooden swings facing the lake on the front porch. Maybe a tractor-looking bird feeder on the rail."

JB glanced out the window at the green swing. The bird feeder.

The man was close. Close as the wind outside.

There was one more thing that had been gnawing on JB's mind. "Hey, when did you contact Landon about coming to Crayton?"

"I left him a voice mail right after you and I talked that afternoon. He didn't call back until about 8:00 the next morning. Why?"

"Then how did he manage to be in my wife's hospital room by nine o'clock that morning? Springfield is a good three hours away. It's almost like he planned everything from the start. What do you think? Why would he do that? Of course, I guess a really smart mastermind would have thought of everything."

JB waited for a response. Maybe that would be enough to goad Wilson into making a mistake. Into taking credit. Make him confess everything now, so the final confrontation could be quick and done.

"I...you're right. Takes a smart man to get away with all this." Wilson paused. "Tell me JB, have you figured out what you did to Landon? What made him want to make you suffer? 'Cause he's sure tortured you these past couple weeks. I couldn't believe he tried to kill your wife right there in the hospital."

JB punched the wall. Hard and to the point. The son of a bitch on the phone had tried to kill Marcy. He'd been the volunteer with room information back at the hospital, planning everything so Landon would take the fall that day. Even so far as setting the stage to allow Leon out on bail.

Calm, play this calm. "Yeah. Like they say, you never know who your enemies are."

Wilson chuckled, low and conniving. "Friends...you never know who your friends are."

"We'll talk about friends and enemies the next time I see you." JB ended the call and tossed the phone on the sofa. Didn't need to talk to anyone else anytime soon. Now, the game centered on the here and now. Him and Marcy.

He knew his friends. They were on their way.

She followed his movements with her eyes. He listened at the window again.

Motioning Marcy to stay quiet, he walked back to her and leaned in close. "You heard me say it's Wilson?"

She nodded.

"I need to see if he's set anybody else up. Get him to admit he killed Jennings. Ratted me out." JB's lips brushed the hair next to her ear. "I need your help to pull off the plan we talked about. Can you do that? Will you help me?"

She bit her lip, then mouthed. "Yes."

"Good girl. You can do this."

She turned to his ear. "What are you going to do?"

He grinned. "Let him in."

After a quick kiss on her lips, JB pushed her behind him. He turned, she turned. Two people...one movement.

A scratch on the back of the cabin caused him to raise

his gun in the direction of the bedroom. Quiet. A lot of quiet seconds. He clocked it on his watch. Cat and mouse sounds or staging sounds? Tiny pecks sounded on the roof like a handful of pebbles being thrown on top. Don't imagine. Don't put too much emphasis on any one thing. Could be the rain. The storm. The wind. Could be any number of things.

He zoned into himself, didn't let his guard down. His back muscles tensed along with his sharpened focus. Adrenaline rampaged through his system. Control. Get the edginess under control. When the moment came, he had to make sure to tell Marcy what to do a second before he reacted.

Wilson had to be outside. Why was he waiting? Didn't matter. They'd wait him out. Play this out on their own terms.

The two of them stood and turned. Stood and turned, for what seemed like hours. His watch showed ten minutes. Only ten minutes, but more than enough time to set a trap. At least he knew the skunk's stripe now. One step closer than when he woke up. He processed through the little he knew of Wilson's routine. Not much there.

Footsteps on the porch. Not quiet. Not sneaking up.

Strong, stomping footsteps. Blunt and in-your-face, I'm-here footsteps.

JB faced the front door, pointed and gripped the Glock with both hands. Squared his stance.

"Hey, JB. Thought you might need help." Wilson banged on the door. "You in there, JB? Marcy? Let me in. I've come to help."

...

Marcy closed the bedroom door then turned on the shower in the bathroom. Followed the plan. She opened the window where JB'd removed the screen last night. She waited for him to give her the final verbal cue to go. Go out the window, through the trees, down to the lake. He'd told her to climb into the boat and push off.

He'd keep Wilson occupied in the house long enough for her to get away. The script hinged on the jerk believing she was taking a long shower. The ploy hinged on JB risking his life to harvest info from a man crazy enough to blow up a building in broad daylight.

A slight quiver ran the length of her body. From the bits she figured out from JB's phone conversation, Wilson intended to make her husband hurt the same way he'd hurt. In fact, this guy would probably look her in the face and truthfully say it wasn't personal as he shot her. Might not be personal to him, but it was mighty personal to her. The idea of JB being hurt in any way was more than she could bear to think about.

She waited.

Getting into the boat frightened her. The idea of being in the middle of the lake by herself scared the bageebers out of her. Sure, she could swim. That wasn't the point. The boat and the water were the fear factor. Rubbing the back of her head, she half expected to still feel the lump from hitting her head on the side of the boat the day it had capsized years ago. If JB hadn't jumped in to save her, she'd have sunk to the bottom.

She remembered fighting the water and herself and him. Water mixed with bubbles. Bubbles from her nose as they headed to the light of the water's surface high above her. Another quiver ran her body. Then another. *Fight the fear.* All she had to do was get out the window, run to the dock, and fight the fear of the water.

"Hey, JB. Open the door." Wilson yelled. "I came all this way to help. Surely you can let a buddy in out of the cold."

"Hold on. I'm coming." JB's voice sounded tired. Fake-tired for the most part.

She heard the slight movement of the sofa. The latch on the door being thrown. Her husband baited the killer into their space so she had a chance to get away. What happened after JB got his answers?

Her heart pounded with each word she strained to hear. If she missed her cue, then the set-up would be a bust. As much as she wanted to stay and help, she'd follow the plan. She would not let JB down.

"Come on in, Wilson. Glad to see you. Why didn't you tell me you were coming?" JB sounded like a guy opening the door to a high-stakes poker party. These stakes were even higher. "I can use all the help I can get."

The stomping boots from the porch walked onto the wooden floors in the living room. She swallowed hard. Her breath shallowed, quickened. Nausea vied against her nerves for first place.

"Figured as much. Cut my vacation short just to help you out," Wilson said. "What the heck took you so long to open the door?"

"Trying to get a little sleep while Marcy takes a shower." JB chuckled. "I swear that woman uses more water than a steam locomotive."

Wilson laughed. The noise filled her mind with visions of elves and gnomes on crack.

The sound of her husband's fake yawn and stretch brought her on alert. Soon. Real soon. She'd do what he planned. JB would handle the rest and make sure they survived. She had to believe that the two of them would be okay. She had to get out.

Out the window. Into the boat. Out of the cove. Had to…had to…had to.

"I haven't gotten much sleep the past couple nights. If you don't mind, maybe you can stand guard while I get some rest," JB said.

"You got it, buddy." Wilson's voice held her attention. Somewhere between crazy and sane, his words flowed like sludge. Slow and heavy. "Can you help me bring in my gear from the truck first?"

The sofa scraped the floor a bit. "Help me move this sofa out of the way of the door." JB's cue. She inhaled deep. Readied herself.

The sofa scraped again. She hoisted herself to the window, looking outside. At least the fog had lifted. Loud and long, the sofa scraped and banged against the floor, slamming into the wall as she climbed outside. Her coat snagged on a nail from the window frame. She pulled. Pulled again. Had she made a noise? She slipped from the coat and left it hanging.

She ran for the trees. Through the trees. Gun. Where was her gun? The gun? Her stomach cramped. She'd left the gun in the coat...on the nail at the window. Maybe she should go back for it. No. Run. Water...where? She tripped. Slammed into a tree limb. Ran again. The thick fog held heavy in the trees as if trapped. Her feet went out from under her on slick mud, and she crashed to the ground. Slid into a clearing in the woods where the sun had found a spot to soak up the fog. Fast, she jumped back up. Finally, she had a clear skyline through the trees to find her way. Where was the dang boat? She stopped, looked around.

No. No, no, no. Not good. She'd run parallel to the lake. Hadn't even bothered to look for the water as she ran. Wouldn't have seen it for the fog. She'd used up valuable time going in the wrong direction. She retraced some of her steps, then turned and started down toward the dock.

Heart pounding, she knelt at the edge of the tree line. Inched forward to the edge of the lake. Moisture crept through the knees of her jeans, coating her legs in icy cold water. JB'd been right. The water was too cold for her to wade to the boat. The storm front had moved in with dropping temperature. Dangerous hypothermia might set in if she got wet and ended up in the boat for any length of time.

That was why the plan had been she walk out on the dock to the boat. That was before she ran the wrong direction and had to circle back. Too much time had passed to assume Wilson wouldn't be looking out the window. The best she could do was stay low and crawl onto the dock. After inching her way to the side of the boat, she eased downward onto the flat bottom and braced her stance. Undid one of the lines.

The front door on the cabin opened, and she crouched down, peering over the edge of the dock. JB and Wilson walked outside onto the porch. She should have already been gone. Laying in the bottom of the flat–bottomed aluminum jon boat, she continued to watch the men. For less than an instant, she saw JB's gaze glance across the dock. The boat. He acted as if nothing were out of the ordinary.

Had he seen her? No.

He had to think she was still inside the cabin. That she'd never made it out the window. Her out-of-control running through the trees in the wrong direction had cost them.

How much? How much had it cost?

...

JB's mind worked to create a new plan. The boat bobbed on the water, still looped to the dock. Marcy hadn't made it out. He'd hoped to gather more insight into Wilson. Try to garner a confession. See if the man had any traps set for anyone else. With enough information, the FBI could stop the threats.

Not now. The situation had changed. One priority remained. Marcy's survival.

She must still be in the cabin.

He stretched. Stooped to retie his bootlaces. Walked down the steps. Played for more time. Time for her to get away. Why hadn't she followed the plan? "Where's your truck?"

Wilson walked behind him. "Not far."

JB angled his trail in the direction of the fallen log. The fireplace poker. He still had his Glock, but a backup weapon added an edge. His instincts shouted the man wouldn't kill him until he made him suffer losing Marcy. JB didn't plan for either one of those scenarios to happen.

Instinct also told him before this walk ended he'd become a wounded prey. His spine tingled with a shot of adrenaline straight to his brain. He needed to react now. Attack before disabled. He couldn't. Couldn't attack until he knew Marcy had escaped.

With Wilson's expertise in explosives, there was no telling what traps he'd placed. Even if she made it out of the cabin, she could be lying somewhere wounded. The man might have even rigged something so she couldn't get out of the window. Out of the cabin. She might be trapped inside.

"That's far enough, JB." Wilson's voice quivered with excited anticipation. "Turn around."

The ruse was over. From now on, everything JB did meant life or death for him and his wife. He felt his nostrils flare. Felt his fingers twitch into their fight rhythm. Felt his will for survival kick into fight-to-the-end mode. He might die today, but he for damn sure wouldn't die easy.

JB turned to face the monster and his weapon of choice.

"Stay right where you are." Straight and fierce, Wilson kept his gun trained on him. He appeared composed. Confident in his madness that he was on the side of right. "Hold your arms out to the sides. Shoulder height. Then use your left hand to remove your shoulder holster."

JB complied. "You don't want to do this. What if you miss a bullet casing? Leave a fingerprint?"

"I wondered how long it would take you to figure this out. You always were one of my best agents. Too bad." Wilson motioned with his gun. "Pull your Glock out enough to release the clip. Then throw the clip in the lake."

"Carla wouldn't want you to do this." JB did as told. Heard the splash as the bullets hit the water. "Go back with me, Wilson. Get some help."

"Tell me, did you figure out Jennings, too? He got a little too close to costing me my money. I had no choice but to get rid of him." The maniac of an agent laughed. "Carla wore her best schoolgirl outfit. Took him in hook, line, and sinker as a snitch. He believed everything she told him. She was being held. Abused. There were others." Wilson's expression oozed of pride. "Got him to the right place for me to pop him."

Confession. JB didn't move. A confession he might never get a chance to relay.

Wilson kept his weapon pointed an inch below JB's Kevlar. The man knew the weak points. "Now the backup gun on your ankle. And that knife you've got on your calf. Guess you thought I wouldn't check your routine. I give you credit for the knife thing. May even use the idea myself."

"Too bad you won't get to see South America. You and Carla." JB pushed the limit. He had nothing to lose. Maybe he could get Wilson to break. To drop his concentration long enough to take him down. One split-second...that's all JB needed. "Oh, that's right. You were late to the party. Too late to save her. That why you want to kill Marcy? To ease your guilt for being late?"

"Shut up and do what I said." The man's face flushed, eyes bulging.

"Late, Wilson. Late." JB goaded with precision and the rhythm of a lullaby. "You weren't in time. Carla trusted you'd be there, and you failed her. That must be hard to face."

Wilson's cheek twitched. His predatory posture fractured for a second. Eyes moistened.

JB glided slowly into a new position. Again and again. Each placement of his feet measured. His body angled for the best blow he could strike. Almost like a ballet where every movement took into account the next position. Wilson didn't seem to notice. He hoped to lull the man holding the gun into a stupor. Anything to slow his reaction time when the moment came.

"It's not too late for you to lower your weapon, Wilson. We can get you some help." JB stared the man in the eyes. "You know I had nothing to do with your girlfriend's death."

Maniacal laughter coupled with a gasping sob spilled into the air. "Girlfriend? How dare you disgrace her memory with such a thought? Carla was my daughter. My. Daughter."

Daughter? JB sucked in air. The situation had changed. A man might be angry over the loss of a girlfriend. Even be a motive for payback. But in all likelihood, he could be talked down. The killing of a man's child was different. Could take vengeance to a whole different level. One that meant blood for blood.

"I didn't know, Wilson." JB shuddered to think what he'd do in the same situation. How he'd get retribution against someone he thought had killed his son or daughter. "Why didn't you ever tell us you had a daughter?"

Wilson shook with anger, his finger set against the trigger and pressing. "Why should I? None of you all ever cared about me. Neither did her mother. I was just a trick that produced a problem. A problem she put up for adoption."

The air seemed to have grown thicker. Made breathing more labored. Life more fragile.

"Didn't even get to see Carla till she showed up at my front door a few years back. She was in trouble with some dealers. Needed my help." The man shook his head. "Every time I got her out of one situation, another came up. Figured getting her...us...out of the country was the only way to give her a new start. That meant money...and...."

"So you started skimming the drugs and money we busted. I can understand the odds you were up against." JB needed time. "After all, you were her father. Who else could she turn to?"

Wilson nodded. "Then Jennings came snooping. Once I offed him, I'd made my choice. Needed to make one big score. Took months to set that meth bust. Then you...you and Landon screwed everything up."

JB angled with his words, hoping something he said would make the man have a second thought. "We didn't know she was your daughter. You should have told us she'd be there. We could have—"

"What? Just what the hell would you two upstanding special agents have done? You sure as hell wouldn't have gone down my path. Besides, I had everything planned. You and Landon screwed everything up." Wilson shook his head, raised the gun straight, and primed to shoot. "You called the go. Landon could have stopped you if he'd been on time. And that turncoat boss of mine... He ordered the bust a day early. He'll get his, too. Him and his bratty kids." Pure venom had oozed in his last words.

In that moment, JB knew there'd be no taking Wilson alive. This had to end today. On this hill. He would not risk other lives to save his own. Either he or Wilson would not walk away at the end of the day. That was all right with him as long as Marcy walked away.

Maybe he could get Wilson to shoot him. Make him think he'd made a direct hit, then come at him from behind when he turned. JB'd seen no sign of Marcy. She still had to be inside the cabin. Okay, she'd be safe there. Backup was on the way. She could barricade herself in until they arrived. Worst case, she had a gun and knew how to use it.

Wilson regrouped, motioning JB to step backward again and again. "That should be far enough." Nonchalant, the man reached in his pocket. "Shame about the cabin."

The cabin? What about the cabin?

The explosion happened like the blink of an eye. One second, the cabin sat peacefully. Blink. The cabin growled into a fireball.

Trees shook. Ground rumbled. The air echoed with the intensity of the bomb. Boulders catapulted down the hillside. What had been logs became sticks, sharp and jagged as they shot through the air. Searing heat blasted across the open ground.

"Marcy!" JB roared louder than the bellowing flames. He plastered a charge of blows to Wilson's nose, his jaw, his kidney. JB dropped, rolled, and came up with the stashed poker from beside the log.

Wilson shot. Shot again.

Hot fire pummeled JB's right shoulder as he swung the iron against the agent's knee with his good arm. He swung again. Landed a second blow. Wilson staggered, then regained his footing. Smashed his fist into the gunshot wound. JB dropped.

The killer stomped the bleeding shoulder and held. "How does it feel to know you'll never hold your sweet, little wife again? Huh? I blew her sky high. If she'd of died back in front of the bank, you'd at least have had a chance to say goodbye."

JB spun out of the hold, crawling to his knees. Wilson back-slashed him across the face with the gun stock.

"You might as well kill me, too, Wilson. 'Cause I'll hunt you down one inch at a time." JB hoisted himself to his feet. "And when I find you, you won't even know what happened."

He lowered his head and charged Wilson's midsection. The man pulled his backup Glock, crashing it across the back of JB's skull. He staggered. Still fought.

Wilson grabbed the poker. Slammed the iron across JB's shoulders and forearm. JB grabbed his arm. No sound. No cry of pain. His arm hung at a worthless angle. Broke.

Still he fought with his good arm. Backed Wilson up with the blows. The agent smashed JB's arm again. JB fell to his knees. Wilson stabbed him with the end of the poker right below the Kevlar.

"One more thing." The crazed man laughed. "Wonder who ratted you out on that last job?"

JB had no doubt. Didn't matter. The man had killed Marcy. That mattered. This fight wasn't over. Wouldn't be over until he took his last breath. "You didn't even have the guts to do the job yourself, did you? Had to hire it out."

"I hated I couldn't be there when they branded you." Wilson's laugh coiled like a snake around his words. "They said you took a long time to pass out from the pain." He raised the iron, fireplace poker over JB's head. "Should only take one hard blow today. Goodbye, sucker."

. . .

"Noooooooo!" Marcy screamed. Stood. She needed to get Wilson's attention. Get him away from her husband.

She worked the rope on the final line. If she could get free, then Wilson would follow her. If she didn't, he'd finish JB. She worked her fingers through the tight knot.

Wilson jerked, facing the dock as he smashed the sharp end of the poker downward.

She squinted to see if the blow had connected with JB but couldn't tell. He hadn't moved. What did that mean? Was he unconscious? Dead? He couldn't be. This couldn't be the end. Not like this.

Wilson never looked down to see if he landed his blow as he yelled with rage. Livid, he threw the poker at her. The iron plummeted onto the ground and tumbled end over end into the lake. Suddenly, he staggered. Fell. Had JB jerked on the man's legs?

Wilson regained his footing, stumbled again, then hollering like a crazed man with no other words, he charged down the hill.

Sinister. Loathing. Rage.

He'd gone mad. All her analyzing in the world wouldn't get her out of this. If he got to her, he'd kill her. And, JB? If he was still alive, Wilson would go back and finish him off after he finished with her.

She struggled with the knot, her fingers scraping against the dry hemp. Hard and brittle, yet set like cement in the twines of the knot. Her hand slipped. Blade-like strands of rope sliced her fingers. Blood coated her hands, the rope. She fought to ignore her reaction to the sight. Fought to push the nausea aside. Widened her eyes to battle the lightheadedness.

The closer he came, the more his face snarled with hate. Then he stopped. Glanced over his shoulder at JB.

Crazed laughter escaped from Wilson's mouth. "Too bad JB's gone on to his maker." He turned back to face her, laughing even louder. "Maybe I'll just take you with me to South America. Shouldn't take long to convince you to cozy up to me. Do what I say…when I say…how I say."

He charged forward. Tripped over his boots. Picked up a handful of rocks and threw them at her again and again. Like an angry child tossing their toy in the corner, he screamed through his sob. He'd gone over the edge of sanity. So crazy he had no idea what he was doing. He charged again.

Why couldn't she get the rope free? Her bleeding fingers fumbled. The more she pulled, the tighter the rope got. Her hand scraped, ripped open. A nail? The rope had snagged on a nail. She tugged the loop upward over the rusted metal till it finally popped free. Looking up at the scene on the hillside, she shoved away from the dock with the oar.

From the corner of her eye, she saw JB push to his knees. Swiping his hand across the side of his head, he struggled to stand. Staggered. Tumbled down the hillside. Grabbed onto the sapling. Bad arm wrapped around the tree, he flung a flat stone aside, grabbing the clip he'd hidden underneath. She watched him claw his way back up the hill toward the Glock. His feet dug into the dirt, pushed. Pushed. Slid. The Kevlar snagged on a log. He shucked out of the vest's protection. Dug his feet in again.

Sirens wailed in the back ground. Closer and closer. She paddled and paddled, but got nowhere. More sirens joined in.

Wilson turned in the direction she was looking. "Sonofabitch. You bastard, don't you ever stay down?" More crazed laughter. "You'll never make it to one of your guns in time." The man waded out into the water and grabbed the bow of the boat, hoisting himself inside, even as she pelted him with the oar. "You're dead, Marcy Bradley."

The sirens stopped. Through the trees, red and blue lights flashed. Shouts from familiar voices echoed through the brush.

She clawed at the man in the boat with all the strength she possessed. Grabbed a buzz bait lure from the bottom of the boat and scraped the hook across his face. "JB. The bait box. Bait box."

The man grabbed her hand and squeezed till she released her hold on the lure. The hook lodged in his cheek, and a trickle of bright red blood edged down his jaw line.

Her husband rolled down the hill, staggered to the bait box, and reached inside for the extra gun. Wilson fired at him. The bullet clipped the wood at the edge of the dock. She walloped at the man's knee JB had smashed before, but Wilson backhanded her before she could strike again.

"Let her go." JB's voice was hard as steel. "Let. Her. Go."

Wilson pulled her in front of him. She watched her husband brace into his stance on the dock. His right arm dangled useless. The gun in his left hand an extension of his straight arm. Wilson raised his gun to fire, and Marcy elbowed him in the ribs. Punched her foot back at his knee. The man flinched in pain, and she spun away.

JB notched down ever so slight. "Dive, Marcy. Dive."

She jumped a split-second before shots rang out.

Two from JB.

One from Wilson.

The water swallowed her whole.

Chapter Twenty-four

JB opened his eyes to a welcome sound. A heart monitor beeped his existence. The last thing he remembered, hot pain had drilled into his chest. He'd stumbled, plunging into the water. Cold, dark water.

His head hurt like someone had banged him with a ton of steel. A groan escaped his mouth when he tried to raise his left hand to touch what felt like a bandage on his chest. Throbbing aches and pains radiated from every part of his body, including ones he hadn't known existed. He let his hand drop back to the sheet. To heck with the bandage.

Warmth against the fingers on his right hand stirred him back to the moment. He looked at the only peaceful spot on his body. Marcy...his wife slept with her cheek resting lightly on his fingers. The only part of his right arm and hand not sheathed in a cast. He flexed his arm muscle, and pain shot straight to his brain. No need to do that again anytime soon.

He wiggled his fingers against her cheek.

Her lashes fluttered. Her eyes opened. Her smile said

everything.

"We seem to be spending a lot of time at the hospital." He sighed with the exertion. "How long have I been here?"

"Three days."

She stood, then leaned and kissed him. Rested her forehead against his. Tears trailed across their lips as they kissed again. Hers? His? Didn't matter.

Marcy drew away enough to look him in the eye. "I thought I lost you."

"I thought I lost you, too." He tried to raise his left arm again, groaned, and let it fall. Even now he wondered if she'd stay by his side or leave for the other room, so-to-say. He'd be content that she was there at the moment. "What about Wilson?"

She shook her head. "You got him. He won't bother anyone again."

JB nodded. His insides eased. The danger was over. Part of him hated Wilson for what he'd put Marcy through. Part pitied the man for the loss of Carla, the daughter he loved.

The bed shook as Marcy reached for the nurse's button, sending a fiery jolt across the side of his chest. How badly was he hurt? He moved his feet. Okay. His legs. Okay. His torso. Hot, searing, razor-edged pain. Not okay.

Dr. Crowley entered the room, followed by the nurse carrying a syringe. She straightened JB's good arm enough to give her access to the IV port.

"What's that for?" JB said.

"You're awake, so I figured you might want something to take the edge off." The doctor grinned. "Now if you don't want the shot, just say the word and—"

"Okay. Okay, I get the picture." Heck, yes, he wanted the shot. Bucking up for this damage wasn't an option. "Only enough to take the edge off."

His wife winked and then nodded. He shook his head. What had they done to him? From the looks of the equipment, the feel of his body, and the grateful look on Marcy's face, they'd done whatever it took to keep him alive. Even doc looked worried.

Dr. Crowley evaluated the wounds. Listened to vitals.

"Well?" JB asked.

Doc charted and conferred with the nurse. She changed his bandages.

"Let me know if any of this hurts, JB." The doctor pushed and poked and prodded at most places not covered by a cast, needle, or gauze.

JB grimaced. Groaned. Nauseated. What was that noise? Himself? Couldn't be. Not him. He could take anything. Always had, always would. Yet the noise he heard spew from his mouth didn't begin to express the agony inside.

"You can stop any time." JB growled.

Dr. Crowley paused. Looked him in the eye. "Does any of that hurt?"

"Yes. It hurts."

"How much?"

JB swallowed, blew out a quick breath. Clenched his teeth. "One heck of a lot."

"Good. We've finally got some honest communication going between us. Not like when you were here after the explosion." The doctor grinned and left the room, followed by his nurse.

Thank goodness they were gone. JB wanted no one but Marcy right now. Wanted to get an idea of where they stood.

She eased her hand under the sheet, rubbing her fingers back and forth on the inside of his ankle, then returned to her place in the chair next to the bed. He missed the heat of her skin against his.

"Why didn't you ever tell me Truman used to be FBI? Still does some work for them?" She shot him one of her gotcha looks.

"I don't know what you're talking about." This wasn't what he wanted to talk about right now.

"Don't pull that with me. My mother and I had a nice, long talk about marriage and the law. You and Truman and my dad." Her voice didn't sound sad or angry, just mater-of-fact. "What gets me is, all these years, I thought she'd played it safe with a simple businessman for a husband, when it was just the opposite. Guess you don't always know what's going on in someone's life."

Not sure of where this conversation was headed, he stayed quiet. He glanced around for a pitcher of water. None. Not even a glass of ice chips. Nothing in sight to ease the pain of waiting for her to get to the point. He guessed a man waiting for the verdict of a jury must feel about the same way. 'Cause his future was in her hands, and her answer might be no. Might already have his bag packed and sitting on the porch.

Well, she had another think coming this time. He might have left easy the last time. But he planned to go down fighting this time. Fighting for her. For them. Hell...why didn't she get this over with and say what she was gonna say?

She covered his fingers with her own. "I always knew you were one heck of a lawman, but these past days have made me see just how good you are. The FBI, the DEA, the...the...well, any of those initialed agencies would be lucky to have you." Her fingertips rubbed against his palm. "I'm so damn proud of you."

Here it was. Her way of pushing him out the door. "So what are you getting at?"

"I just wondered if you had considered staying in

Crayton." She fidgeted with the edge of the sheet.

Stay? Of course he planned to stay. With her? Depended on Marcy. He was who he was — the law — now and forever. If that wasn't good enough for her, then so be it. He'd never doubt himself again. "You trying to go back on your promise to show me how much you care?"

She tilted her head and stuck out her tongue, crossing her eyes. "No. It's just, before Landon left town yesterday, he asked the doctor when you'd be able to get back to work."

"Sounds like he was in one damn awful hurry to leave Crayton." Couldn't the man see the police department might need a little help at wrapping up the case?

"That's not it. He got a phone call that his wife wasn't doing well, and he needed to head home." She blinked, then rapidly batted her eyes. "Did you know she has cancer? They found out the day he was late to that past assignment you worked together. The one that started this whole thing."

JB hadn't thought he could feel any worse, but he'd been wrong. Cancer? Diagnosed that day? Explained a lot...one hell of a lot. "I didn't even know he was married."

Was that how he wanted to keep living? Always keeping your personal life secret. Trying to protect your family by never sharing the bad times with others. Not even the good times. At least if you had a community like Crayton around you, there were people who cared enough to be there as you celebrated accomplishments. And there to see you through the pitfalls.

As soon as the fuzz of pain and medications got out of his body, he'd call Landon. See if there was anything he could do to help the guy.

"Anyway, I figure you'll be going as soon as you're well." Marcy brushed her fingers against the sheet covering his legs. "Seems the FBI doesn't want you to quit. They think you'd be perfect for some position in the Springfield office."

JB rolled the idea around in his head. Kept coming to the same conclusion. He and the FBI needed to part ways for good. But he still planned to work in law enforcement. "Do you want me to go, sugar? I mean, I did make you a promise."

"No. I don't ever want you to go." She laid her cheek against the hospital gown covering his chest. "That's one promise I won't hold you to."

"I guess if you need me that much…" He gave a fake put-upon-sigh. "…then I'll have to stay." That should rile the Marcy he loved.

Her head popped up. "Need you that much? I don't need you. In fact, you can leave any time you want." A mischievous expression belied her words. "Go ahead. Leave. See if I care."

"I think you care more than you say." He grinned and reached for her with his uncast arm. If she could feel the pain that small movement caused him, she'd know how much he cared.

She came to him willingly, taking in his tongue as it swept against her lips. Gave as much in return.

"I care a lot. So no matter where you go, no matter what you do, I've decided to go with you." She poked his shoulder, then laid a kiss on the same spot. "No matter how much you aggravate me."

"What if I get hurt?"

"Look at yourself, JB." She palmed her hands up in front of her and gave him the once over. "Do you think you could be hurt any worse than this and survive?"

There was the crux of the situation. Might as well lay the cards on the table.

He formed the question first in his mind, then took

as deep a breath as he could muster right then. "So what happens if a bullet finds its target, and I don't get up?"

"I faced that possibility, Jean Bernard Bradley. Back on that hillside when Wilson slammed the poker down at your head, I couldn't tell if you were still breathing or not. And as I jumped into the water, the sound of the guns exploded around me, and all I saw was the jerk of your body on impact." Big tears spilled from her eyes and rolled down her cheeks unabated. "I thought you were dead."

She swiped the back of her hands across her cheeks. "I was sinking in that cold, dark water, and all I could think was that you were dead. That I'd drown because you weren't there to pull me out. But, I fought…I fought to reach the air again. To live. And one stroke at a time, I made it to the top. I survived, because I kept fighting to live."

He longed to reach out to her but knew she needed to walk through this emotion on her own. He'd done the same last year when he thought he'd die. When he discovered he wasn't invincible and that all he could do was fight till the end. His own survival back then had made him see that no matter what, he just needed to get up one more time. Throw one more punch. Struggle for one more breath.

"Guess I'm stronger than I thought." She smiled.

"You always were. I've just been waiting for you to figure that out." Now that she had, JB wondered what effect that would have on their future. Was she so strong she wouldn't need him at all? Or strong enough to let him be there for the good times and the bad? "You still haven't answered my question. What happens if I don't make it off the ground one day?"

"Well, it all goes back to what you said about the hazards of being a lawman. We'll face that if and when that ever comes." Sucking in an extra-extra-extra-deep breath, she managed a tiny upturn of her lips, then kissed him sweetly. "Besides, loving a man like you is already one damn big hazard in itself."

He couldn't argue with her there. Except he'd like to go on record that she wasn't a walk-in-the-park herself. But he wouldn't. He lived for her sassy comebacks and stare-down arguments. Besides, she only called him by his full name when she was stone-cold serious.

"That sounds good, sugar. But I was thinking—"

"Don't you dare try to talk me out of this," Marcy focused her eyes on his and lifted her chin, then lowered the rail and nudged him to move over. "You're my husband, and I belong with you. We can go to Springfield or St. Louis or all the way to Washington, D.C., if that's what you want."

With what strength he had, he scrunched himself across the bed till he rested against the other rail. "I was trying to tell you that I'm never leaving you, sugar. Not even if you pack my bag and set it on the front porch. And for now, let's just stay in Crayton. Soon as I'm well, I plan to talk to Sheriff Davis about getting my old deputy job back."

She jerked a quick nod, and smiled. "Good. That means you can be the new sheriff."

"Sheriff? What about your uncle?"

"Says he's calling it quits. Gonna let the younger guys carry the load." She fluffed every pillow on the bed. "Deputy Evans says they couldn't pay him enough to do the job. He and Kennett have already endorsed you as their choice."

Sounded like he'd been the topic of conversation as he lay there knocked out the past few days. Sheriff? Maybe.

From what he'd heard around town, Crayton was getting a new factory next year and an expansion on the medical center, plus an outlet mall had just broke ground midway between the lake and the city limits. The town was ripe with growth, and he was ready to settle into a police department that needed his background.

Funny how life gave you what you wanted if you managed to stay alive long enough. JB held the covers back and motioned Marcy to climb in beside him.

"Do you think it's okay?" His wife glanced at the door.

"Do you think I care if it's okay or not?"

She shook her head and giggled, then shimmied into the space he'd made between him and the rail. Every shake of the bed jolted shots of pain through him. First one spot, then another. She finally settled in. Nestled her head against his chest. Cuddled. Nestled again.

He grimaced. Groaned. Clenched his jaw.

"Did I hurt you?" Her voice already eased into a sleepy mew.

"Nope. You're fine." Dang, her settling worked his pain threshold. About a twelve on a pain chart of ten. No matter. Marcy was beside him, and the pain meds would kick in soon. The nurse would have a fit. The doc would call this highly improper. Too bad. Feeling her against him was the best medicine he could imagine.

"JB?"

"Yes, sugar."

She leaned up on her elbow. "I've also decided to scale back on my marriage counseling business. Not entirely, but a little."

He bit back a smile. "But you're so good at it."

"True. But I'm going to diversify, as big business would say." She nestled against his chest.

He grabbed the rail and gripped. Gripped tighter and tighter till she stilled. He blew a long breath of air. "How?"

"Huh?"

"Diversify how?"

"Oh." Her body relaxed into her dreams. "First, I'm going to volunteer at the women's shelter over in the county seat. Second, I've decided I need a hobby. You may not have noticed, but sometimes I can be a little intense. So I've been studying the horticulture book and have decided to grow things. You know…like tulips and tomatoes and…" Her fingers pressed against his chest. "…babies."

Babies? The meds must be kicking in, because everything she said made sense. Babies. Yeah, he could see them with a few kids. They'd need a bigger house.

"I love you, JB."

"I love you, too, sugar."

His mind and body eased into a pain free float as she jiggled closer. They were both alive. And even though he'd been hurt worse than ever before, here was Marcy. In his bed. Snuggled against his side. She'd even offered to go with him any place he ever wanted to go.

He tucked his cheek against her hair and grinned. His risk of a lifetime had paid off.

Allow us to

IGNITE

Your passions and imagination…

Did you love this Entangled Ignite novel? Check out more of our titles!

And for exclusive sneak peeks at our upcoming books, excerpts, contests, chats with our authors and editors, and more…

Be sure to like us on *Facebook*

Follow us on Twitter

Acknowledgements

To think that I'm an author who gets to share the story of my hero and heroine with you is just a little exciting, so please bear with me as I thank a few of the wonderful people who made this all possible.

First and foremost, I want to thank my always supportive family who's been there with me through all the ups and downs, writes and rewrites, wins and losses. Without their encouragement and belief in me, this path would have been harder to follow. You are my bright and shining stars, and I'll love you forever. Thank you, thank you, thank you.

Then there's my fabulous romance critique group (Cosmos With A Twist) who's not afraid to tell me when my alpha heroes are acting a little too beta. With a special thank you to Michelle Sharp and Linda Gilman who've been with me on this book from my first brainstorming session at the lake. You two rock!

Thank you to my amazing agent, Melissa Jeglinski of The Knight Agency, who is always there when I need her, and sees my goals for the future right along with me. A special thanks and super-much appreciation to my editor Tracy Montoya who pushed me to be the best I could be; with your help I found a level of emotion and writing expertise that was hiding deep inside me. And thank you to the entire Entangled Publishing family including Nina Bruhns, who took a chance on my manuscript, and Terese Ramin, who continues that support.

Finally, I'd like to acknowledge everyone who has guided me along my writing path including Coffee & Critique, Louella Turner, and Donna Volkenannt; mentors B.J. Daniels and Jeannie Lin; beta readers Kathy, Noelle, and Heather; MORWA members and speakers; and the KOD chapter's great classes on writing suspense. And I'll be forever grateful to Nancy Bartholomew who gave a writer's prompt in a class she taught at Wildacres Writers Workshop that made this story take seed in my mind.

My husband, the love-of-my-life, said I should quit work and write my novels, so I did. We laughed and hugged and celebrated when I completed my first manuscript a few months before he passed away. He may not have been here in person as I wrote *Risk of a Lifetime*, but I'm sure he's read every word of this novel looking over my shoulder. Thanks for believing in me and my dream. I miss you.

About the Author

Claudia Shelton thought she wrote mainstream when she began writing, but before long, a critique partner told her she sounded more like romance. Since then, she's focused on happily-ever- after with a splash of suspense, always featuring Alpha males and the women strong enough to love them. Her advice, always remember that a warm cup of cocoa in the winter or a cool drink by the water in the blazing heat will make your day a little brighter. She is a two-time finalist in the Daphne Du Maurier (Unpublished) awards for excellence in mystery and suspense. Visit Claudia at: http://www.claudiawriting.com/

Sign up for our Steals & Deals newsletter and be the first to hear about 99¢ releases from Claudia Shelton and other fantastic Entangled authors!

Reviews help other readers find books. We appreciate all reviews, whether positive or negative. Thank you for reading!

VILLAIN SCENE (EXTRA)

The Villain walked past a row of six empty booths before easing onto the green cushioned seat in the last one. His back against the wall, he checked out the going-ons of the diner. Got his bearing. A television droned the 7:30 AM news above his head. Most people would sit far enough away to get their morning fix of 24/7 news.

He didn't need to know the news. He needed to know where JB and his feisty little wife were stashed.

Letting them get away had been a mistake. A challenge was always good, but he should have realized JB would know the ins-and-outs, the up-and-downs of the woods. The guy wouldn't need to follow procedure since he grew up running in the woods around Crayton. Running for his life wouldn't be any different.

The Villain clenched his jaw, fisting his hand. He had no one to blame, but himself. He'd lost them in the woods. He'd find them in the woods. Might take a little time, but then the game would be over.

Carla's retribution was within his grasp. The Villain's gut clenched with the prospect of having Marcy in his grasp. Paybacks were hell and he planned for JB to see every bit of her suffering. The expression on JB's face when he realized he couldn't save her would be priceless. Pained and priceless right up until he blew both of them away.

The villain laughed. Grimaced. Had someone heard him? He glanced around, then refocused. If someone heard him laugh for no reason, they'd think he was crazy. He wasn't crazy. He was Carla's revenge.

The sheriff's cell phone contact list had been a bust.

Just a bunch of local-yokels phone numbers. The wife. The restaurant. The doctor. The veterinarian. The drug store. The bank. The cops on the local force. Cops on the Highway Patrol. Cops in Jefferson City. Other cities. Other jurisdictions. Other states. Cops, cops, cops and half the town of Crayton. The do-gooders. The behind-your-back slackers. The howdy, good-morning friendlies.

He'd like to blow the entire town of Crayton to smithereens. How much plastic would that take? If one more person said he fit in like a native, he planned to knock them from here to New York and back again.

"Coffee?" The same waitress, wearing the same black slacks and beige knit shirt, asked him the same opening question she had yesterday. And the day before and the day before. Every morning the same smile, the same friendliness, the same question.

His nerves wound tighter. "Yes. Coffee. Black."

"You want your usual?"

Had he been there so much he was known by country ham, five scrambled eggs, double order hash browns, large orange juice? "Yes. My usual."

Once he finished off JB and Marcy Bradley, the last thing he'd do before leaving town would be to leave a well-placed package in the last booth. A package with enough explosives to blow Dee's Morning Diner and Joanie's Pizza, Pub and Pool Room across the street, clear off the face of Missouri.

In fact, when he got settled in South America, he'd take an advertisement out in the Crayton Gazette. One that told the yokels how stupid they'd been to welcome him in like one of their own.

Deputy Evans and Cain Connery walked into the diner. Both took stools at the front counter, their heads tilted, their mouths moving fast as they talked. Appeared to be a serious. Maybe there'd been a change in the sheriff's condition.

The Villain knew Leon was a dead. What made that small town bully think he could blackmail someone so far above his caliber? Not gonna' happen. Popping Leon had been a breeze. Staging the cab of the dump truck to look like suicide ranked as pure genius. Sheriff Davis had been another story. Climbing down the side of that hill to get the phone had nearly cost the Villain his own life. He thought the last blow to the sheriff's head would have done the guy in. From talk around town, Davis was a tough old bird though. Still hanging on over in Jefferson City. At least he hadn't woke up to talk yet.

Focused on the screen of his laptop, the Villain ignored his surroundings as he waited for breakfast. He flipped through his file of photos. Photos of him and Carla. Their dream of big money and an even bigger yacht had been within arm's reach. Only a few more sales. A few more kickbacks. A few more kilos disappearing from the evidence room.

The waitress sat his usual in front of him and refilled his coffee. He ate without focus, his mind struggling to think of anything that might lead to JB Carla's death shouldn't have happened. If JB had waited for him, she would have been protected when the SWAT team went in. His plan to whisk her away, shuffle her out of holding and onto the street backfired though. The takedown imploded on itself. So what if orders had been given by his own superior, JB should have waited.

A couple walked back to his area and took the booth in front of the Villain. When he glanced up the old gentleman nodded, he nodded in return. More of that stupid town friendliness. Evans and Cain pushed off their stools, paid at the register and then walked out the door. Good. The entire time the deputy and Cain were in the restaurant, he'd hunkered down in his seat. Now he could leave uninterrupted.

The Villain patted himself on the back for his artful deceptions. In fact, his phone planted in Jefferson City for anyone checking to locate by its GPS had been pure genius. He'd took a big risk coming to Crayton this morning, but so far the risk hadn't paid off with a clue to JB's whereabouts.

The waitress brought the Villain his bill and he paid, finishing off his coffee as she went for his change.

"Wasn't that Cain Connery with the deputy?" the older man at the next booth said to the grey-haired lady with him.

"Believe so." She peered out the window. "I think his old man died."

"No. JB's dad died. That's why he came back to town to wrap up the estate."

At the mention of JB, the Villain perked up. At this point any mention of his quarry deserved his attention, so he zeroed in on the couple's conversation.

"I think you're right. Let me see if I can think of why Cain's in town." The grey-haired woman sipped her coffee, staring off into space. Suddenly she tapped her fingers on the table top. "I remember now. Cain's back in town to remodel the place his dad gave him. Getting it ready to sell, I think."

The old man nodded. "Yep, I believe that's it. Of course, I'm surprised we haven't seen Cain around town more. What with the house he's remodeling being a couple blocks from ours."

"From what I hear, he's been staying out at that lake cabin his dad owns. It's only been the past couple days I've seen him around town."

Cabin? By the lake? In the woods? The Villain had seen

JB and Cain talking once before. Could be what Cain and the deputy were talking a few minutes ago. Might be worth looking into because a cabin would make a perfect place for JB and Marcy to hunker down. Maybe the Villain's luck had started to change.

He dawdled over his empty cup, waiting for the waitress to hand him his change before asking for a refill on his coffee. The he waited...sipped the strong brew of caffeine... and waited some more.

Like an old married couple, the elderly man and woman glanced back and forth between the stools at the counter and the outside. Quiet. Content. He gulped down the last of the bitter drink. Must have been the bottom of the pot. He deserved better.

"Didn't you and Cain's dad go hunting together years ago?" the grey-haired lady said to the silver-haired gentleman.

Across from her, the old guy smiled. "You know come to think of it, we did go hunting one year. Even went fishing a couple times the next summer before his dad got into one of his wandering spells."

The waitress delivered the couple's food. There'd be no more information, now that their breakfast arrived. Should the Villain chance staying longer? No, he's already overstayed his usual time. He slid out of the booth. Close, so close to an answer, but he felt his chance slipping away. What could he do? He didn't want to be obvious, but there had to be some way to find out more.

Taking a chance, he stopped at the couple's booth. "Excuse me, I couldn't help but overhear you talking about Cain Connery being back in town. I've been meaning to take the boat out, stop by his old man's cabin to see if Cain's staying there."

The lady kept right on eating.

Meanwhile, the gentleman watched him with an evaluating look. "Wife says that's where he is."

"Was." She grimaced at her husband. "I said he'd been staying out there, might be in town now." She glanced up. "You just missed him. He left as we walked in."

"Well, I'll be." Smile. Be friendly. The Villain braced his arms on their table until he saw the man flatten his expression as if some invisible line had been crossed. Okay. He stood up. "You know for the life of me I can't remember the mile marker of that cabin. Wasn't it the...the..."

"The eight mile marker." The old man motioned the waitress for more coffee. "Right around the eight mile marker."

"Right. Now I remember." He tipped his head to the couple. "Enjoy your breakfast."

The elderly man grabbed hold of the Villain's arm. "You be careful out there on the lake by yourself this time of year. Supposed to be a rain later today. Maybe a storm. Lake water's none too warm heading into winter."

"Thanks for the warning. Maybe I better drive in." He fake chuckled and eased his arm away. The answer had fallen right into his hands. JB and Marcy didn't stand a chance. The clock on the corner chimed once for the half hour, 8:30 AM. Plenty of time left. Plenty.

He stepped from the diner out into the brisk air, his breath fogging before him as he walked to the county court house. A cold front had moved in during the night. Good thing he had plenty of flannel in his car's trunk. Without thinking, he followed the hallway path to the Recorder of Deeds Office.

"Good morning." The perky, young blond behind the receptionist desk smiled. "You're back again. Still trying to find a piece of property to buy?"

He forced a grin. Yesterday, he'd scoured the records for any places the police department, or JB might use for a safe house in the local area. "Right. I love it around here."

"Well, we sure like having you around, too." She leaned toward him enough to give him a view of her ample breasts. "What can I do for you this morning?"

The low-cut tank top beneath her jacket jarred his thoughts for a moment. Maybe he should ask for her phone number. Hell, maybe this barely-passed-jail-bait age woman would like to take a trip with him. No. He deserved someone with experience. Besides, all the money he had stashed in the Argentinean bank from the bribes the past five years would have more than enough women jumping into his bed.

The young lady before him cleared her throat. "I said what can I do for you this morning?"

"Sorry, guess I'm a little distracted. You smell mighty good today."

She blushed. Giggled. Jiggled.

He brushed the side of his finger against hers as he laid his hand on the counter. That should be enough to get him his information. "I heard somebody over at the diner talking about a cabin on the lake. Somewhere around the eight mile marker. Said it might be coming up for sale."

She led the way to one of the microfiche viewing machines. "Which side? East or west?"

"I'm not sure." He steadied himself on the chair. "Maybe you can help me. They said it belonged to Cain Connery's old man. Can we look it up by the last name?"

"Well, yes." The young lady frowned. "Except there's a lot of Connery's around here. Let me ask someone who's lived here a lot longer. I'll be right back."

He nodded.

"Want me to bring you a cup of coffee?" She leaned again, winked.

A door slammed behind him and he jerked. Sounded almost like a small bomb blast. The clock on the wall caught his attention, 8:45. He turned back to the receptionist. "No. No coffee. I'm kind of in a hurry."

Ten minutes later, she returned with a small stack of microfiche. Brushed her fingers against his as she handed him the film. "There you go."

His insides quivered at how close he was to the final piece of the puzzle. Closer than ever before. Wait for the answer. Don't rush.

"The clerk says Cain's old man was James Connery. There are a few deeds in the county with that name, so I brought them all." She smiled.

"Fine. Thank you for your help." He touched her arm. "I'll stop by sometime next week and take you to lunch."

He wouldn't. He didn't need her any more. His fingers trembled as he inserted the first film. Leave. Get out of my way, girl.

He winked. "Or, maybe dinner."

"I'd like that. Well, I better get to my work." She sashayed toward her desk, then glanced back. "If you need anything else, let me know. Anything at all."

The Villain eased through the slides through the microfiche reader...stopped...grinned. He keyed the address into his phone, figuring the GPS would be his friend today even if JB never turned his phone on again. The Villain breathed a sigh of relief. All he'd had to do was wait for the right information to fall into his hands. Retribution was close now...real close.

He tapped in to the airline and purchased a one-way ticket to South America for this evening. That was just the first leg of his journey to disappearing for good. But the faster he got out of the country, the better. And once he had a little fun with JB and Marcy, he'd be gone. Gone for good.

They'd be gone, too.

THREE MONTH FOLLOW-UP CHARACTER INTERVIEW
Marcy and JB Bradley

1) What is your favorite time of the year?

Marcy: Spring...and I'll tell you why. I love to see the tulips and daffodils and crocus pop into the world with all their bright colors. I've already got some bulbs to plant in the flower garden. Oh, and I love listening to the birds sing once they come back.

JB: "Fall."

2) Which side of the bed do you like to sleep on?

Marcy: "Whichever side JB is on. Of course, sometimes I guess that might be considered the middle. Then again... we've been known to fall asleep cuddled on the sofa until one of us rolls on to the floor."

JB: "Left."

3) What is the first thing on your grocery list?

Marcy: "Depends on what I feel like cooking. You see I'm not much of the chef-type, but I am good at soup. And cupcakes with chocolate frosting—lots and lots of chocolate frosting."

JB: "Coffee."

4) What is the last thing you do at night?

Marcy: "Kiss JB goodnight."

JB: (He glanced at Marcy and grinned.) "Next question."

5) What would you look for if you bought a different house?

Marcy: "There should be at least—"

JB: "Five bedrooms, three-car garage and a big wrap-around porch with a swing to sit on and watch the stars with Marcy each night."

Marcy: (She touched JB's hand and smiled.) "That's right...every single night for the rest of our lives.

6) What do you like on your pizza?

Marcy: "I used to like everything except mushrooms and onion. I even liked pineapple on top. But lately I haven't been feeling too well." She held her palm against her tummy. "So cheese is the best I can do for the time being."

JB: (Again he glanced at Marcy and grinned.) "No more questions for now. Marcy needs her rest."

Why I Wrote Risk of a Lifetime

Water has always been a part of my life, whether it be weekly trips to the lake when I was young, summers spent at the pool as a teenager or actually living at the lake which I've done as an adult. So what better place to center RISK OF A LIFETIME than in a small town, on the verge of expansion, in a lake community?

Add to that, miles and miles of shoreline filled with points-of-land and backs-of-the-cove settings. Places where water laps gently against the rocks as it springs fresh into the lake. And others places where the depth is more than I want to consider. Hills and crevices adorned with pines and cedars, oaks and maples, dogwoods and mimosas provide the backdrop for the four seasons.

Since my town is fictional I can make this setting anything I want, so this was the perfect place to drop in bad guys and suspense. Which meant I needed Alpha heroes and tough, sassy women to battle the elements, the unknown and each other. Plus I figured this small town needed a touch of the outside world inching into their friendly community, bringing new life and a way to expand its horizons.

My options for fun and excitement plus those all important romantic moments are endless in the imaginary world of Crayton, Missouri. And if I decide to revisit these characters in this small town, you'll be the first to know.

Enjoy your summers and making memories,
Claudia Shelton
www.claudiawriting.com
claudia@claudiawriting.com
Twitter: @ClaudiaShelton1
FB: https://www.facebook.com/ClaudiaSheltonWriter

10 Things I Like About Living On A Lake

1) View and view and...oh, did I mention the view?

2) Swimming till you're waterlogged.

3) Fishing whether you catch anything or not.

4) Sand squished between your toes.

8) Wind in your face as you speed across the lake in your boat.

5) Smell of barbeque floating through the air.

6) Sound of waves lapping against the shore.

7) Glow of the moon as it makes a path across the water.

9) Reading on the deck with a nice cool drink close at hand.

10) Waterfront restaurants with music that floats across the lake.

I always know the smell of suntan lotion—anytime, anyplace, anywhere—will take me back to enjoy the memories of living on a lake!

IGNITE YOUR PASSION WITH THESE SUSPENSE TITLES...

HER DESERT TREASURE
by Larie Brannick

Inheriting her grandfather's ranch is the perfect opportunity for Meg Reynolds to begin again. The land is her only chance to hold on to the last bit of family she had. But Jake Matthews has other plans. Despite the heat blazing between them, he'll do whatever it takes to get what he wants. When someone threatens Meg and seems willing to kill her for her land, she doesn't know who she can trust. And when she's kidnapped, Jake wonders if he'll ever be able to let her know he cares more for her than the land that stands between them...

PRETTY RECKLESS
by Jodi Linton

Deputy Laney Briggs has long been considered reckless, but when a dead body turns up and her ex, Texas Ranger Gunner Wilson, decides to stick his boots into the town's first murder case, she'll be damned if she lets him trample all over her turf—and her life. His ability to undermine her libido is only outdone by her constant urge to butt heads with him. But when the bodies pile up, Laney needs the lethal bad boy's help. It might not be the best idea, but Laney has always been pretty reckless...

You Again
by Ashlee Mallory

In high school, Allie McBride thought the sun set around her friend Sam Fratto's smiles. Now she's older, wiser, hotter, and teaching at the same school they grew up in. When Sam joins the faculty, she has a chance to make good on the crush that got away. But when a dead body turns up on school grounds, they realize there might be a murderer in their midst. The heat keeps getting hotter between Allie and Sam, but more might be in danger than their hearts…

Lie by Night
by Cathy Marlowe

Cole Stewart's mission to protect close friends from a criminal mastermind takes an unexpected turn when Emma Bailey runs head first into his investigation. He once spent a single night falling in love with her, but now she's not only a danger to his heart, but her brother is a key suspect. In their race to keep the people they love safe, Cole and Emma betray each other's trust time and again, not realizing that trust—and their growing love for each other—is the only thing that can save them all.

Between the Sheets
by Genie Davis and Linda Marr

Erotic romance writer Jenna Brooks finds herself drawn into her own stories, literally. When the seductive, mysterious Riley Stone rescues her from an attempted hit and run, she's plunged into a reckless, wild relationship unlike anything she's ever experienced—except on paper. A drug kingpin, a billion dollar development scheme, and a hostage situation have Jenna and Riley running for their lives. As Riley struggles to keep Jenna safe, the romance they've woven could force them to pay the ultimate price: admitting they've fallen in love—for real.

Hearts Under Siege
by Natalie J. Damschroder

Molly Byrnes has loved Brady Fitzpatrick forever. As his best friend and a de facto member of the Fitzpatrick family, she holds them together in their crushing grief. But as a member SIEGE's ground team, she doesn't buy the official line about Brady's brother's "accidental" death and launches her own investigation—only to uncover a shocking secret that she and Brady must get to the bottom of before their target finds them. Can Molly trust the possibility of a future with Brady...or if they can count on any future at all?

Risking it all for her Boss
by Sharron McClellan

When the scientist Eva Torres is guarding is kidnapped, she turns to Quinn Blackwood—her former lover and the man who broke her heart. Quinn taught Eva about secrets, sex, and lies, but sacrificed his relationship with her for the job. Now, Eva and Quinn have to work together before entire cities are destroyed, a hard task made more difficult when they find themselves fighting both the enemy and their growing desire for each other. Can they accomplish their mission without reigniting the passion between them—or will passion be the salvation of them all?

Made in the USA
Lexington, KY
13 February 2015